Also by Isabel Cooper

BLOOD
AND
EMBER

ISABEL COOPER

sourcebooks
casablanca

Published by Sourcebooks Casablanca, an imprint of Sourcebooks
P.O. Box 4410, Naperville, Illinois 60567-4410
(630) 961-3900
sourcebooks.com

Printed and bound in the United States of America.
OPM 10 9 8 7 6 5 4 3 2 1

To my parents, Daniel and Kathleen Kunkle; my sister and brother-in-law, Emily and Benedicto Gell; and my nephew, Felix. You all mean the world to me, and I'll let you know which pages you need to skip.

Part I

The attacks resumed today. This first was only a test of our guard: a score of twistedmen and five of the trance-birds. We drove them off handily enough. The spell that Hanyi and your Gerant came up with at Oakford shields our minds well, and our mages have been diligent about applying the sigils. Injuries were light, casualties nil, and the new fortifications hold well.

Still, the air here has changed. None, not the Order nor the soldiers from Criwath nor even the reinforcements from Heliodar, fresh as they are, can mistake the meaning of this attack or be in any doubt of what will follow.

For eight months, we've discussed what deviltry Thyran might be up to out in the forest, where we have no strength to reach. We have come to no conclusions.

I suspect we're about to find out.

—In the Order's Service,
Vivian Bathari

The Traitor that humans call Gizath murdered his sister's lover, they say, because he thought it a disgrace that a goddess should lie with a mortal. Over the centuries, his hatred for mortal life has expanded far beyond that.

One hundred years ago, Gizath's servant Thyran slew his wife and her lover out of jealous rage, and then his own servants to seal a pact with the Traitor God. Jealousy swiftly became spite: anger that the world did not give him what he believed was his by birth and blood.

In the north, when he called those of like mind to him and merged them with demons, perhaps they too wished to order the world by their standards. Perhaps even then Thyran had the same ambitions.

After a hundred years and two losses, I suspect his desires may have shifted.

He may strive still for conquest, if such a mild word can describe a world ruled by him and his twistedmen.

If he is thwarted in that, I think he will turn his sights to annihilation. And he will do so quickly.

—Lycellias, Knight of Tinival, "Musings in a Time of War"

Chapter 1

THE DREAM LEFT OLVIR COLD IN THE DARKNESS. SWEAT coated his limbs, cooling rapidly in the spring night. He tasted blood in his mouth: he'd bitten his lip again.

None of it was new, but it was worse this time. His heart was thudding between his ribs and his chin. Images danced evilly in front of his open eyes. Not even the sound of three other knights snoring could make the memories seem as unreal as Olvir knew they were.

Dreams, he told himself, as Edda had told him when he was far younger. Nightmares had been different then: shapes outside the window, ghouls behind the house, the sort of stories youth repeated and parents could generally dispel with warm milk and a few words.

Olvir doubted that soothing words would've helped completely. He'd long since grown to prefer whiskey to warm milk, too, and a liquor-mazed head was the last thing he'd need the next day, particularly considering the quality of whiskey that went around the front lines.

It was a myth that Tinival's knights never surrendered. The training was very clear about recognizing lost causes. Sleep, at that moment, was among them.

He disentangled himself from his sweat-dampened bedroll as quickly and quietly as he could manage. None of his companions stirred. It was funny: their alertness was legendary, but any experienced warrior grew accustomed to certain sounds. In camp, these included both snoring that could shake the earth and the noises of a tentmate trying to make a stealthy exit in the middle of the night.

Tinival hadn't given them heroic bladders, after all.

Putting on armor would be more likely to rouse his tentmates, so Olvir simply tugged on his breeches, then picked up his boots and tunic in one hand. He carried the belt with his sword on it in the other. The camp was relatively peaceful, no attack expected, but there was no point tempting fate.

Edda had taught him that long before he'd entered the Silver Wind's order as a page.

He stumbled outside into a chilly gray predawn. The remains of fires made the camp a little brighter but, at that hour, mostly just added smoke to the air. A flash of Olvir's dreams sprang from fading memory to vivid detail with the odor. He sat down hard on a rock.

Vomiting would only waste rations, and the army had a strictly limited number of those. Screaming would only wake soldiers who had too little rest as it was. Olvir scrubbed his hands hard across his face, wishing that he could do the same to his mind, trying not to look too long at his hands themselves. They had been the worst part, and that had been a new element of the dream.

If your thoughts are sour, turn to deeds. It was another of Edda's sayings. And Olvir was already sitting down. Getting dressed was the obvious next step.

He pulled on his boots, listening to the sounds near him. The camp was mostly still abed, but not entirely. Out of the three thousand or so souls who defended that part of Criwath's border, fifty-odd were assigned to patrol the fortifications. Olvir could glance up and see two of them walking behind the wooden palisades, peering through cracks too small for arrows as they tried to spot any activity beyond. He could certainly hear their footsteps, regular drumbeats behind the irregular noise of snoring sleepers and shifting horses. Their presence was reassuring, but he'd have been a fool as well as an oaf to distract them.

A few rows of tents behind the defenders, the wounded slept

restlessly. The Mourners, noncombatant servants of the Dark Lady whose domain included healing, kept their own vigil among them, watching for sudden declines. Letar's priests were good company as a rule, but Olvir didn't want to disturb the Mourners on their duty either.

There was always practice. The few sets of pells were barely holding together after rounds of recruits had trained with them, so by common agreement, nobody used them except those who truly did need help hitting their targets. Fighting the air, however, required only space. Olvir stood up and turned to retrieve his tunic.

A woman stood a few feet away from him.

That itself wouldn't have been a surprise or a problem—a relief, though he wouldn't have wished it, to find another who couldn't sleep—but Olvir hadn't heard her approach. Coming on top of his dream, it was more than he could reason through calmly. Before his brain caught up with his body, he'd hissed in a wary breath and reached for his sword.

"It's a shade early for a duel," she said.

As usual, Olvir recognized her voice before her face. He knew the tone in particular: soothing amusement. The words beneath the words were *we can laugh about this, we're laughing already, we wouldn't be joking if it was any great matter.*

He'd used that manner of speaking before, when the minutes before battle bit into the throat like wire, but he'd heard it most often from the woman in front of him: Vivian Bathari, commander of the Sentinels who held the border.

As was usual with the Sentinels, her clothes—dark, plain wool beneath a mail shirt—gave no indication of her rank. The gold-worked hilt of a greatsword over her shoulder, and the eye-sized sapphire set in it, made a striking contrast to that austerity.

The sword marked Vivian as a Sentinel. Its stone housed Ulamir, a spirit hundreds of years old.

Vivian's face showed the other signs that she belonged to the Order of the Dawn: a half-circle of bloodred tears beneath each gray eye, glowing against her light-brown skin. The gods had reforged her, like they did all of her order, turning them into weapons. None who'd been through that process ever looked fully human again.

None, in truth, were.

Many feared the Sentinels, even as they relied on them, believing them too close to the monsters they killed. Olvir hadn't been nervous around the Order's members in more than a decade. He'd known Vivian for nearly half that time and depended too much on her to feel the slightest alarm once he recognized her.

Embarrassment was a different story.

———————

How easily he startles, said Ulamir.

"Everyone's jumpy right now," Vivian replied, "and no wonder."

She spoke in the murmur that she'd spent eighteen years using with her soulsword. Most people couldn't hear it unless they were trying to listen.

Olvir nodded, then contrived to appear even more awkward than he had before. He carried it well, as always. Being tall and square-chinned with big hazel eyes helped. "Not talking to me, were you? Though you're right. Or Ulamir is."

"I forget I have to be careful around the knights," she said, with unspoken acceptance of his equally unspoken apology. "I'm still too used to people with normal hearing."

Should your memory slip around any of them, he's the safest, Ulamir put in. *What could you say to him that you didn't say in the Myrian lands, when that undead sank its teeth into your leg?*

"If you have any dark secrets left where I'm concerned," Olvir echoed, "you didn't give them away just then."

"Oh, good. I'm sorry for sneaking up on you, by the way. And for keeping you from getting dressed."

She wasn't entirely sorry for the latter. Vivian had seen Olvir with his shirt off on a few occasions. The sight had always been pleasant, particularly when he wasn't bleeding. Tinival's knights trained well, and Olvir's appearance in particular suggested that he'd spent his mornings lifting small cows over his head.

Still, it wasn't polite to say she'd be glad to keep him shirtless. The morning was a little cold too.

Vivian started to turn away.

"You weren't seeking help when you came across me, were you?" Olvir asked, making her turn. The tunic slid down over his broad back and narrow waist, concealing his head for a moment before his close-cut chestnut hair emerged. "If you'd be able to use an extra hand with any task, I'm more than willing."

"No, but I do thank you for offering. I woke up and couldn't get back to sleep, so I hoped a tour of the camp would help."

"You too? Not that it's so unusual, given the circumstances."

"I'm surprised there's not a crowd of us. Ample hard work or rotgut must be effective for the others."

Olvir turned toward her. His belt was fastened, and his sword on it—"girt to his side," as the old stories had said. He mostly fit the picture of an upstanding knight, but far more worried than they generally appeared in tapestries. "Forgive the question, but you haven't been having dreams, have you?"

"I have," Vivian answered him slowly, "but only what you'd expect. And you sound like you mean another sort."

"I'm afraid I'm not sure what I mean. I've never been a prophet, so I doubt it's that, and yet they repeat more often than any dream I've ever had."

There was a memory connected with his name, one more tactically significant and less personal than their missions together or the taverns afterward. It started rising in Vivian's mind as Olvir mentioned dreams: an official document, one of a few hundred she'd read since the war started. She'd been startled to read the mention of Olvir, but the report, whatever it was, hadn't seemed immediately relevant. It had gotten lost in a thousand tasks.

"I don't want to pry," Vivian said. "Or, rather," she added, because she was talking to a servant of Tinival, whose dominions included truth, "I do, but only as far as it might be tactically significant. Tell me more?"

Olvir squared his shoulders, a man confronting an unpleasant duty. "I'm in different places," he said. "It was the village where I grew up in this dream, but in the last one, I was at the chapter house where I trained. It's always a place that I'm fond of. And it's always burning. The smell of smoke is very vivid. The screams are too."

"I haven't studied the mind," said Vivian, "but that doesn't strike me as so out of the ordinary to dream about, given all of this." She gestured, indicating the campfires but also the palisades and the army and by extension the war. "It sounds like you put it a few degrees away rather than using memory straight out, but... minds do that, probably."

"So I thought. But"—he swallowed—"tonight I saw where... I saw that I was lighting the fires. My own hands were piling the wood, spilling the oil." Olvir held them up and out in unnecessary illustration, or perhaps to try to get them as far from himself as he could. "I tried to stop. It didn't make any difference."

Chapter 2

Talking didn't actually help very much, which came as no surprise to Olvir. Knights were trained to meet fear boldly, both when it came from outside and when the source was inside their own heads. If he'd only needed to confront his dreams to make them stop, he would've done so months before.

He'd harbored a small hope, as he began describing them to Vivian, that putting words to the images, the crying and the odor of smoke and flesh, would define them and thus trap them. That didn't happen either—the dreams remained, as nebulous and unnerving as ever. Olvir sighed, then waited for Vivian to state the conclusion he'd already turned over and still believed possible: worries about command, or about the war in general, nothing more.

She stayed silent. While the fires smoldered around them and sentries' footsteps thumped out the moments, Vivian frowned, stared, and didn't speak a word. She didn't move either, adding to the sensation that gripped Olvir, a feeling of being looked not just over but *through*.

Vivian didn't resemble cheerfully profane Emeth and her earnest lover Katrine, who Olvir had spent the most time with in the months since Thyran's return, or any of the other half-dozen Sentinels he'd met more casually. In that moment, facing her clear gaze, he experienced a little of what the uninitiated must have felt in a Sentinel's company. Training helped him not to study the dirt or fidget, for which he was profoundly glad.

"You were at Oakford," she finally said. "You played a major role, unless I misread the reports."

"I was." That line of reasoning had also suggested itself. "But the dreams started long after that. I've only been having those for a handful of months. There could be a correspondence, I suppose, but—" He shrugged.

"It's not a clear connection," Vivian agreed. "If you don't mind, I'd prefer to hear what happened in your own words. You know what reports are."

"It was late in the siege," he said, remembering a different set of walls, other sets of companions who likely wouldn't all survive the next few days. Had it been more desperate? Perhaps, but a different sort of desperation. "Thyran himself came out to face us."

Nightmare had spawned nightmare then. They'd all heard that Thyran—the most famous servant of the Traitor God Gizath, the man who'd locked the world in winter for years when his previous attempt at conquest had failed—had somehow come back. Olvir had thought he'd faced that fact until he'd seen the bone-crowned figure on his walking throne of corpses and looked into the rotting inferno of his eyes.

"I didn't know him," he told Vivian, a year later and not a great deal wiser, despite a fair amount of scholarly effort. "Not in the sense people mean that phrase. I grasped his…frame, his pattern. A familiar tune, but not the whole of the song. I tried to find out more," Olvir went on, gesturing to the badge on the shoulder of his tunic, where a blue sword signified Tinival, "and saw blackness, shining blackness in pieces, before I lost consciousness."

"The contact disturbed him too. Did I read that correctly? Darya, I think, said he seemed pained."

"If Darya said it happened, I believe her," said Olvir. "I was in no state to observe anything."

"That was all?"

"On that occasion. Later…" Olvir rubbed his chin, uncertain of the precise wording. Most of the magic he knew was the power Tinival granted his knights. Until a year before, he'd been content to let others attend to all else. "Gerant, Darya's soulsword, cast a spell to extend his protection to General Amris and to let the three of them speak directly."

Vivian nodded, with a quick breath of resigned laughter. "It's a pity that the spell doesn't work outside of their circumstances and that those are so unique. If I could give Ulamir's power to any lover I took…" She laughed again, a surprisingly light sound, clearly at a comment from her sword, then waved a hand. "Please continue."

"A few of us made a circle for them. We ended up connected. It was less intense for those of us on the outside, but I was aware of the others in a manner that I wasn't before."

"I take it that wasn't part of Gerant's goal."

"No. And Darya said it hadn't happened when the three of them had done the spell before."

"She and Gerant aren't—weren't—precisely used to having others nearby, to be fair. Her preference for the remote is unusual even among us."

"That's so," Olvir admitted, "and she said so. Silver Wind's truth, I have no idea how closely any of these incidents are related, except that the second and third almost certainly are, and Gerant said that he thought the third had to do with me. Forgive me… I'm getting ahead of myself."

A bell chimed in the distance: five slow, measured strokes. A fresh—relatively speaking—sentry headed to the wall, sparing a quick glance at Olvir and Vivian but no more. Their focus was already turning outward.

"At the end," Olvir said, "Thyran tried to kill General Amris and me with magic. I saw Gerant's protection taking a fraction of it. It wouldn't have been nearly enough to save us. I knew that. I…" He brought back a memory he'd repeated until the words had worn holes in what he'd once known. "I felt as though I was being torn apart. I don't recall what I was thinking, if I was thinking at all."

"Hard to be coherent at such times," Vivian agreed. "But you turned Thyran's spell back on him."

"I suppose so. All of us who'd been involved in casting the shield seemed to join in, but Gerant said my presence might have been the deciding factor." A year later, and it still felt like boasting to say it. "More likely it was the god's."

———

"It's possible," said Vivian. She'd never heard of Tinival working like that. She assumed that none of his priests had either, or one would have long since provided the clarity the god was known for. On the other hand, how often did a knight confront Gizath's champion, let alone with all the magical complications Olvir had described? "He may be behind the dreams too."

Olvir looked politely doubtful.

Naviallanth wouldn't veil his message, Ulamir said, using the stonekin's name for the god, *nor would he have any need of obscurity with his chosen.*

Doubly reproved, Vivian switched angles of approach. "I take it you had yourself inspected by all the correct people."

"As many as we could find, before the war called me away. The Dark Lady's Mourners said that my life force was normal, and her Blades couldn't find any corruption in me." Olvir made the fourfold sign of thanks, touching forehead, eyes, and mouth quickly with the fingertips of his right hand. "The mages said that my spirit had been altered somehow, shaped, but they couldn't tell why or whether it'd taken place before or after Oakford."

One or the other need not be the only choice. All gems are cut before they're polished.

"Fair point," said Vivian and explained, "Ulamir says the initial shaping could've taken place before Oakford, and then those events could have brought it out. Do you know when it might have happened?"

"No," he said, politely but promptly. Obviously he'd given the same answer a few times before. "I've had an active life, but no mysterious incidents with mages."

"And your childhood?"

"Infancy, maybe. I was only a month or two old when my mother found me, and she would've told me if it had happened since she was a dedicate of the Silver Wind herself. It had been many years since she'd held a blade, but the oaths don't vanish."

"No, they don't."

Vivian hadn't sighed, and she believed she'd looked suitably casual, but a trace of her thoughts must have gotten through. Olvir's large brown eyes briefly met hers in a moment of connection that had nothing to do with the war or his dreams. He was at least ten years younger than Vivian but old enough to have reached the point where a warrior, even one molded by the gods, had to see the ground shifting ahead. Slower reflexes, fragile bones, and all the other frailties of mortal flesh were still mostly in the future, but not nearly as far away as they'd been at sixteen.

A soldier or a mercenary without a vocation might have started considering small farms, or inns, or ceremonial posts with nobility. The paths were different for the servants of the gods. Vivian had just begun to wonder about that when the war had really started. Now it was anyone's guess how many of them, god-touched or not, would see that terrifying age.

"That raises possibilities," she said, pulling the conversation back to practicalities, or analysis, which was the next best thing, "but only those."

It happens at times that my people bestow gifts on likely humans, said Ulamir, *but such favor is rare, and no land near here is missing a prince.*

Olvir shook his head. "No. If we'd had more time and could

have consulted additional mages, possibly, but I was more use with a sword than as a curiosity."

"You're right on that point."

"Thank you…and thank you for listening."

"I wish I'd been able to help more," said Vivian.

The camp was slowly waking up around them, with quiet groans and mild profanity drifting through the air. Those who hadn't had Olvir's dreams, or the normal nightmares of the battle line, had to return to a world of unwelcome facts: they were still here, the war was still going on. *Bugger it* was a frequent response, with no effort to be specific.

He shook his head. "I couldn't have expected it of you and been reasonable, any more than I'd have expected you to have the same dreams. I only thought, well, it's always worth asking."

"It is," said Vivian and then heard footsteps behind her, less regular and more purposeful than the sentry's.

Olvir saluted. "Good morning, General. You seem to have a mission in mind. Can I help?"

"Morning." General Magarteach had a light, efficient voice. "Glad I caught both of you together."

"Glad to be of service," said Vivian, turning to see the newcomer. The general was broad of shoulder and bosom, with red hair running to gray in streaks. Magarteach was roughly her height, which was not inconsiderable, so that the general effect was of a moving wall. Right then, it was a troubled wall. "What's today's complication?"

"Those clouds," said Magarteach and gestured to the north, where the thick gray sky was taking on a darker shade. "I don't like them. More to the point, the mages don't either. I suspect we may have hoped in vain for spring, Sentinel. I'm sure we'd best start getting the camp battened down."

Chapter 3

WIND SHRIEKED THROUGH THE NIGHT. CLOUDS BLOTTED OUT the stars, dumping snow by the bucketload onto the border camp, and the air was painfully cold, even when the wind didn't whip it into a sandstorm of ice. It had been spring two days before. Now it was midwinter again, hard and bleak.

Out beyond the walls, magelights shone stark white on the snow, bright enough to blind any watcher who didn't shield their eyes, but making sure that any figure approaching the palisades was visible right away. Thickly wrapped soldiers escorted the wizards out three times a day to keep them shining.

Vivian watched the ground before her from the thin slit in her bonemask, blinked to clear her vision, and cast her gaze over every inch of the snow that she could see. The obvious figures of twisted-men, Thyran's shock troops, weren't the only danger. Movement could mean tunneling. She watched for the slightest change, analyzing each shift of the snow to see if it went against the wind.

The cold was fine. Poram and Letar had both blessed her at her reforging. Now Vivian could face the blizzard with no worse than mild discomfort, just as she could stand in a fire for an hour and come away with no worse than a nasty sunburn. The monotony of the watch itself was the danger, and the weather made it worse. Snow clouded the sharpest vision after a while. Visions appeared in the cold. Voices rode the wind. It would have been easy to lose herself.

She did lose track of the time, until another figure approached her position on the walls.

Only the Sentinels and the knights had the endurance to be sentries for very long in the storm. Not many of those had blessings to match Vivian's. Katrine was wrapped in wool and fur until she looked twice her size. Only the amethyst-hilted sword at her waist would have given her identity away if Vivian hadn't known who else was out there with her. She still shivered.

"All calm on your circuit?" Vivian asked.

"All calm. You make an excellent landmark, Commander."

"I do my best." Vivian peered at the other Sentinel, observing what she could between fur hood, wool scarf, and bonemask. Katrine was pale, but she'd always been pale. The droop in her shoulders was more indicative. "You've reached your limit."

"So have you," said a voice from the stairs behind them.

Vivian didn't turn when she recognized the speaker. Nor was she surprised that she hadn't heard the approach: Emeth was the most silent-moving of the Sentinels she knew, particularly when snow muffled her steps. "Well—" she began.

"Well, you've been out here two shifts, and you'll be no damn good if you fall asleep on your feet. Katrine, love, you're damned near blue. Alyan's about ten steps behind me. We'll be fine while you two get some blood into your fingers."

"I'll ignore the insubordination, then," said Vivian.

"Good. Olvir said his tent'd have stew ready in a couple minutes if you want to stop in."

I wouldn't trust your fingers near a carving knife just now, Ulamir put in.

Vivian's aide was skilled in many things. Cooking was not one. "I'm told I make illustrious company," she said and let Katrine take the lead.

Wizards took care of the inside of the camp as well as the outside. Down off the walls, the wind was already less fierce, but a transparent, faintly yellow shield blocked the rest of it, leaving only the air necessary for breathing. Glowing saffron-colored crystals every few yards served as anchors. A head-sized garnet sphere sat at the middle of the camp, radiating heat to two circles of tents.

The wounded and those who cared for them got the closest spots to the flame orb. The healthy soldiers took the outside, supplementing magic with braziers, fires, and body heat.

Olvir's tent was large, lit within and full of song. The smell of cooking food drifted out along with the music, making Vivian's stomach growl. It *had* been a long watch.

"Come in, please!"

She'd always admired Olvir's voice, which had the clear depth of a great horn. It was perfect for shouting orders across noisy battlefields. Now it cut cleanly through the wind. In its own way, it was as much welcome—as much shelter—as the light and the scent of stew.

―――――――

Swords often gave Sentinels away. Bonemasks and layers of furs could conceal other people's identities, but a Sentinel's blade was hard to mistake for any other. The amethyst in Katrine's Coran glinted in the brazier's light, and Olvir only took a moment longer to connect the sapphire with Vivian.

He'd seen her here and there since they'd talked, but both of them had always been very occupied with their duties as the camp prepared itself for the storm. As she pushed back her hood and unstrapped the bonemask, leaving her charcoal-rimmed eyes bare, Olvir found himself at a loss for words. Having spoken of weighty matters, it was hard to find his path to the lighter ones.

Fortunately, singing took care of it. There were five others in the tent, and two of them were silent, but Morgan and the two baritones with her were vigorously making up for the lack.

"O that my love were in my arms," the verse wound to a conclusion, the singers' low tones providing a comforting counter to the high shrieking of the wind beyond the walls, "and I in my bed again."

"Not that I'd insist on a bed," said one of the men, tipping Morgan a wink.

Vivian laughed. "That's the difference between twenty and forty, good man," she said. "I'd take the bed in a heartbeat right now, with love or without."

"So would I, if I'd been standing out for a day," said the other man who'd been singing. He dipped the ladle into the stew and held it up, offering the handle. "Come get 'round a bit of turnip and let's-call-it-bacon."

The two women stepped forward, but then Katrine stopped and turned, peeling off her bonemask in the meantime. She tilted her head slightly, in the manner of a hunting hawk, and studied the men who hadn't been singing. "I'm afraid I need to ask who you are."

Olvir hadn't recognized them either. They'd come in with the others, back from refreshing the lights. Their faces looked vaguely familiar, but he couldn't place them, particularly as they'd kept their hoods raised and were half-buried in piles of fur. He'd thought the cold must have lingered for them—some felt it more easily than others—and hoped they'd feel better after stew.

"Why?" asked one. He had a strange voice, low and clotted. That might have been his wrappings or an earlier injury, but given the way Katrine was acting… Olvir rose to his feet.

"I'm Jan," the other said quickly, his voice similar. "He's Bres."

Morgan and the soldiers around the stewpot had been watching quietly, but now the man who'd winked at Morgan placed the ladle in the stew, shaking his head. "Nobody named that in our outfit," he said.

"It could be a simple mix-up," said Olvir. He didn't reach for his sword, but he became aware exactly how quickly he could draw it. "The storm confuses things. Which regiment are you from, gentlemen?"

The one who'd given names sucked a wet breath through his teeth. "Criwath."

"There's a lot of Criwath," said Vivian. "I think you'd better take those hoods off. A peek at your faces could clear up a fair amount."

Olvir couldn't be certain what gave the "men" away. Insight didn't bother listing its reasons. His sword was out when they changed.

It only took a second. Their features crumbled like the snow outside. Red muscle glistened beneath, apparently bare of skin. Jaws and arms stretched too long, claws shot through leather gloves, and mouths gaped to reveal three rows of black barbed teeth. These were the twistedmen, Thyran's creatures, emerging from disguises that they'd never worn before.

Ignoring everyone else in the tent, they both rushed toward Olvir.

Chapter 4

ONE OF THE TWISTEDMEN BATTED A SOLDIER OUT OF THE WAY as the man was trying to scramble to his feet, an almost casual blow from the outsized arm sending him flying into the tent's canvas wall. Olvir glimpsed red and smelled blood. He couldn't tell any more, because the monster was on him then.

He slashed out, equaling the thing's speed. It was too close—the blow was awkward and half-strength—but it opened a line down the right side of the twistedman, enough to give most such things pause.

This one didn't care. Like the wild boars in the Criwath forest, it simply snarled and charged forward, slashing down with its talons to seek purchase in Olvir's guts. He blocked one blow with his sword, stumbled sideways to dodge the other, and banged his side against the burning brazier. Immediately he corrected his course—setting the tent on fire would only make the situation worse—and retreated over a bedroll that wanted to tangle his feet, as if the tent and its contents had themselves sided with Thyran's forces.

Olvir dodged around the tent's central pole. That brought his shield within reach, so he scooped it up to meet the next strike. He used the force to pivot and twist, stepping around the debris on the floor. As the creature advanced, he swung the blade up through its rib cage.

The thing shrieked. Blood poured from its mouth, but the black sockets of its eyes flamed.

It leapt, driving Olvir's sword deeper into its chest as it threw its whole dying weight against his shield. He staggered back, trying to shove it away. Its breath on his face was blizzard-cold and reeking.

"Soul…" it gurgled. The maw gaped again. The long neck twisted.

Olvir jerked his head to the side just in time. Barbed teeth grazed the skin over his jugular and snapped together on empty air. The twistedman sank its claws into his shield, seeking better purchase.

Silver Wind, take my spirit, Olvir called out silently, struggling to get his sword arm free of the weight, *for I have always tried to serve you.*

The monster lunged.

A set of gloved fingers grabbed its skinless skull, then yanked backward. A dagger sank deep into the spot where that skull met the neck beneath.

The twistedman's jaws shut on air. They stayed closed.

"That," Vivien said as the dead creature slid down Olvir's shield to become a vile heap on the ground, "was profoundly unexpected."

━━━━━━

Vivian stripped off her gloves. At least one of them was probably ruined. Both stank. So did her coat, but there were more layers between that and her skin.

Her mood had been worse, but those times had been few and far between.

For their sakes, you must be a wall, Ulamir reminded her. *Show no cracks.*

It was good advice. Already she saw fear in the faces around the tent—not yet panic but the potential for it. One soldier was kneeling by his friend, pressing a cloth to the man's wounds. The other knight was picking themselves up from where the second twistedman had thrown them with its dying blow. Katrine was cleaning her sword. Although her hands were steady, Vivian recognized the lines near her mouth.

They'd both fought more enemies, and more deadly ones. They all had, by that point in the war. None had taken them so much by surprise, though, or sought a lone target with the single-minded, suicidal focus Vivian had recently seen.

She commanded at least one person there. The only one who might match her for rank was Olvir, who'd just nearly had his throat ripped out.

"Good work, everyone," Vivian said, deliberately dropping her voice down further into her chest. It was more reassuring that way, she'd found. "All alive? Should I go and fetch a Mourner?"

"No, no," said the wounded man. His voice was pained but strong. "Bastard got me in the shoulder. Be a while before I can fight, worse luck, but Kev'll bind it up fine for the moment."

"Good man," said Olvir. He sounded only a touch out of breath. Vivian wasn't shocked, given how well the knight had maintained his composure the rest of the time she'd known him, but she admired him for meeting this latest and worst test so readily. "I'll help you over to the tent when we're done here."

"Are *you* all right?" Katrine asked.

"Yes. Thanks be to Tinival, and to all of you as well. I'd bow, but I fear I'm likely to fall over."

"No blame to you if you did," said Olvir's fellow knight. "I'd no idea you were such an appealing target."

"Neither had I." When Olvir spoke, Vivian noticed a series of red lines marking the right side of his winter-pale neck, evidence of how close the twistedman had gotten.

"And they were in here with us all the while," said Kev.

"I'd imagine their plan was to wait until Sir Yoralth left, then slip out after and ambush him, or to bide their time until the others took their leave. Katrine ruined that idea neatly. Well done," Vivian added.

"So the gods forged me," Katrine said, the traditional answer in such circumstances—not that there were many circumstances similar to those they were now in.

"But you were the one who heeded their call," said Vivian. She went to run a hand through her hair, realized that the hand in question was coated with twistedman blood, and allowed herself a grimace. "I'll have a word with Magarteach and the others. It'd be best if we established signs and countersigns when our forces come in, now that we know they can resemble us."

"A rough resemblance, but yes," said the knight. They frowned suddenly. "Do you think there are more? That they've gone after others?"

"I doubt it," said Vivian. "We'd have heard the noise, just as I'm sure others have heard ours. We'll have company soon. And they seemed to ignore the rest of us."

"There've been"—Olvir actually blushed a little, as if he was afraid they'd think he was bragging—"strange things about me since the war started. Since Oakford. Thyran might have wanted to get rid of a threat, or get revenge."

"It spoke to you before it died, sir," said the unwounded soldier. "What'd it say?"

"'Soul.'" Olvir's broad forehead wrinkled. "But I've never heard of the twistedmen eating those. The dalhan, yes, but...do you think Thyran's combined the two?"

"No." Memory stirred in Vivian, like the memory of Oakford when she'd spoken to Olvir a few days earlier: words breaching the surface of a sea of reports. "I think there may be another meaning. I'll have to check, but we may both need to go talk to a few more people soon."

Chapter 5

"Sir Yoralth." Magarteach eyed Olvir with no particular sign of recognition. Olvir wasn't surprised. There were a thousand people at the outpost. "Seems you've made things interesting."

"Not my intention, General, I assure you."

The general had offered a camp stool. Olvir had preferred to stand: the attack had been a day ago, and the god-touched healed quickly. He'd realized, too late, that standing made him feel like a criminal on trial—or a two-headed calf at a fair. He tried to trust in Tinival, as well as his knowledge of his own innocence, as he took stock of the yurt's smoky interior and the people gathered there.

Lord Marshal Nahon, his direct commander, sat on one end, frowning. He'd known about Oakford, of course, but the war transformed events from a mere six or eight months before into faint historical notes. Now his strange knight's strangeness had become a matter of immediate concern, and he clearly didn't enjoy the development.

Next came Magarteach, then Vivian, and finally a priest who wore the gold robes of Sitha over sturdy travel clothing. They were short, thin, and bleached-looking, with a not-quite-present cast to their pale-gray eyes. By those signs, Olvir recognized a senior member of the Golden Lady's clergy—and knew he hadn't seen them in camp before. He didn't want to consider the significance of that too closely.

"It could be to our advantage, in the end," said Vivian. Olvir could tell that she wasn't trying to reassure him, which was itself more reassuring than otherwise. "We've discovered, with no fatalities, that the twistedmen can assume some semblance of human form. If that was all, that would be useful. It isn't."

"No," said Nahon, "but I wouldn't call the rest 'useful.'"

"It may be," said the priest. "And it may need to be." They exchanged glances with Magarteach. "Have you told them?"

"No. I haven't had the opportunity since you told me. This is Gwarill," the general said. "He's come from the western shore, from Amris. Got in with the storm on his heels."

In a moment, Olvir stopped being the most interesting thing in the room. General Amris had gone to the western shore to advise the Princess-Regent of Kvanla on defenses, in case Thyran was planning an attack by sea. Gerant was consulting with the wizards there about potential methods of stopping Thyran's various magics.

Messages between Kvanla and Criwath were unreliable at the best of times. Gwarill bore the first news they'd gotten in weeks, and everyone hung on his words.

"I was sent," he said, "to collect information but also to give it, and this is no occasion for gentleness. This storm isn't natural. Poram's archpriest had been sensing disruptions for a while, but he's lately become certain. Thyran's started his old spell working once again."

Magarteach hissed in breath like they'd suffered a physical wound. Nahon whispered Tinival's name. Vivian was completely still. Olvir watched all of them and himself from a mile away, noting the twisting sickness at the pit of his stomach without really feeling it. They'd all known of the possibility. They'd all feared it. Every snowstorm in the winter had been the subject of talk among the whole camp. There had been no point in the speculation, no definite conclusion they could come to, but everybody had talked regardless.

Now it was fact.

The five of them sat and stared, partly at one another but mostly off into space. Olvir thought each of the others was hearing childhood stories again or seeing the worst parts of history books. He certainly was.

A hundred years in the past, the storms had gone on for years.

They'd been bad enough at their peak to kill off all life outside shelter in some places. People had frozen, starved, or worse. Many had survived because Thyran hadn't totally succeeded: Amris and Gerant had cast him into a hundred-year sleep, letting the storms out of his control before they could build too much strength.

The odds of that happening again were low.

"What can be done?" Nahon asked.

"Amris and Gerant have some notions of shelter and preparation," said Gwarill. "No idea how the spell could be stopped, except by the same methods as before. It's not likely we'll get that chance. My order no longer has the knowledge to construct the spell of stasis, for one thing."

"I've started plans," said Magarteach. "Food, shelter, defense. I'm still struggling with the details, so I'll likely need to consult with all of you."

"I'll do what I can, of course," said Olvir, "but, Brother Gwarill, what else did we learn in the attempt on me that we can use? If there's any way I can help prevent this or keep people safe—"

"I have no doubt of it," said the priest. "I've heard you had dreams. Repeating ones. When did they start?"

"A little more than two months ago."

"So I would have expected," said Gwarill. "Sentinel, perhaps you'd best take over."

———

Vivian had taken notes, once she'd had a few hours to go through her correspondence. She thanked both the gods and her past self that she had, or she might have lost her conclusions entirely in shock at Gwarill's news. She was grateful to Olvir, too, for bringing the conversation back. The end of the world was too large to take in at once—with a nibble at a time and other subjects in between, she might be able to handle it.

"This comes from Heliodar," she said, "from Sentinel Branwyn and the Mourner Zelen, who was previously Lord Zelen Verengir. Last autumn, they discovered that most of the Verengir family had worshipped Gizath for several generations. Those living were dealt with appropriately. Among the evidence they found were notes that the previous generation had incarnated some or all of what certain stonekin legends refer to as the Sundered Soul, the Remnant, or the Heart of Gizath."

She saw Olvir sway backward. It was a slight movement, before his discipline kicked in, but it contained all the revulsion she could ever imagine. He'd worked it out already. In some ways, that would make the rest easier.

Speed would be merciful now, said Ulamir.

It was more mercy than Vivian had been able to give herself. She'd learned quickly to sleep when she could, no matter what the state of her mind, but that hadn't held up the night before. Ulamir had been with her when she'd stared into the darkness, trying to reconcile what she'd learned with the man she knew.

She'd reached no peace, just an inescapable conclusion. Now she made the final blow as swift as she could.

"Either Gizath gave up his heart to kill his sister's lover, or she splintered his soul when she attacked him in revenge. Whatever the fragment is, it would likely be extremely powerful."

"And the Verengirs tried to make it a person." Magarteach rolled their eyes. "Heliodar. What happened?"

"A fire. A number of deaths. That evidently gave one of their servants second thoughts. He stole the child and vanished."

"And that's me, isn't it?" Despite the silence of the yurt, it was hard to hear Olvir. "The child with part of the Traitor God in him?"

Nahon was shaking his head before Olvir had finished. "It can't be. You took an oath. Tinival would have denied you, or worse."

"Yes, if hosting Gizath's fragment meant you shared Gizath's fall," said Gwarill, hitting the *if* heavily. "The shard may be what Gizath could have been—the potential for good that he left behind in the moment when he struck. It may only be power. I can't say, but I would suspect that Verengir was hoping for innate corruption or simple power. Thyran, quite probably, does likewise."

"Then why would Gizath's followers want Olvir dead?" Nahon asked, abandoning one line of attack and switching to the next.

Vivian wished he'd convinced her, or that she hadn't thought of the counterargument already. "To start over," she said.

Magarteach stood up. "Maybe they expect they won't have to." They took a poker and went to stir the fire. "From the sound of it, they did this before Thyran came back. His presence makes things different. You die now, maybe the rest of Gizath goes to him."

Even though Olvir was staring straight ahead, he met nobody's eyes. "My death wouldn't serve our purposes either, then," he said, toneless.

"Quite the opposite," Gwarill replied. "You may be our best chance at thwarting Thyran's spells."

Olvir's self-control abandoned him then. He turned an incredulous gaze to the priest. "How?" he demanded, "I'm sorry, Brother, but... I've tried to repeat what I did at Oakford. Half a dozen wizards have inspected me, and priests of all the Four. I meditated. I prayed. All that ever changed were those damned dreams."

"And that may be for the best," Nahon said, brows drawn inward. "If this is true, it could be more danger than help contacting that thing inside you."

Gwarill glanced around the yurt, pausing at each face in turn, then reached for a metal case by his side. "That's the other reason I'm here," he said. "There are no mortals equipped to judge the best path forward. We must let the Golden Lady do what she can for us."

His heart beat in his ears. Olvir listened for an off note.

That was stupid. He'd been examined many times: regularly by the Mourners as he grew, thoroughly when he'd begun training and then before he'd taken his vows, as part of his healing for every serious wound, and most recently after Oakford. Nobody had ever listened to his chest and run shrieking into the night. Nobody had said they'd heard the slightest strangeness.

What would it have sounded like anyhow? An extra beat? An evil laugh instead of a pulse?

He took a breath. That was the same too. It felt almost like a betrayal—*ha-ha*—that his body continued working the same way it had or that it had put in nearly thirty years of working exactly like that of a normal man.

The Sundered Soul. The Heart of Gizath. It had been sleeping within him for his entire life, if Vivian and Gwarill were right. Olvir couldn't come up with any reason they weren't.

Sitha's priest lifted a small gold-and-silver cube to his lap and undid unseen latches. It happened at a distance, in a room where another man stood.

All four sides of the box opened. A gold-furred spider with a body the size of a man's fist sat inside, raising its forelegs as if in greeting. Maybe it was saying hello. Sitha's creatures were supposed to be fairly bright, in addition to their other powers.

"Sir Yoralth, please come forward," said Gwarill. "Hold out your right hand."

Aware of the others watching him, of Vivian most of all, Olvir extended his hand and kept it motionless as the spider climbed onto his open palm. Small, furred legs tapped against his skin, tickling but not unpleasant. Eight eyes regarded him, each ink-black with a tiny golden sphere in the center.

The spider was the only thing moving in the room. It held its place for a while, its legs tapping steadily as though to send a message or to judge him for some internal quality: soundness, perhaps, or ripeness. Then it scurried up his arm to his shoulder, leapt to the beam supporting the yurt's roof, and finally dropped down on a long golden thread.

It dangled there and began to spin.

Chapter 6

Gold letters took shape, encased in a scant circle of web. The spider moved in long, slow drops and reverses, each line seeming to take considerable effort.

Prophecy is heavier than mountains. It's a small creature to bear the Golden Lady's burdens, said Ulamir.

Everybody is, Vivian thought.

The first word formed in the web as they watched: *heart.*

"Thyran's heart? Olvir's?" Magarteach asked. "Or is it confirming what we suspected?"

Gwarill didn't look away from the web when he replied. "Both. Either. Neither. I have no more means of knowing than you. If she has the strength, we'll see."

The spider plunged down, looped around, and swung back, attaching silk in motions too quick and small for Vivian to track. A *B* formed beneath the *H*, then an *A*.

"Battle," said Nahon. "The heart of the battle? Or a battle within the heart? I… Wait. There's another letter forming."

They'd expected *battle,* but not the *F* after it. None of them were in any doubt after they saw it, however, even before the *I* appeared.

"Battlefield," said Olvir. "Heart of the Battlefield."

There were many battlefields in the war, with many hearts. There'd already been many others in the world when Thyran came back. Vivian knew which one the spider meant despite all that. From the others' faces, she knew that they did too.

The Battlefield.

Olvir had heard the story growing up. Everyone did. There were variations, depending on what had been passed down and how much patience the mother or priest or nurse telling the tale had, but the basics remained the same.

Once upon a time, the gods had walked the earth with mortals. There hadn't been humans yet, but the waterfolk and stonekin had been present. Letar had been the goddess of healing and love, death, and fire, but vengeance hadn't yet entered her domain. There hadn't been any need for it.

She'd fallen in love with Veryon, one of the stonekin. Her youngest brother hadn't liked the idea of a goddess consorting with a mortal, so he'd lured Veryon to what had then been a pleasant grove, ambushed him there, and killed him.

Gizath hadn't reckoned with his sister's wit. She hadn't fully realized the extent of her brother's evil. Letar had followed him and Veryon, expecting to intervene in a fight. She'd arrived to see her lover fall with Gizath's dagger in his back. Then she'd launched herself at her brother's throat.

Gods had never tried to kill each other before. It didn't work particularly well. When the other three arrived, Letar and Gizath had only managed to wound each other slightly, but they'd devastated the land for miles nearby. That, as much as Veryon's death, had convinced the other gods to leave the mortal world after they'd banished Gizath.

The place where they'd fought, the Battlefield, was still there beyond the northern mountains. Even before Thyran, when the north hadn't been so cut off, travelers and tribesfolk alike had given it wide berth. Olvir had never heard of any living being coming out, certainly not of anybody going in.

"What would I do there?" he asked.

Nobody answered. Nobody could, except the spider, which dropped down from the web and onto the floor of the yurt. It landed on its back, legs curled against its belly. The sight pulled Olvir out of his own distress.

"Poor creature," he said. Kneeling down, he reached gently for her. "Can we help her?"

"She's come to the end of her strength," Gwarill said, sounding only a trace regretful. "There are many paths to the future. Seeing so far as to reliably select the best action is hard on flesh, even such altered flesh as the Weaver's creatures possess. The prophet will return to Sitha and be reborn."

The spider was already fading, literally. Her golden shape shimmered, became transparent, then began to vanish from the ends of her legs inward. "Is she in pain?"

"No."

The web still hung in its place. Olvir got to his feet and looked at it, wanting the message to change but not foolish enough to hope it would. Then he turned his attention to the rest of the room.

All the other people there were watching him. Some were probably expecting tears or anger, perhaps flat refusal. Olvir had all those impulses. He was a normal man. He'd done his duty every day, and while he'd made mistakes, he'd always tried his hardest. This was his reward, it seemed.

All he could do was try to be better than what he carried.

He turned to Gwarill first. "It's more than I'd have known otherwise. Thank you. Praise be to Sitha, the Builder."

The rest of the impromptu council echoed him, high and low voices blending together in a quiet chorus.

"We can equip you, once the storm's properly over," said Nahon, shaking his graying head as he spoke. "The twistedmen may not notice one man by himself, or there may be a path to the mountains that'll keep you hidden. Your Sentinel, Emeth…" he added, looking to Vivian as sudden insight struck him. "She talks to the beasts. Perhaps she could find him a clear route?"

"If there is one, she's the best person to find it," Vivian said, and then, without changing her tone or drawing a breath, as though she were reporting the watch schedule for the day, she went on. "She'll be doing so for both of us, by the way."

———————

One of the good things about Vivian's present company was that it was disciplined.

None of the other four in the yurt shouted, leapt immediately to denial, or demanded a full explanation in the wake of her announcement. Gwarill simply nodded; Vivian wondered if he'd known in advance what she'd say. Nahon lifted his eyebrows but looked relieved.

Olvir and Magarteach spoke, essentially at once.

"You don't have to," he said. "It's my duty."

Magarteach asked, "Why, and why you?"

"Physical dangers aside, we have no clue what the Battlefield does to people who get near it or how the…fragment…will react. You could go into a trance," she said to Olvir, "or simply fall over, as you did at Oakford. That strikes me as a bad situation in general, doubly so out in the middle of the north."

"Oh. I hadn't thought of that, but you're right," Olvir frowned. "You're needed here, though."

"Katrine is fully as capable of command as I am, only slightly junior."

Very slightly, said Ulamir, to whom five years had meant as little as a single dawn even when he was alive.

Vivian suppressed a laugh and continued. "At my reforging, Poram gave me the ability to find any place I concentrate on. I'm fairly confident that it'll be useful in Sir Yoralth's mission."

"Damn well would be," Magarteach said, "even if the mountains are pretty obvious. I'd bet the Battlefield is, too, once you see it from above."

"That is only so much help from the ground," Gwarill replied.

"Finally, Ulamir, my soulsword, was stonekin. He lived on this side of the mountains, but he was one of the older peoples, with their affinity for the land."

Your praise would make me blush if I yet had cheeks to do so.

Vivian gave the others a moment. They were unlikely to sway her, they didn't have the authority to stop her, but listening did no harm.

"You would be valuable company," said Nahon.

Magarteach sighed. "You're right about Katrine too. I don't love losing two of you, but from what you're saying"—they jerked their chin toward Gwarill—"if you don't succeed at this, my front won't matter a whole lot regardless."

"That's a simplified view," the priest replied, "and incorrect in a few notable aspects. If they fail and the protections we create hold, those here will need to face Thyran's troops. If they succeed, there's no guarantee that Sir Yoralth will be able to stop the army, only the storms. All the same, I think the Sentinel should go."

"And you?" Vivian asked Olvir. "Even if you only have a gut feeling, you should say so."

He focused on Vivian for the first time since she'd revealed his nature and managed a small smile. "No, no feelings," he said. "Except that I'd be glad to have a companion, and even happier if it was you."

Affection made her smile back, despite the guilt twisting her chest. She'd provided three reasons. The fourth was best left unsaid.

Chapter 7

Melted wax poured red onto the oiled paper, spreading out like lifeblood. Vivian pressed the ring on her right hand into it. It left a capital V with stylized guard towers on each side.

"You may as well take the ring too," she said to Emeth. "Where I'm going, the best it'll do is make me lose a finger." Once she was certain the seal had taken shape, she stripped off the gold band and laid it on top of the small parcel.

"Are you taking any gear, other than the clothes you're standing up in?" Emeth asked.

She and Katrine stood in Vivian's tent, which now showed little sign that anybody had lived there. Vivian's pack and bedroll stood waiting in a corner. Katrine would inherit the tent itself, along with the brazier in the center. Emeth would come with her—probably getting rid of the need for a brazier altogether, at least until the next storm hit.

The rest—a bundle of letters, a small portrait in a silver frame, and a few bits of cheap jewelry from the towns Vivian had passed through—was tied up in the parcel she gave to Emeth.

"Two changes of linen, for both of our sakes and so that my scent doesn't draw every tracking beast in Thyran's army. Rations. Rope. Spikes. Flint and steel. Crossbow. Bedroll. The usual."

She'd debated the bedroll, but while cold wouldn't kill her, it'd slow her reflexes and wits if it was bad. On the mountains, in a storm, it might well be.

"And a knight," said Emeth.

"He's taking her, if we're being accurate."

"We're traveling together. He has the maps," said Vivian. The others had been informed only that he had a mission in the Battlefield. Nobody save the Sentinels, the highest-ranked priests, and Magarteach had been told that much. "Katrine, do you have any questions before I leave?"

The blond Sentinel shook her head and recited her previous briefing, obviously reassuring herself as well as Vivian. "Armies from the west should be here in a day or two. We can expect an attack roughly then, depending on how soon Thyran gets word that they're coming and that General Amris is with them. We're currently reinforcing the walls."

"That'll take some of the attention off the two of you at any rate," Emeth added. "If it'd help, I'll try to look like a bigger target."

"And how would you do that, exactly?" Vivian asked, feeling a corner of her mouth lift.

"Get a mage to make me glow as Kat does when the bastards show up. Or just make faces and yell rude remarks. Haven't really decided yet."

"I'm sure you'll weigh all sides of the issue."

"You know me, Vivian. Always a woman for careful consideration."

"I could tell a different story," said Katrine.

Emeth chuckled. "You could tell many stories, Kat. Commander…" She lifted a shoulder, leather armor creaking. "It keeps sounding odd to say that. Look, I don't have a damn notion what you're doing, but I hope it works and I hope you live through it."

Neither outcome was ever a guarantee when a Sentinel went to work. Neither had ever been certain, war or no war. The gods had reforged the Sentinels, but a different god had touched most of their prey, with less concern than the Four had to have for mortal minds and bodies. Vivian knew very few members of the Order who'd made it to their fifties.

"Much obliged," she said. "I hope so, too, and that you both do well out here while I'm gone. If you do and I don't—"

Emeth tapped the parcel gently. "Toriat, the farm of Ioan Wheelwright. West of the mill."

She recited with the same air that her lover had, which made Vivian smile and ache at once.

"Precisely," she said and held out her hand. "I can't thank you enough, either of you, and for more than these present duties. You know that."

Emeth grasped Vivian's forearm firmly. "Things have to be done, so we do them. Be careful out there."

"I'll pray for you," said Katrine when it was her turn for the arm-clasping. "Not that I doubt the gods will be paying you plenty of attention as things stand, but I prefer to believe I'll help."

"If they use you as a focusing lens, I'm sure they'll do as much as remotely possible," said Vivian.

She let go, turned, and picked up her pack. The mission didn't let her stall. She was glad of it. There would always have been something else to say, one final question, a last check, but it was time to go.

———

"No," said Olvir. "The impulse is generous, but I can't travel with too much weight, and I wouldn't want to take too many provisions away from the front. Honestly, we have a better chance of hunting food, or finding it, than you all do."

Nahon couldn't really argue that point. Foraging parties ventured a little way into the forest at times, when Emeth's bird scouts said that the twistedmen were nowhere near, but only for brief periods.

"This side of the mountains, perhaps," he said. "I don't know that much grows on their peaks. As for the Battlefield, I wouldn't eat any plant or animal within three days' ride of that spot."

The storm had stopped. Spring had reasserted itself quickly, with blue skies above the yard where Olvir packed, and warm breezes carrying birdsong to his ears when Nahon stopped speaking. Over near the base of the palisades, a few purple buds showed that crocuses had made it through. Olvir wanted to take all those things as good omens, but he understood too much to let himself.

He understood, also, both layers of what his commander was really saying. One he knew from his own command: *Let me do something. I can't protect you from your fate, I can't share it, but there must be a way I can help.*

Nahon tried to hide the other, but the knights had never been good at subterfuge. It had been a day since the meeting in the yurt. Olvir's commander had spoken with him a few times, always putting more distance between them than he ever had before, then moving a few inches closer when he realized it.

They'd known each other since Olvir had started his training, a lad with weedy arms and a constantly cracking voice, and the marshal had been a rawboned young knight with the first shine remaining on his armor.

Now it was an effort to look each other in the face.

Nahon wanted him gone, hated himself for it, hated the practicality of it more—and so kept making the offer.

Olvir would have said yes, whatever the motive, under normal circumstances. Extra supplies were never really a bad thing. There were the other soldiers to consider, though. As Gwarill had said, they'd still be facing the twistedmen if Olvir succeeded. If he failed, food would be worth more than gold.

"Two days' extra, then," he said, compromising. "And thank you for it."

"It's an important mission," said Nahon. "I wouldn't spoil a good horse with old shoes."

"I suppose there's a reason they put you in charge here," said Olvir, his own throat thicker than he'd have liked. He glanced down at the bag he was packing, once again going through his mental list to be sure he hadn't left some important item behind.

He was taking few belongings. Cleanliness—illness could be as deadly as the twistedmen, and some of them tracked by smell—dictated a few changes of linen, a flask of liquor for cleaning wounds, and another skin of fairly sour wine for purifying any water they found. Nahon's extra rations would make five days' worth of food. Then there were light blankets that rolled up into a small bundle, a few bandages, flint, steel, and a short coil of rope. The marshal had given him two maps as well, both painstakingly constructed copies of those that had been drawn a hundred years earlier.

Olvir would wear his light armor, the chain muffled with strips of cloth, and carry his sword, shield, and knives as well as a short bow and a quiver of arrows. He'd already painstakingly dulled the shield he'd equally painstakingly polished a few nights before the storm.

He had checked all the details, keeping his mind clear while he did so. He'd been a warrior and a knight. Now it was time to be human. He met Nahon's eyes squarely, seeing the tears standing there and letting his own fill in response.

"You know how much I owe you, I hope," he said. "For leading here, for helping me along my path. For being my friend. Tinival's blessed me, but I couldn't have come so far in his service, or lived so long, without you."

He couldn't say *I don't blame you*, or *I wouldn't trust me entirely either*. Tinival valued truth, but some truth would only cause more trouble than it was worth. On Nahon's face, he saw all the words the marshal couldn't speak. Nahon embraced Olvir quickly instead, his mustache rasping against Olvir's cheek with the kiss of friendship.

The knights' missions weren't as regularly deadly as the Sentinels' or the Blades', but they went into danger often enough.

Olvir had said goodbye to friends when none of them had been certain they'd meet again. He'd only known the odds against it to be nearly so long once before, at Oakford, and that had just been his body at risk.

He didn't know what it would mean to return from this mission.

All the same, that departure was very nearly the same as others had been when one or all of the people involved was going into danger. Words could never fully contain love, fear, or grief, and all three mingled at such moments. Tinival had given speech to mortals, but even his knights couldn't say all that was in their hearts.

So Olvir reached for the old phrases that everybody made do, and which, by virtue of everybody knowing that they would never be sufficient, went as far as speech ever could. "Silver Wind be at your back, my friend and comrade."

"May he give strength to your arm, your mind, and your heart," said Nahon. He stepped back from the embrace. Rather than giving Olvir the salute of a higher-ranked knight to a lower, he bowed as if to his lord. "Know that you go to serve his truth and that the love of your fellows goes with you."

———————

In a small tent off the main infirmary, Vivian and Olvir met with Gwarill one last time. They didn't bother with light, but the priest's gold robes still shone.

"You have not tried to contact the fragment of Gizath?" he asked Olvir without preamble. It was barely a question. "Not knowing what it is."

"No. I meditated after Oakford, of course, but nothing happened. Last night—"

Vivian didn't look at Olvir. It would have been too awkward to witness either what he felt or his efforts to conceal it.

"It seemed too dangerous," he finished.

"Wise. I would do so when you reach the mountains and not before," Gwarill said. "Physical distance is less…distant… where matters of the gods are concerned, but it still can have influence. The closer to the Battlefield you are, the more likely it is to work, and the farther from Thyran you get, the safer you're likely to be."

Olvir bowed. "I hear and treasure Sitha's wisdom."

"I have faith in your valor, Sir Yoralth. Sentinel, stay behind a moment."

After Olvir left, Gwarill remained silent until they heard his footsteps growing fainter. Then he picked an object up off one of the cots and handed it to Vivian. "This is from Mourner Dale, chiefly, though I contributed as well."

It was a carving the size of her palm, made of smooth-sanded pale wood: yew, Vivian thought, though she was no expert. A woman's weeping face had taken shape under the carver's knife. Painted tears ran down her cheeks, black and red alternating.

Powerfully enchanted, said Ulamir, *or as much so as human arts can manage on short notice.*

"He'll need to touch it," said Gwarill, "and swear to his identity. Neither of us can be certain what it will do if that oath is false in any sense, but there will be some reaction. You understand."

"I do," she said.

She had knives in her boots and up her sleeves, Ulamir by her side, and the gods' gifts in her speed and strength. In addition, she knew Olvir both in and out of battle. That was all the advantage any of them were likely to get.

"His death serves no purpose unless we're desperate," said Gwarill. There was a consolation in the reminder, but then he went on, stripping even that away. "But the nearer you get to the Battlefield, the more likely that the fragment will simply return there rather than going to Thyran. I can't tell you the moment when the risk balances toward one course of action or another,

Sentinel, or the signs that his potential for destruction outweighs his use. We must all trust your judgment."

Duty had been heavy at times. Command had weighed the world. There was no comparison for this.

Vivian only nodded and found all the words she had. "If the need arises, I won't hesitate."

Chapter 8

THE PALISADE FACED THE FOREST WITH A ROUGH BUT ALMOST seamless front studded by makeshift towers. Large forces had to approach from the back, since rock outcroppings blocked the side, but small parties could use a door beneath the rightmost tower.

Wind stirred Vivian's hair as she waited there, watching the sky for Emeth's messenger. Olvir stood by her, and near them Kev, the soldier who hadn't been wounded during the assassination attempt. All of them were trying to act as if this was no different from any other hunting expedition. Vivian hoped she was succeeding. The others weren't.

If the twistedmen can read your countenances, you have a great deal more to be concerned about, said Ulamir.

There was that. Her father had used to say that such-and-so flaw in appearance would never be noticed from a trotting horse. Vivian supposed it was the same thing, only likely to be more lethal.

Olvir was the first to spot the speck in the blue sky. "There," he said, pointing as it grew bigger. "Is that what I think?"

"Likely," said Emeth. She held out her arm. The spot soared downward, taking on wings, a long tail, and a head with a high crest. Up close, it was lavender-blue above and white below, with black markings. It regarded all of them with an expression that Vivian thought was derisive as well as suspicious.

The twilight wren landed on Emeth's wrist, emitted sounds like a rusty gate swinging back and forth, then waited, head cocked sideways.

"Thyran's keeping his creatures an hour or so away," she told her human companions. "Building siege ladders, it looks like, which means trouble for us soon. I'll spread the word once we're back. But this is our moment."

"Then let's use it to best effect," said Olvir. He opened the door.

Vivian and Emeth went out first, not running but moving briskly over the plantless swath of ground between the palisade and the forest.

The land was dark, bare, empty except for the four of them. Their feet pattered across the packed earth. No voices escaped the wall. Noises from the forest were still distant. It was an alien feeling, but an advantageous one—any attacker would give them plenty of warning.

Slowly the fortress, Vivian's home for the past year, receded. The trees loomed up ahead. Darkness spread under their leaves. That was a point in their favor, too, but Vivian had to remind herself of the advantage.

"Head left," said Emeth quietly. "There's a game trail. Takes us through some underbrush."

They veered to one side, passing beneath the first branches that the defenders had left intact. Vivian spotted the trail Emeth had mentioned, which was barely more than a slightly worn spot in the undergrowth. Most animals had stopped coming so far out months before.

She took the lead, Olvir falling in behind her. Branches were their greatest danger at first, and Vivian used Ulamir to great effect, slicing off any bit that threatened to put an eye out or snag on their clothing.

As they went on, alert for movement on any side, their passage did get easier. Game was scarce here, so close to both humanity and the twistedmen, but elk, bear, and larger beasts had roamed freely once. The path still bore the tracks of their passage. Moreover, the deeper shade farther into the forest killed off most of the underbrush.

It would have been a pleasant walk in other circumstances. Leaves were unfurling on the trees that weren't evergreens, blue sky occasionally showed through the cracks above, and sunlight filtered down in small patches. Alert as Vivian was, her body responded favorably to new sights and sounds, to freedom from the same walls and people she'd been looking at for weeks, and to the chance to stretch her legs without actively being in danger of losing them.

The body was fundamentally illogical. There were many times when this was unfortunate, but a few when it came in handy. Trouble would be in good supply in the future. For the moment, there was the forest, the day, and for some variety of last time, her friends.

Vivian kept her sword out, kept watching the trees for movement and listening for sounds, but let her chest ease and her breathing deepen. When a smile snuck onto her face, she let it linger there.

All was not well. It never was. She'd learned, over the years, that it didn't have to be.

Vivian's shoulders had a slightly jaunty set to them as the group went onward, Olvir noticed. He wasn't observing her most of the time, trying to scan the forest for threats instead, but she was ahead of him. Forming an impression or two was inevitable.

Therefore Olvir noticed that Vivian walked as though she were really on a hunting party on some noble estate rather than the middle of hostile territory. He also noticed the firm roundness of her backside and the length of her pleasantly curving legs, clearly outlined by tight gray deerskin, but quickly brought his attention back above her waist, doing his best to be respectful.

They hadn't had to travel much when they'd worked together before, so Vivian's long, light stride hadn't made an impression on

Olvir. Now he took note. Emeth had something of the same pace she did, which meant it was likely part of the Order of the Dawn's training, but Emeth was shorter, her body more angular and her motions choppier. She darted from one spot to the next, while Vivian glided.

Granted, Emeth also had a shorter journey in front of her.

It wasn't very long, in fact, before she stopped and held up a hand, bringing the other three to a halt. They stood in a small bare patch, not quite big enough to be a clearing worth the name, with spots of dark-green moss and yellow-green celandine breaking up the brown of the dirt.

Emeth reached into a pouch at her waist and came out with a palm full of wheat kernels. Looking up into the trees, she pursed her lips. The sound that emerged was exactly like the calls of greenwings that Olvir had been hearing every spring of his life. A young member of that species promptly flew down, ate a few of the kernels, and sat on Emeth's wrist.

The Sentinel let out another series of chirps and trills. Vivian chuckled. "Sure, she can talk to every creature but the nobility," she told Olvir and Kev.

"Why would I want to?" Emeth asked, not taking her eyes from the bird until it flew off, its feathers matching the celandine almost perfectly as it rose against the forest's shadows. "With luck, this won't be long. They're some of the quickest around by day."

"We must seem very ponderous to them," said Olvir.

"Oh, yes. I'm a slug to most of the creatures I talk to."

"Do you talk to slugs, Sentinel?" Kev asked.

"Tried a few times but didn't get much of a response. Birds and bats are easiest of the wild things. Wolves aren't bad either, but not useful right now and probably asleep."

"I wouldn't mind a wolf or two for company," said Vivian.

"You know they wouldn't go with you."

"No?" Kev asked, though he hadn't looked like he liked the idea at all when Vivian mentioned it.

"Beasts don't understand about Thyran. His Twisted hunt them for sport when they can catch them, so wolves might attack the bastards when they encounter one another, but leaders far away make no sense to them. They wouldn't come fight beside humans or seek out Twisted to kill. And I can't make animals—or anyone—do what I want against their will. That'd be Gizath's arts," Emeth added and spat through her fingers in a gesture of aversion. Kev did the same.

Vivian made the fourfold sign instead, and so did Olvir. It was a reflex after twenty-odd years. He was more than halfway through before he thought, and then hesitating would have drawn attention.

He went on, alert for any odd sensation, then felt foolish when none occurred.

Naturally. He'd been making warding signs almost his whole life, and all that time he'd been…

Possessed? Infested?

A variety of words had suggested themselves to him over the last day or so. He'd never quite managed to distract himself from them, no matter how much he tried to concentrate on preparation instead.

Silence was all but impossible in a forest, even one as inhabited as the woods near the Serpentspine Range were these days. All four of the people standing there stopped talking, though, stifled not just by awkwardness but by mention of the enemy behind Thyran—the enemy that, Vivian and Olvir knew, was partly among the four of them.

The woods provided refuge, as they often had for Olvir, with a patch of gold-streaked blue mushrooms at the bottom of a tree. Gathering them was a straightforward task, one that kept him from trying to tell if Vivian was watching him. "Coins-in-the-ocean," he said, because the quiet had taken on too much weight. "They let you go a little longer without water."

"You should take them, then," said Emeth. "No wells where you're going."

"We don't know that," said Vivian.

"None that I'd want to drink from. I talk to frogs, but I don't want to be one... Ah," Emeth said. Olvir heard the motion of wings in the air, then chirping.

When he rose, with the mushrooms wrapped in a cloth, the greenwing was just taking flight from Emeth's arm again.

"Keep on the path a little longer," she said. "It'll split around a big dead oak. You'll go right. He doesn't see Thyran's forces out there. Doesn't mean a few might not wander that direction for sport."

"Thank you," Olvir said and bowed.

"Keep your nose clean, Sir Paragon," said Emeth. "Stay out of the bars and the brothels if you can manage it. Ember, come back before Kat gets used to bossing me around."

"I doubt I can manage *that* turn of speed," said Vivian with a small smile and a suspicious shine in her eyes, "but I'll do my best. Be safe, both of you."

That was all they had time for. The bird's report had been true in the moment it had flown over Thyran's army, but gods knew how long it would stay so. Without another word, Emeth and Kev turned back toward the camp, continuing to watch the undergrowth along their path.

Only Olvir and Vivian remained.

Part II

Our losses in the fire are naturally a setback. The fire itself, nonetheless, bodes very well indeed. If the Heart, newly incarnate and in a feeble infant's body, could cause so great an effect, what may He not be capable of when properly grown and trained? Surely those present fulfilled the roles our god gave them by allowing this demonstration of His might—the might of but a fragment. We should not mourn them but rather honor their sacrifice.

The treachery of our servant is another matter. Even now we seek to find him. We will retrieve the Heart and its host. We already have taken steps to ensure no further such defections— and our manservant will learn correction at our hands.

—Janayal Verengir, Notes (In the Custody of Tinival's Temple, Heliodar)

Those peoples in the forest beyond Klaishil are warlike and vigorous, for so their lands do make them. Sundrie creatures inhabit those woods, and many are fierce and will prey on man as readily as other game. My guide speaks of the greycat, nine feet long, which slips between shadows to seek its meals. It fears no fire, and its coat in most places is dense enough to turn all blades but those wielded with extraordinary strength.

He tells of other beasts as well...

—Bestiarie of the North, Author Unknown

Chapter 9

THEY TOOK THE PATH AS SILENTLY AS POSSIBLE. VIVIAN FOUND the need for quiet a relief. Conversation had been fine while they'd been with the others, but too much awareness had swiftly filled the space Emeth and Kev had left. All she could have come up with to say in the first moments of their absence was either *Fine day for a suicide mission, isn't it?* or *So, if you were to measure it from one to ten, how treacherous are you feeling today?*

It was better to stride along, listening to birds calling to one another, making sure that the rustling in the trees came from nothing larger than squirrels, and covering as much ground as she could at a step without putting herself in danger of tripping. Sentinels healed far faster than normal people, but a broken ankle would be a hindrance.

The oak Emeth had described loomed ahead before long. To the left, the path they'd been on kept going, as narrow as always. It widened on the right. Vivian could spot the remnants of flat stones beneath the ground cover. A hundred years ago, a road had been there.

That gave them better footing but almost certainly meant increased danger. Packs of twistedmen often strayed from Thyran's main forces, seeking food or amusement. The road would be as convenient for them as it was for Vivian and Olvir.

She watched the gaps in the trees carefully, alert for a glimpse of red, skinned flesh that would signal Thyran's normal forces or the rot-bleached white that meant his scouts. Ulamir's hilt was solid in her grip, the sword's balance a comforting known as it had been since nearly childhood.

In life, I was wont to travel this road, said Ulamir. *We remember each other yet. I cannot say how far out I would sense the presence of the Twisted, but I suspect it would stand out to my senses before even your vision, O Fireshaped.*

Vivian sent silent thanks. Communication through that method was never complete from the Sentinel's side, but it got easier the longer a bond with a soulsword lasted. There were some rewards to being old.

The Heart-Host travels well, said Ulamir, making Olvir sound like a type of dried fruit. *A relief.*

It was. Once, he and Vivian had worked together when undead were attacking a village, and they'd joined forces again when a man had summoned demons to kill off his family's other heirs. Neither had involved travel, and the knights were generally less mobile than the Sentinels. How Olvir would manage on the road had been one of her many concerns.

He didn't tromp, despite his size and armor, and he kept pace with her easily. It was an excellent start.

No few years have passed since we've traveled with companions. Never have we taken them from outside the Order.

It was a novel experience, Vivian agreed. Olvir could defend himself as well or better than she could, depending on the foe. He'd been at war as long as she had. Despite acknowledging that, she kept wanting to make sure that he was all right. The knights aided those in distress, which meant fighting as often as not, but they weren't the hunters the Sentinels were, nor were they as used to Gizath's monsters.

His nature would sorely tax any who bore it.

And then there was that.

The road split again. The path they didn't take was broader and in better shape, though that was a relative term. It went to Klaishil—the city where Thyran had made his then-final stand and been caught out of time, the city where Darya had found Amris a hundred years later, the city from which the whole damned mess had started again.

For Vivian, Olvir, and Ulamir, the trail led away, much further into the past.

―――――――――

Sticks crunched between Olvir's boots and ancient paving stones, giving forth sounds that had made him flinch the first few times he'd made them. He walked as quietly as he could, but he was a large man in armor. He could only help so much—and so, as he went on, he'd put what he couldn't control out of his head, breathing in the steady four-count that he used during temple services until his footsteps blended into the forest's general noise.

The walls of his new world were mixed shades of green: lighter shades of unfurling leaves against the jagged darkness of pine and fir, dull lichen hanging from the trunks and deep-green moss coating rocks. Brown and gray appeared in patches, with the brighter colors of flowers or birds occasionally flitting through, then vanishing as Olvir or what he was seeing moved on.

Slowly the old road wound northward, as the light faded into the rich gold of afternoon, then went violet with evening. That was the only way Olvir could mark the hours. His feet kept moving, his arms ached from the weight of sword and shield, and then the ache faded into just another part of his circumstances. Once in a while, they paused to drink water or pass it. Any one of those moments was mostly the same as the one before it. They never talked.

He spotted the clearing as darkness was falling. It was a clearing in truth, not like the patch of ground they'd stopped at to leave Emeth and Kev behind, and it was slightly off the main road. It also wasn't immediately visible from there—a large, moss-covered rock meant Olvir was halfway past before he realized what he was looking at.

"Vivian," he said quietly and pointed when she turned. "There?"

She hesitated, eyes unfocusing as her soulsword expressed some opinion, then nodded. "I'll take first watch."

"Cold camp?"

"I think so. I'll eat while you sleep and vice versa."

There wasn't much camp to their camp, only the necessities to keep even a god-touched body working reasonably. Olvir spread his bedroll on a relatively flat, rock-free bit of ground, knelt by it, and went through his evening dedications to Tinival.

It was a simple prayer, suitable for nights in the field: *Silver Wind, Your servant salutes You. May all things I do be in accordance with Your will. May You guide my arm, clear my eyes, and give me courage.* Olvir looked up through the pattern of tree branches over his head while he prayed and saw, in the dark patches visible between them, a few scattered stars.

Olvir's prayers the night before had been at once rote and frantic. As he'd recited the words, trying to hold on to the deeper meaning in phrasing he knew by heart, his mind had been incoherently screaming: for help, for advice, simply for the god to *make this not be happening*.

He'd known there would be no answer. He'd been in no fit state to hear one, and he'd dreaded what else might answer.

In the wilderness, with a day of hard walking behind him, it was easier to quiet his fear. He shaped each word with care, too mindful of Gwarill's caution to seek beyond the customary phrases for the presence of either Tinival or any other.

As the words fell into the night, though, Olvir could believe that Tinival heard them. At any rate, lightning didn't strike him down, nor did he even feel any sense of rejection. He would take that.

Afterwards he rose, removed his boots, his armor, and his belt, and lay down, keeping his sword close.

Vivian had settled herself on the ground nearby while he prayed, legs folded neatly beneath her. She took dried meat and bread out of her pack, unhooked a waterskin from her belt, and began to eat in quick bites. Between swallowing one and beginning the other, she stopped and waited, judging the silence for any danger.

She was as motionless as the stars otherwise, yet Olvir knew from experience how quickly she could move, with how little notice, when the need arose. He watched her as his eyelids grew heavy, as he felt his muscles relax and the weight of his body settle down onto the earth. The last thing he could remember seeing was the glimmer of starlight on the hilt of her sword.

It was slightly past midnight when he awoke to the pressure of Vivian's hand on his shoulder. Moonlight was slanting through the gaps in the trees. Her face, a little way above his as she knelt, was calm, so Olvir sat up and pulled on his boots without undue haste before he reached for weapons and armor.

After he stood up, Vivian gestured at the blanket where he'd lain and gave him a questioning look. Olvir was proud of how quickly he figured out her meaning, considering how late it was. He nodded: if they were switching watches, there was no point in getting out two bedrolls.

He took Vivian's place on the rock. Small noises came from behind him as she undressed as much as either of them were going to under the circumstances, then lay down. Olvir, eating and drinking with a hand free in case he had to quickly go for his sword, heard Vivian's breathing deepen toward sleep.

He didn't deliberately watch her. The woods, and respect for Vivian's privacy, demanded that Olvir keep his focus turned outward. He did look across the clearing regularly, though, as the night wore on and walked slow, quiet circles around it once he was done with his dinner, and thus the figure in his blankets made an impression.

Vivian slept on her right side, cheek pillowed on the crook of her arm, legs stretched out.

The sight of her stirred feelings more personal than comfort and more tender than lust. Silence had enhanced that closeness rather than detracted from it. After most of a day without speech, Olvir was better attuned to the quiet messages of face and body, as well as shifts in breath or the weight of footsteps. Blending into the forest, maybe, had brought them more in harmony with each other.

Night sounds went on outside the clearing. It was too early for the cricket choruses of high summer, but Olvir heard the rustling of small furred creatures, the peeping of frogs in the river not far away, and once or twice the hunting screams of owls. The moonlight shone on moving shapes in the undergrowth at times, none so large as to cause alarm, all passing quickly on to the business of wild things.

Olvir walked circles, stopped for a bit to let silence fall, listened, then resumed his circuit. He tried not to contemplate what could happen or could lie ahead or to wonder about his nature. He tried to be purely in the moment and alert to the ways it could shift. He didn't manage it completely, but he came close enough.

Having Vivian at the center of his pacing helped.

Chapter 10

Sleep was a matter of balance. Four hours would keep Vivian going. Her reflexes wouldn't appreciably dull until she'd spent a week or two on that schedule, and she could keep going past that. She remembered that from training, not to mention a few missions in her past.

Keeping it in mind when Olvir woke her an hour or so before dawn was difficult. The world was clammy. Trained as she was, she ached—a day-long walk used different muscles than months of fighting inside a stockade—and her mouth felt like a squirrel had died in it.

Oh well, she was alive to be disgruntled.

Vivian gave Olvir a quick appreciative nod and suppressed a grin as she watched him run a hand through his auburn hair, which stuck up in uneven places when he first woke her. Hers curled too tightly to present that particular issue, though she had to finger-comb a few pine needles out of it.

The world mostly broke down into a series of tasks. There were boots, and she put them on. There was armor, and she shrugged into that, too, doing up the fastenings on her leather jerkin with still-stiff fingers while Olvir rolled up the bedclothes and packed them away. They left the grass where they'd lain in turn a little crushed, but Vivian doubted that the best tracker could make much use of that. Smell was another story, one neither of them could particularly help.

Olvir's wasn't at all bad, she'd noticed. Granted, they hadn't been in extremely close contact, but stench usually came off on blankets. Olvir's had smelled mostly of leather and faintly of sweaty man, unavoidable but decently clean, so not unpleasant. They'd still been warm when she'd lain down too.

He would probably be warm if she leaned against him now, Vivian thought, glancing over to watch Olvir close his pack. There was the armor, of course, but she'd found she could ignore that with the proper incentive.

It would have been pleasant. Many things would have been pleasant.

She wished she'd taken an hour or two for any of them in the past. There had been moments, after battle or late at night in taverns, when she could have reached out and drawn Olvir closer to her. Vivian didn't think he'd have objected—but it had always seemed too momentous, too fraught with the potential to change the nature of their friendship. *Perhaps another time*, she'd always told herself.

Now she knew he housed a piece of the Traitor, they were in the middle of hostile territory on a mission to gods knew what end, and they had no time to linger.

Her past self had been a fool.

Packed and ready, Olvir came up to her side and gestured to the road, then to himself, then in the direction that they were going.

After a moment to figure it out, Vivian nodded. It'd be better to switch who took point. Different positions, when possible, kept people alert. She made her own gesture, a go-ahead motion, then followed Olvir out onto the road.

They went on in that fashion for three days and as many nights without exchanging more than a few whispered words at once. Quietly they exchanged watches, unpacked at dusk and packed at dawn, stopped at noon to eat and drink, and kept on walking.

One night was cloudy. One day, a deer bounded across their path, but they didn't bother trying to shoot it; it would take too long to dress or cook.

Such small features shaped the hours. Otherwise, there were only the forest, the creatures in the forest, and Vivian, all of whom remained constant.

The road began to slope upward as the days wore on. It shrank, too, though it never got as narrow as the game trail had been. The creatures that had cleared it had been smaller than elk or bear, but they'd built their works to last. They'd only mostly failed.

It was a gloomy notion, one that went well with the crumbling stones Olvir walked on and the hazy white sky above. People had planned the road, cleared the forest, laid the stones, then traveled it. That had lasted for hundreds of years and vanished in fewer than a dozen.

Criwath, Silane, all that people had managed to preserve and all that they'd managed to rebuild since then, could disappear in less time. If the spells Gerant and the others in the west had developed were very good, and if the armies facing Thyran held very successfully against the full strength of his forces, some pieces might remain, but Olvir knew that the losses would be great unless he succeeded.

He still didn't know exactly what that would entail.

The dreams hadn't returned.

It had been easier to walk without thinking on the first day, when their journey had just started and the camp had been close behind them. The immediate circumstances had been new enough to command all Olvir's attention. Four days in, the wilderness had become normal. He stayed aware of all his surroundings, breathed as he'd been taught, but couldn't keep his mind completely clear.

They went on, walking a road whose creators had likely never imagined its sad end: pitted and overgrown, no living people left in the places it had once connected, inhabited by animals, monsters, and a pair of desperate people. Long ago, its builders had acted with high hopes. Nothing they'd done had lasted in the end.

If the forces opposing Thyran won, would that last? Would whatever task he had to accomplish on the Battlefield let the world rest and mend its wounds in peace? Or would Olvir merely throw Thyran back to try another horrible trick? Might he clear the way for Gizath to bring forth an even worse champion?

All things pass, Edda had told him in his youth: when he'd fallen and scraped his knees as a child, when he'd been twelve, mourning his first dog, and when a fire had killed two of his friends from the nearby village. *Time makes us all unrecognizable.*

He kept realizing how much she'd known, in different ways, throughout his life. Walking over the stones laid by people whose names he'd never learn, toward a fate he didn't understand, Olvir found a new truth to the words.

———————

The bones of the world rise closer to the surface here, said Ulamir. *We have left the path that I once traveled. Now I know our road only from my own senses.*

Now, when she wasn't as caught up in the strangeness of the trip, Vivian wondered why Ulamir had been going north so frequently. It hadn't been his home: he'd been born in the southeast, in jewel-studded caves below the plains that surrounded Nerapis.

Vivian kept her curiosity to herself. That was mostly the best approach when talking with soulswords about their pasts. Death healed some wounds, but lingering to watch the world change opened others. She trusted Ulamir to tell her information that would make a difference. Otherwise, she listened.

Either he caught the edge of her question or he felt disposed to explain. *Once, my father's sisters dwelled under the mountains north of Klaishil,* Ulamir said. *Guests were always welcome to their halls, stone of their veins or no. They were a merry lot.*

He spoke with more wistfulness than pain. Vivian returned sympathy nonetheless.

The stonekin in the north had been Thyran's first targets after he'd acquired his allies. Gizath bore Ulamir's people a very old grudge. His servant had been thorough in acting upon it.

She and Ulamir let that knowledge lie between them as they went on. It filled the silence among the forest's sounds, the space between her footsteps and Olvir's. Ulamir had known the loss firsthand, Vivian from histories, but it weighed on them both.

In the days before, he said eventually, *my cousin said that the wind wept at night when it blew over the mountains.*

That made sense to Vivian. She couldn't hear the elements the way the stonekin did, but if she'd been the wind, crossing such a place would have probably set her crying too.

Before much time passes, the truth of it will become clear.

Vivian's thighs could have told her that they were approaching the mountains. The trees were thinner, shorter, and fewer, too, which didn't make the walk any easier. More branches were at eye level, and the increased light had let a small second forest of briars sprout. She did enjoy being able to see more sky.

She reflected once in a while on their progress as it would've appeared on a map. The land, the one the stonekin had called Mortera, was shaped like a snake with butterfly wings. From Silane in the south, a traveler could follow the Larykan River upward, past Heliodar's marshes and through Criwath. Rivulets fed it high in the Serpentspine, flowing cold from tiny springs.

Past that—the Battlefield.

Nobody living could say what else. Nobody had left any records that Vivian believed. Even the old peoples, the stonekin and the waterfolk, had left the northeastern lands after the Betrayal. Some stories said they'd fled south to escape too many memories.

Others said that the gods' fight had turned all the ground to black glass where nothing would grow or cracked holes in the world that monsters had come through.

Nobody had been fool enough to go and look. Before Thyran and his storms, there'd been barbarian tribes in the northern forests, who'd sometimes climb the slopes with their herds, but Vivian had never heard of anybody going to the Battlefield itself.

If they won and lived, maybe she'd be proud of breaking new ground. She suspected she'd have too many other feelings to notice it.

She went on through the forest, careful of her footing among moss-slick stones and half-hidden sticks. There was a knack to walking that way: motion coming from the hips, heel hitting the ground first, weight settling gradually through the ball of the foot once Vivian was sure of her balance. It came back quickly, even after months of confinement. So did the art of drinking and eating one-handed, without breaking stride, in small helpings that she could swallow swiftly at need.

If their scouts were correct, they'd passed the majority of Thyran's forces—or those he'd sent toward Criwath at any rate. Outliers were possible, but the invading army tended to stay a day's march away from the human camp. A day's journey for one knight and one Sentinel, traveling light, was much farther than for a whole army.

The forest bore that out. Birds called more raucously. Small animals darted more freely through the underbrush—not fearless, but with no greater fear than any wild thing lived with in the normal course of its life. Once in a while, a louder sound signaled that a deer had caught their scent.

Vivian wasn't initially alarmed when she heard another animal pushing through the forest. It sounded bigger than a deer or even an elk, but it could have simply been closer than those animals had previously gotten to them.

She stopped anyhow. So did Olvir, with no need for her to get his attention, though he glanced over his shoulder beforehand to make certain he didn't take her by surprise and cause a collision. She nodded to show that she was all right.

The next sound was closer, louder, and definitely not a deer. Vivian couldn't hear any footsteps or hoofbeats, but the sound of snapping brush was clear, loud, and low.

It's no creature of Gizath that approaches, said Ulamir. *But it is large.*

She drew the sword swiftly and turned to face northwest, where the sound was coming from. Olvir had his shield up when he followed her motion. Vivian heard the metallic *shing* as he drew his own sword. There was no time to do so quietly.

A roar from the northwest shook the trees. A heartbeat later, a mass of green and gray fur, topped by a blocky head with four red eyes, crashed through onto the road.

The time for staying quiet was definitely over.

Chapter 11

Flight was impossible.

The thing that charged through the trees toward Olvir and Vivian was a bear in basic shape, but it was as tall as Olvir at the shoulder. Even if they climbed a tree before it reached them, which was doubtful, he was reasonably sure it could knock most trees down, just as he suspected it would easily catch them if they ran.

Thus he braced himself, shield guarding neck and vitals, sword up and ready. Olvir also let out a deep, full-throated yell, not really hoping that it'd scare the creature off but figuring he had nothing to lose.

The beast reared up on its hind legs, bringing its ears level with most of the treetops. It waved all four of its claw-tipped arms— two in the expected place, two others sprouting from its back, just below its shoulder blades. Its mouth opened as it roared again, giving Olvir a good view of curving yellow fangs that looked very sharp.

"Geisbar," he said, the name coming to him out of stories. Then he couldn't talk. The bear lunged forward, grabbing for Olvir with the lower two of its arms. He dropped and rolled, feeling razor claws pass right above his head, and rose on the geisbar's side.

Vivian had flashed into place while he was moving. Ulamir slashed down on what looked like empty air, but the geisbar jerked back, snarling. Blood ran from the mottled green fur of one paw.

"Three feet to the right," she said without looking at Olvir, then leapt backward from foaming jaws that snapped on the air where she'd been.

The bear had dropped to all fours. Olvir took a swing at it, not lacking for a target. He sliced open its shoulder as it turned, but its hair was thick and the fat beneath thicker. The geisbar didn't so much as flinch. It used two other arms to swipe at Olvir, who ducked one blow. The other hit his shield with arm-numbing force. Worse than that, he felt the steel bend under the bear's weight.

Holding ground was only going to work a little better than fleeing.

Vivian was pulling Ulamir out of the creature's body. She was frowning, not unusual in such a fight, but shaking her wrist a little as well; she'd hit a rib rather than any vital organ.

Olvir hoped for a second that the geisbar would see sense. *Run*, he thought at it as it bellowed with pain. *We won't chase you. We can all come out of this alive.*

The bear sprang instead, maddened by its wounds or perhaps sick to begin with. Olvir leapt to the side himself, just in time to avoid four sets of claws landing on top of him. The force of their impact made the ground tremble.

He went to one knee, catching himself hard on it and his shield arm. Later he'd feel the impact—assuming he was alive later.

———

Metal hummed in Vivian's grasp, and the stone that anchored Ulamir's spirit to the sword flashed in a quick rhythm. She yelled as she rushed the geisbar, a short, sharp sound from the top of her lungs. As it turned from Olvir, the sapphire's glow struck its eyes. It bellowed again, cringing back.

The god-power took it then. Ulamir called it *fault lines*. Vivian didn't have a name for it: it was what she did, what Letar's and Poram's power combined to let her do. The past flowed over the geisbar's body, finding all the old scars, the broken bones that had since healed, the ancient wounds, and making them fresh again.

A series of claw marks ran down the bear's neck, dripping blood through its fur. Near its muzzle, a red hole the size of Vivian's hand opened up.

It roared again, shaking the trees, and cringed backward. Vivian darted in. The neck wasn't exposed, but the side was a decent target, if she could avoid the ribs this time. She lunged.

She didn't see the paw until it struck her. There was only the blow, a disembodied force that sent her flying backward at what felt like a horse's gallop.

The geisbar charged toward Vivian as she scrambled to get her legs under her. When it opened its mouth to roar again, its breath streamed hot and rancid across her face.

She rolled sideways, away from a paw that nearly struck off her head, and saw a disjointed series of images. The geisbar snarled in frustration, then reared up in pain. Olvir appeared at its back, sword deep in its side. He turned to give momentum to the blow, as graceful a motion as Vivian had ever seen, and pulled his blade out dark and dripping.

A bad wound. A fatal one? She didn't know. The geisbar didn't seem to know either, only that the small shining form in front of it had caused it more pain than it had experienced in its whole life. Angered, it went for Olvir, grabbing for him with two of its fore-limbs and whipping its head down toward his face.

He ducked and lunged. Vivian came up to her knees, raised Ulamir, then drove herself forward.

No ribs blocked her. Ulamir slid smoothly into the bear's chest. On the other side of its body, farther up, Olvir's sword slammed into its neck, which split under the power of the stroke. Skin and muscle parted, the spine split, and the geisbar's muscles locked, holding it in place in a final moment of shock.

That wouldn't last long. Vivian whipped Ulamir back, dodging the spray of blood that followed, and sprang clear of the bear. Olvir was dashing out of the way, too, though the path of his retreat was straight down the road. Vivian glimpsed his broken shield on the ground.

When the bear fell over, almost headless, bleeding in a thousand places, the ground shook. The forest was silent in the aftermath.

———————————

"Are you all right?" Olvir asked.

Vivian stood on the other side of the bear's giant corpse. She was breathing and had no grievous wounds that he could see. With the Sentinels, that generally meant any other problems were temporary.

All the same, it was a relief to hear her respond, "Essentially. You?" and to register that she sounded a little breathless, as Olvir had himself, but not in pain.

Simply hearing her helped in other ways. The silence had initially been companionable, nothing to object to even when Olvir's own thoughts had started troubling him. In the aftermath of the fight, with the bear's final pained roar echoing in his ears, he welcomed a quiet, reasonable voice speaking words.

"In one piece," he said. The dead bear was blocking the road, so Olvir began to pick his way between the trees on the side, heading toward where Vivian stood by a thick-trunked evergreen. She was cleaning Ulamir, pouring a little water from the skin at her waist onto a cloth, then wiping the blade clean of blood. "Though I'll miss my shield."

"It served its purpose well." She wiped her own hands and face clean, then took a second, dry rag out of her belt pouch and started to dry her sword.

Olvir reached her side and began the cleaning process himself. "Sitha rest it, it did."

"So did we." Vivian assessed the hulking pile of fur and meat that lay across the road and pursed her lips in a silent whistle.

"I'm glad Thyran hasn't managed to warp any of these to his will. They're bad enough as it is."

"The baron's son where I grew up lost half his face to a bear," he said. "That was only the regular sort." Hunting a common bear, the smaller sort that had four paws and was where it appeared to be, took four or five people, on horseback, with dogs. Even then, things went wrong, as young Faltienne had learned.

If Olvir and Vivian were more resilient than most mortals, they also had to be. On their mission, any wound worse than a few cuts and bruises would be a much greater hindrance than normal. "I'm glad there were two of us," Olvir went on, "and that you knew about those beasts."

"I can't say I'm an expert," said Vivian. "Nobody I know has fought one. They're among the creatures you hear about in training, but there are plenty of those. I wouldn't have recognized it if you hadn't told me the name."

There was a trace of awkwardness in her smile that Olvir recognized. If either of them had been under the other's command, it would've been an occasion for praise. Since they'd each spent the last few months commanding other people, it would've felt condescending to say *good job*, as though either of them were in a position to approve of the other or to seek the other's approval.

It felt good to have hers, despite that, as much as he could infer it.

"We should check each other," he said, changing the subject before the moment could get too uncomfortable. Deep enough cuts might not hurt, and the blood might not show under their armor.

"Good thought," said Vivian. "Let's get a little distance first, though. The noise may have drawn some attention, and the smell certainly will before long."

Chapter 12

IT STARTED RAINING AS THEY BEGAN TO WALK AWAY. VIVIAN, who'd had things on her mind other than the sky, blinked when the first drop hit her, then looked up to see gray through the trees and got another drop directly in her right eye. She sighed. Under the circumstances, it probably wasn't worth putting her cloak on. She'd just have to take it off again after a little while, and in the meantime, it'd get covered with bear blood.

The rain did help with that, she had to admit. And it'd probably hide their scent. The traces of the road would keep their tracks from being too visible. Poram was likely being kind, all things considered, which was especially gracious of him since they'd killed one of his creatures not long before.

"It's a shame we can't stay to make use of it," she said, glancing backward at the giant dead lump.

"Other creatures will," said Olvir, rather than pointing out how heavy the fur would've been or how long butchering the thing would have taken, either of which Vivian would've expected. "The earth doesn't waste."

"You sound like Emeth."

"Thank you. Though I'll try to be less irreverent."

"I'd find *reverence* unnerving," Vivian said, laughing quietly. They'd have to resume their silence soon, but the fight with the bear and the squelching of their footsteps meant it would do no good just then.

"Maybe less profane, then," Olvir suggested from behind her.

"That's between you and your conscience."

"Have you known her long?"

"Five years, maybe six," said Vivian. "She was taking her vows in a chapter house in Silane when I was there healing up. We encountered each other off and on since. That's generally the way it goes with us."

"That must've been quite a battle," he said, "if you had to stay in a chapter house to heal."

"It was," she said. "Hunger-ghost."

Olvir recognized the term. Vivian saw him wince. The hunger-ghosts weren't *directly* Thyran's creation, but they were more common in the years since his first wave of storms. People had gotten desperate for food, so desperate that they'd turned to acts they'd never so much as consider otherwise. That left marks on the nature of a place. Some of those scars drew forces from outside.

"Had it raised many dead?"

"About a dozen. Mostly animals." She glanced back again, but the bear's corpse had vanished behind a bend in the road. "It was the same problem I had just now, but more so—old wounds didn't trouble them particularly. On the other hand, my major blessing was useful."

Olvir, who knew her blessings as well as the other Sentinels she worked with, groaned. "You didn't."

"Set myself on fire? Not *directly*. Or not at first. I put together some incendiaries, then plunged in after the ghost once her minions were more or less ablaze."

"I…don't know whether the phrase I want is 'nice work' or simply 'ouch.'"

"Both. I wasn't precisely in wonderful shape when all was said and done, thus the chapter house. And speaking of being in wonderful shape—" She glanced around, saw no impending threats, and suspected that the rain would go on for a while. "This is as good a place to check as any, I think."

Olvir stopped. "Yes. Though I feel somewhat silly about asking, now that I hear you've thought nothing of running into a mob of flaming undead."

"I thought plenty of it, believe me. And I wasn't good for much afterward, which proves your point," Vivian said. "Besides, I've heard as many stories about the knights. We just serve different purposes, mostly."

"The same purpose with different methods, I'd say, but…" He waved a hand back and forth, dismissing the whole thing as philosophy. "Would you care to go first, or should I?"

"I'll have a go." She eyed him for a moment. There were no obvious bloodstains, but the rain would disguise that. It certainly had rendered his shirt and trousers more formfitting. Vivian cleared her throat. "Mostly back, I'm guessing? The rest seems quite easy to check ourselves."

"I'd add the head and the sides of the neck, if you don't mind," said Olvir. "I'm not sure what we can do if either of us has cracked our skull, but…"

"Better to be aware," Vivian agreed. "All right. Stand still. Tell me if I hit anything sore. Nonviolently, if possible."

He'd made the suggestion very practically. It *was* common among knights to inspect each other for injuries if they couldn't get to a healer at the end of a battle, and for good reason. Olvir had seen people walking on broken legs for hours. It hadn't ended prettily.

So he'd proposed that he and Vivian take the same precautions. He didn't exactly regret it. First of all, it was still a good idea. And second—

Well.

When he'd turned to face Vivian, he'd seen raindrops shining on her eyelashes like captive stars. He'd noticed the way her full lips moved as she spoke. Although he'd tried to focus on her face, which presented all the above problems, her tunic was wet and clung. Olvir was a knight, not a saint.

He should probably, given all that, *have* regretted his idea, or at least its necessity, or his inability to discipline his thoughts. That sort of detachment held no appeal, however. It made the world feel grayer simply to contemplate it.

Matters did not get any simpler when Vivian walked behind him. Olvir was no less aware of the woman for not being able to see her. He heard every quick step on the wet earth and each light breath. Neither the rain nor the breeze that came with it hid those or kept him from feeling the shift in air as she passed him. He felt as if he could sense the heat of her body even with inches between the two of them.

No, if he was trying to keep his mind above his waist, his lack of vision was no help at all.

Olvir waited for her touch, and the waiting itself set him more on edge. Anticipation mixed with the hint of danger he felt when anybody stood at his back, no matter how much he trusted them. He concentrated on breathing normally. He also thanked Tinival that his armor came down to midthigh.

Vivian's weight shifted. Before Olvir felt her hands on the backs of his calves, he heard her breathing near his waist, which sent a flood of images into his mind.

"Don't worry," she said. "I won't stab you."

She mostly sounded amused, but there was another element in her voice, one that made it a shade less steady than normal. Olvir was tempted to believe it was desire. That was as likely as not wishful thinking.

"No blood at any rate," she went on, as she ran her fingers lightly but thoroughly up his legs. "And I can't feel any bones out of place. Pain?"

"No." He thought he got the word out casually. He hoped so.

There *was* a sore spot on his right thigh, probably a fair-sized bruise that would linger for a while. Olvir welcomed that discovery. Right after that, Vivian was inspecting his backside, and although she did so quickly and respectfully, he wasn't sure he could've stood motionless at her touch if not for the earlier pain.

Up she went, passing Olvir's waist, giving his spine careful attention. He controlled himself enough to say, when she was at his shoulder blades, "I hope the chain's not too hard on your hands."

"No," she said. "Not as long as I'm not hurrying, which I shouldn't be. I'm not sure how much I can feel through the armor, though."

"I can feel you, and that's a good sign." Olvir shivered as Vivian's breath blew past the back of his neck. "Ah. Sorry."

"My fault." Her fingers followed her breath, then combed through his hair. "No injuries. Or they're well-hidden ones."

"Thank you," he said.

For the sake of his dignity, he was glad when she stepped away, but the rest of him mourned the loss of her touch.

———————————

The rain wasn't nearly cold enough.

Vivian turned as soon as she'd made sure Olvir's skull was intact. She was reasonably good at keeping a neutral expression on her face, but she didn't want to test her skill just then. Touching Olvir, who felt like warm iron through his armor, had left her more than a little heated herself.

"I know I've got a slice across the back of my right leg," she said, trying to distract herself, "and a couple on my side. None of them feel very deep."

Olvir cupped her right leg. "This one doesn't strike me as bad," he agreed after a moment. "It's still bleeding, though. I could clean it out, but I'm not sure it would be very helpful while we're walking through this storm."

"No matter. Our wounds always heal cleanly."

"Oh," he said. "I should have known that, I suppose, since I never see any of you with the herbalists. I'll bandage it at least."

That was a quick process. He was deft at it, too, tucking the trailing ends into the top of Vivian's boot afterward. Her other leg came next, her thighs and arse after that, while she stood with locked muscles, wanting the process to go on even though she didn't think she had the discipline to go another minute. Although there were layers of wet leather blocking them, Olvir's hands left a trail of spreading sensation along Vivian's skin.

She heard him catch his breath once. Because she was vain, and because she liked that particular method of self-torment, Vivian wondered if it meant he appreciated what he felt.

More pain bloomed in her side when he prodded that. "I'm sorry," said Olvir when she hissed. "I don't *believe* your ribs are broken, but it's a near thing. No surprise either. When you landed, I thought… I didn't think you'd get up again."

"I wasn't sure I would either," she said. "Bleeding?"

"Not very much. I expect that it should be all right without a bandage. I can't swear you haven't torn some bit of your insides loose, mind."

"Nothing to be done if I have."

"I suppose that's true," he said reluctantly and went onward.

Vivian was doing all right until he reached her neck. She'd assumed the…well, not the worst, most certainly not the worst, but the most demanding part was over once they'd gotten above her waist, since Olvir was only working on her back. The pressure on her spine was nice, granted, but the knots in her muscles there took priority over arousal. She'd begun to relax.

Then his fingers traced up her neck, over a spot that had always driven her a little mad under the right circumstances. These were not them, but her senses didn't give a damn. Olvir's touch, without the barrier of wet leather, drew a gasp from her that the sound of the rain did nothing to hide.

Naturally, Olvir stopped. "Did that hurt?" he asked. He was likely trying to ask an honest question, but his voice came out lower than normal and with a smoky quality to it.

"No," Vivian said before she realized that lying would have been a better idea.

"Ah."

Silence followed, hot and awkward.

"I'm sorry," Vivian said. "You know how it is, I'm sure. Survival instinct, attractive companion, and so on. I should've had more self-control, though. We can ignore all this."

Her skull was probably fine, she decided. She'd started to turn when Olvir spoke again. "That's, er, a situation I'm very well acquainted with. As in, one I have present experience of, I might say."

It wasn't the most explicit statement Vivian had ever heard. She had no doubt at all about its meaning all the same. His voice didn't allow for any. Neither did the expression on his face when she did turn: color high on his cheekbones, his eyes wide and dark. Hunger had never looked so stark to Vivian.

Risk paled in the face of that desire: the man had doubtless bedded other people after all. Whatever would get the fragment of the Traitor to emerge, it probably wasn't a few hours of pleasure. "Then," she told him, "I'd say the time for ignoring things has passed."

Olvir's hands closed on her upper arms. He didn't grip hard or close the few inches between them, but Vivian understood the restraint it took for him to hold off.

"*Vivian*," he breathed.

"Yes," she said, then sighed. "But…you know it can't be now."

"No." Olvir groaned softly. That alone was enough to make Vivian catch her breath. "Not for days, like enough," he went on, the softly burred accent of southern Criwath creeping back beneath the polish he'd clearly learned in the knighthood. "Gods, after that fight we probably shouldn't sleep tonight."

"You're not wrong." The bear, and the noise they'd made, would give enemies a point to start tracking them. They needed to get significantly ahead of any such pursuit, even if they didn't know it existed. Vivian wouldn't feel truly safe stopping for the night until Ulamir had returned from the place where he rested after the fault lines.

Olvir grimaced. "I really had no need of another reason to loathe Thyran. For the future, then."

He leaned forward. Their lips met, lightly, gently, but with a world of tension on both sides. To let go would mean distraction, and letting go was damned tempting. Vivian allowed herself to cup Olvir's face in her hands as her mouth opened beneath his to slide her tongue along his lower lip, to twine her fingers into his tangle of wet hair, but no more.

That brief embrace nonetheless left her aching when she pulled away.

"That should keep me warm for a few hours," she said. "Very... tactical."

"It would be," Olvir agreed. He flushed as he went on, but he did go on, and there was a glint in his eyes that let Vivian know he was more than simply flustered. "But my difficulty walking could make it a wash."

They were laughing, quietly, as they went down the road again.

Chapter 13

Sentinels and knights—all the god-touched, in fact—could see in the dark. Colors were a little dimmer, shapes a trifle less distinct, but night journeys were never a problem, at least not as far as vision went.

Exhaustion was a problem. Cold was a problem. Wet clothing that chafed and never truly dried was a gods-cursed problem. If Olvir had hated Thyran more for keeping him from Vivian's arms, he doubled that after they'd been walking for a few hours, when the sun had gone down and Olvir was worried that he'd be too sore in some areas to so much as think about enjoying himself with any woman ever again.

Tactically speaking, discomfort was better than lust. He could focus more on staying alert when he really wanted to ignore his body. Being philosophical about that would have taken a far better man than Olvir ever had been.

Whatever part of Letar's Halls geisbars went to, Olvir hoped it was unpleasant.

The rain itself stopped shortly after nightfall, leaving the forest a dark, dripping mass. Mud squelched below their feet. The footing was not wonderful. Neither was the wind that came up after the rain. *Raw weather*, people had called it in Olvir's childhood, the sort that often led to illness.

He and Vivian had donned their cloaks, which helped somewhat. Mostly they kept moving, eating and drinking in shifts while they trudged forward. They fell into silence again as they tried to stay undetected. After a while, Olvir felt as though he'd known nothing but the rhythm of their steps and the dark, wet crowd of trees.

The forest grew sparser as the old road took them uphill. Olvir couldn't have named the spot where it ended, exactly, but at some point in the night, he realized that they weren't in it any longer. Trees still stood on either side of the road, but they were dotting a hilly plain, not flanking a path through dense woods.

Enemies would find them easier to spot now. Olvir couldn't help liking his wider field of vision all the same, not to mention the marked decrease in branches trying to break his nose. Fewer trees also meant fewer leaves to drop rain down his neck when he brushed against their branches.

Ideally, too, they'd left Thyran's army behind a while ago. Olvir kept one hand near his sword nonetheless and added the loss of his shield to his list of grudges against the geisbar.

The night went on. Eventually, the sky turned from black to coal-gray, then from coal to smoke, with a bit of light breaking through in the east. Then it was day. The path dried out, as did Olvir's boots and Vivian's, until their footsteps no longer sounded squashy.

Birds started their chorus. Many were the ones Olvir had known from childhood, but there were other calls among them: a series of four long trills that repeated, a lower *one-two-three-ONE* rhythm, and a single piercing scream that sounded like some variety of hawk but too wavering to be any of those Olvir had heard.

That was the first sign of life since they'd reached the plains— other than the trees, Olvir supposed, and those seemed like simply taller versions of the tumbled rocks that rose from the earth in spots.

He also guessed that he and Vivian counted as living beings, though that was more knowledge than feeling. Physically, Olvir had walked for longer and put himself through worse, but there was a disconnected sense about the night that he'd never had before, born of rain, silence, and darkness. Even though he could see, he'd noticed the faded colors and the lack of light.

Ghosts came to mind. So did echoes or footprints: tracks of passage, untethered to the thing passing. Olvir thought of the journey's end, as little as he was able to speculate about that, and felt as if he was leaving the world in addition to the forest.

———

You yet live, do you?

It was an hour or two after dawn; Olvir was striding ahead of her with what appeared to be unceasing if solemn vigor. While that notion might have set her mind working in pleasant ways when they'd started walking again, she was just inclined to resent him for it by the time Ulamir spoke. Vivian was inclined to resent everything, in fact, and was continuing to walk mostly out of anger at the earth beneath her feet.

Still, she was glad to hear Ulamir's mental voice again. He sounded rested, too, which was an asset as well as a source of profound envy.

She sent him her thanks for his assistance.

Performing my appointed task is always an honor. Did the beast die at your hands, did you drive it off, or did the two of you simply escape?

She filled him in as best she could without actually talking, skipping the part where she and Olvir had nearly been carried away by lust. Ulamir had never been unaware of her lovers, but as with most Sentinels and soulswords, actually managing liaisons was always a slightly awkward business. He tactfully vanished to the place where he went to rest as soon as he knew any sort of dalliance was happening. Vivian tried to give him advance warning and did the best she could to keep him unaware of the details.

It more or less worked, like most parts of life.

You were wise to press on, Ulamir said at the end of Vivian's story. *I would advise going until sunset, if you can manage it. Tonight I'll keep the sole watch.*

Vivian hesitated. The soulsword was generally aware of what happened near him, but he saw better through her eyes.

The stone is closer here. Should you cover the ground today that seems likely, by night, it will be closer still. What comes across it will be known to me, and you know I can wake you at need.

That had happened a few years ago, when the inn where Vivian was staying had caught fire. She decided she'd exhausted all the arguments she was obliged to put forward, so just thought her thanks again.

Ulamir was right about the stone being closer. Huge purple and blue rocks, worn smooth by age, stuck out of the ground without any apparent pattern. Even when Vivian couldn't see stone directly, the soil looked thinner and the trees smaller.

The wind picked up, passing her face in a flensing rush that made her eyes water. Vivian left her hood down anyhow, knowing that it wouldn't have stayed on in that blast unless she'd laced it so tightly that it impeded her hearing.

It was breaking up the clouds, that wind, but the sky it revealed was a washed-out sort of blue, as though the rain had drained all the life out of it. The land was wide and bare, the trees stunted compared to the ones Vivian and Olvir had recently passed through. They stood lonely or in isolated little groves, casting long shadows on the dark earth.

Vivian couldn't deny that the walk was easier, despite growing more and more uphill, that her field of vision was better, or that nothing was dripping on her head. But the place was bleak. Even the birds sounded harsh and far away. The small animals, with too much ground to cover and not much shelter, flicked nervously from tree to rock to den, rarely visible.

Nomads had lived there once, until Thyran's first war. The land might have been more cheerful when it had been full of tents and horses.

All its former inhabitants had vanished, traceless. Bloodlines survived from those who'd been visiting other lands or in descendants of those who'd been on friendly terms with travelers. So did some of the stories, a few of the traditions, maybe a scrap or two of what those customs had meant.

Most of the rest had died or joined Thyran, as humans from other countries had done when he'd been gathering his armies. Many of those who'd chosen alliance might still be with Thyran in some form. A very few might have had a choice in their shape—rumor had it that the lords of the twistedmen, Thyran's lieutenants, got to pick Gizath's effects on their flesh.

Everything else was gone. After a hundred years, the land didn't even hold on to bones.

Time devours all, said Ulamir. *Thyran only helped.*

━━━━━━━━━

Noon was a pale wash of light above them. Olvir doffed his cloak, and his clothes slowly dried. He spotted flowers clustered near the roots of trees and the bases of rocks but recognized none of the bright-blue and yellow blossoms as edible.

The animals might have been, but there'd be no time to cook them. They moved too fast to hunt anyhow, almost too fast to see. Olvir glimpsed hares, small anteaters, and a squirrel with a scaled, barbed tail, but they were all on the run, dashing into cover almost as soon as he noticed them. Once, a silver-furred marmot bolted up from a patch of grass when Olvir got too close, then stood on its hind legs to stare at him and chitter loudly.

Once Olvir recovered from the shock, he started laughing silently, partly with relief at being a little more certain, on a gut level, that he was alive. He doubted marmots had much to say to ghosts or echoes at least.

"It's probably good that Emeth isn't here," Vivian said from behind him, snickering. "I doubt that you want to find out what he's saying."

"My deepest apologies for disturbing you, sir," said Olvir. He bowed to the marmot, as elaborate and courtly as he could make the gesture while on the road. "I'm sure you're right about everything."

He heard Vivian laugh again. That was another line thrown out, stronger than the marmot: Olvir was truly present, truly alive, connected to the rest of existence. He was shaping the world, not only echoing it.

"I think we can talk now," he said, surveying the rocky, bare land. "Our steps will carry as loudly as our voices on this earth, and we'll be able to hear anybody approaching. Or so I assume."

"Thank the gods, Ulamir agrees with you. He says he'll take tonight's watch too."

"That's generous of him."

"It is," said Vivian, "and he's extremely doubtful about my skills out here when I haven't slept. Or he thinks that nature's trying my patience as it is. He'd be right in both cases."

"I heard you were all at home in the wilderness."

"Oh, we're all trained in the basics. I can manage when I have to. But when I could, I took the kind of missions I was on with you, the sort where I could clear out the undead in a haunted castle or lure ice-apes away from a village. Darya and Emeth are better at places where people don't live."

"And when there's no mission, you prefer to stay indoors?"

"Horseback, if I can help it, or with a dog pack, or out in a garden. A walk in the woods on a nice day. Outside is wonderful; it's just the wild that I don't enjoy. It's too…wild."

"But Poram gave you his blessing?"

"He's also Sitha's love. The gods seem reasonably complicated."

"Or they understand that we are," said Olvir, recalling the vigil at his initiation.

Vivian gave him a split second of careful regard and then asked, "Have you ever been in contact with yours—with Tinival? That kind of communion isn't generally one of our gifts. They reshape our bodies, but they mostly leave our spirits alone."

"When I took my final vows." Olvir said. "I couldn't put it into words, really, but I felt Him. I realized that nothing I'd ever do would measure up to…" He lifted his hands and dropped them, trying to express that sense of perfect balance, exact knowledge of the best path—not the one that would benefit him most but the one kindest to most people—and calm perspective. "But I knew that He knew I was trying my hardest. I knew that it mattered to Him."

"That must be nice," said Vivian. "That certainty."

The Sentinels did useful work. Nobody disputed that—but many people, especially those with generally peaceful lives, kept their distance. Olvir had heard the Order spoken of in terms that ranged from "helpful, certainly, but damned strange" to "as likely as not to turn on us if they don't find prey." If they had no contact with the gods on top of that… He wanted to offer sympathy and suspected Vivian wouldn't take it well.

"It's been very helpful to me," he replied instead, "especially these last few weeks. Like Marshal Nahon said, Tinival saw all of what I was, and He let me serve him."

"Has he rejected candidates before?"

"Oh, yes. Not many. Usually it'll be pretty obvious if you're not cut out to be a knight, long before the vigil happens. But there are stories—a squire who cut his rival's stirrups in a tournament, for example. Nobody had discovered it, but he came out of the vigil chamber weeping and confessing, with a red mark like a sword blade covering his face and his hair pure white."

"Very dramatic."

"Very. And that was merciful. Edda…my mother…" He didn't expect Vivian to quibble over the word but brought it out defiantly anyhow. Edda had deserved the term. A long-dead Verengir cultist never would. "She said that she saw a woman die during her vigil once. Didn't see it exactly, I mean, but opened the door and there she was. Just sitting there, Edda said, staring at nothing. Nobody ever found out what she'd done."

Vivian made a thoughtful noise. "I could hazard a few guesses, but it doesn't really matter. People don't make it through reforging sometimes," she added, serious but matter-of-fact, "but that's generally nothing to do with their behavior."

"Can their bodies just not take the change?"

"For the most part. Sometimes it's the mind or the spirit that breaks under pressure. That's usually to do with the minor blessing or the offensive one. We're channeling some part of the gods then, and they're a lot to contain."

Olvir glanced down at his chest, where his heart beat steadily with exercise and his other nature rested silently. "That they are."

Chapter 14

THE MOON WAS A SLIM CRESCENT OVERHEAD BY THE TIME THEY stopped. An elbow in the mountain's ridge, where the road technically ended before switching back to ascend in the other direction, held a wide spot with a small grove of pine trees.

"That's as good as we're likely to find for a while," Olvir said. Vivian agreed.

When she blinked or turned her head, pink and green shapes lingered in her vision, afterimages of what she'd been looking at. She had to silently tell herself what to do in small sentences, once they'd stopped in the grove and Ulamir had taken watch: *Open pack. Take out blankets. Put blankets flat on ground. Sit down. Take off boots.*

"I'm not sure whether a fire would be safe or not," she said, unbuckling her sword belt, "but I'd probably lose a finger if I tried to cut any wood."

"Picking up fallen branches might be a wise idea tomorrow." Olvir peered up at the mountain's expanse. "In case. It probably does get cold up there." He pulled his armor over his head and glanced sideways at Vivian. "For tonight, if you wanted, we could keep each other warm. I mean that literally. I'm afraid I'm three steps from dead and no use as anything but a hot stone."

"A hot stone," said Vivian, "is exactly what I need right now. I'll take you up on that offer with thanks, Sir Yoralth."

"Thank you. I wasn't looking forward to a cold bed either. And…" Olvir turned to put his folded armor by his boots, but Vivian suspected it was easier for him to speak without meeting her eyes. "I'll sleep easier when I can touch somebody else living. Better that it's you, you understand. Much better," he added quickly, with an embarrassed little laugh.

"Easy. I'm not a maiden in a bad festival play. I know what you mean." Vivian ate a few bites without tasting any of what she chewed, an advantage where rations were concerned. "It's lonely country out here."

"I wouldn't say it's the country."

The facts of their mission—its uncertain destination and still less certain goal—dropped down between Vivian and Olvir with those words. Jokes, practical details such as fire, and even lust could only be distractions for so long. Eventually, conversation always circled around to where the two of them were going and why.

"No," said Vivian. "Not entirely."

They sat with that knowledge, eating and drinking what they knew they needed, watching the night beyond the trees. Moonlight shone down on them, bright but cold. Branches turned into fingers and clutched at the dark sky.

After a while, Olvir knelt, palms flat on his thighs and head uplifted, to murmur his prayers. His face shone with devotion, outdoing the moonlight in his eyes. The sight was a model of faith or futility, depending on where the mind of the watcher was inclined to go.

Vivian wished she could have faith. The gods were far away, across the Veil of Fire. The world depended on their mortal tools, which broke easily.

Sleep, said Ulamir. *You do no good to yourself, nor the knight, nor the land. Sleep.*

Olvir, who didn't have a swordsoul in his head, blinked when Vivian stretched out on her bedroll. He caught on quickly, though, and just as quickly closed the space between them. Then he hesitated, which was the cue Vivian needed to curl herself against him like a snake on a sunny rock.

"Ahh," she said, not meaning for it to be aloud but not really minding that it was either. Large men had considerable merits where radiating heat was concerned.

Her head rested against the hard muscle of Olvir's chest. While the fabric of his shirt was slightly damp and more than slightly scratchy, Vivian had slept on worse pillows. She could hear the steady beat of Olvir's heart, too, as soothing as the tides.

When he stroked her hair, Vivian was a little surprised at the gentleness of his touch, but only a little. She remembered him kneeling in front of the dying spider, reaching for it with calm sorrow.

It had been a long time since anyone had thought to treat her gently, longer since she'd thought to want it. Now Vivian welcomed tenderness despite herself. It might—probably would—make the end of their journey hurt more, but to hell with that.

All things turned to pain in the end. Trying to avoid that only made them hurt from the very beginning.

Sleep came quickly. Vivian's sword keeping watch played a role in that, as did Olvir's complete exhaustion. The weariness made Vivian's presence in his arms an aid to sleep, in fact, while it would have been anything but if he'd had more energy.

As tired as he was, Olvir felt heat in his groin at first. Parts of him responded before other, sensible regions reminded them that he'd been walking all day and the previous night, fighting before that, and, further back, doing yet more walking. If he tried to act on the stirrings below his waist, he doubted he'd live through the experience.

Muscles he'd pushed almost past their breaking point began to untwist themselves. The soles of his feet throbbed, but in almost a comforting way. The regular dull pulse of discomfort meant that

Olvir's weight was off them, and it would remain so for a while. Vivian was heat against his chest, long legs tangled with his, the soft, regular in-and-out tide of air a little above his collarbone.

Nobody, even people who liked them, would have called the Sentinels ordinary. Emeth and Darya, even Katrine, would've laughed at the description. Vivian probably would have too. Not being normal was practically their duty. The woman who lay beside him, pliant in sleep, felt like a small piece of the everyday world nonetheless.

Perhaps it was all relative. Vivian had been part of Olvir's life when he'd been simply another knight. She'd known him when they'd spent their days on familiar ground, around their comrades in arms. She was also solid to the touch, with breath and a heartbeat like any other living being. After hours of stumbling through a ghostly landscape, that reality was valuable too.

Night wind ruffled Olvir's hair. It was cold, but with blankets over him and Vivian's warmth beside him, that barely made an impression. Neither did the calls of birds or the wolf's howl he heard in the distance. Ulamir would warn Vivian about any threats. She'd wake Olvir, and together they'd stand off whatever came.

He wouldn't have been able to have that confidence with a normal woman, Olvir reflected, even another knight. Maybe a normal woman wouldn't have banished his disconnection so effectively—Olvir's nature might have kept distance between them. Vivian, unusual herself, met him halfway.

Reasons didn't matter, he decided. Lying against her, he was part of the world again.

The mountains and the Battlefield still lay ahead of them. He didn't know what waited there. Many of the possibilities, good and bad alike, ended with his death. As Olvir's weary body relaxed and darkness slipped over his mind, he could examine each potential ending without either fear or sadness, considering it and then laying it aside.

He slept without dreaming, without stirring. Night passed between one blink and another.

———

Vivian woke with Olvir's chin on top of her head. He was still holding her close, despite sleeping quite soundly as far as she could tell. At some point during the previous night, she'd thrown one leg over his thighs.

She had not, thank all the gods, drooled on his chest.

Ulamir was keeping watch, his attention on whatever threats might approach. He wasn't as fully in Vivian's mind as usual, but she sensed his presence at a distance and was grateful for it. It let her wake gradually, rather than snapping into instant alertness as she did when it was her turn on sentry duty.

Her muscles ached faintly, and she was not thrilled about the sun coming up already, but Vivian felt a hundred times more like a person than she'd done the night before. Simply not walking for eight hours or so had done wonders.

With rest came sensation. Vivian noticed every detail that she hadn't the previous night, when she'd been too tired for anything but vague impressions. For instance, her face was pressed to the hollow of Olvir's neck, which was surprisingly soft in contrast to the firm solidity of his arms. Cloth provided only a faint barrier to her perception. His biceps, like his chest, were unyielding, his stomach hard and flat. Rising up against it...

Oh, he was more energetic in the morning, too, asleep or not.

A slow hunger began to uncurl through Vivian, a lassitude that was yearning at the same time.

She stretched, shifting her hips forward to bring her sex snug against Olvir's thigh. The motion slid *her* thigh against a very large and insistent ridge. It twitched in response, and Olvir gasped in his sleep, so Vivian repeated the motion.

The noise he made then was approximately *mmm*, not quite a sigh or a moan.

Still apparently without waking, he slid his hand from her waist, fingers grazing her spine. Vivian's shirt might as well not have been there: she felt every tiny motion. When he grasped the side of her arse, gently but quite firmly, it was her turn to moan.

She was quiet. She'd been trained soundly, and lust didn't erase that. The noise she let out wouldn't have drawn undue attention from the wilderness.

It did wake Olvir. His eyes opened a crack, then completely. Vivian saw the sudden recognition of where he was, who he was with, and exactly what his hand was about. That hand went suddenly still, but Olvir didn't pull it away.

"Ah." Desire painted itself across his features, all the sharper because he was awake. "Good morning."

"Considerably better than yesterday's," said Vivian, skin tingling at the breathless depth of his voice. The rational part of her, the Sentinel who had learned her duty by heart, was waking, observing that the sun was rising and they needed to be on the move. She ignored it long enough to flick her tongue over Olvir's earlobe.

Life was difficult. Pleasure was important, whether or not she could see it through. She basked in his groan and the way his hips bucked, let herself have that, then added, "But not as good as it would be if we could linger here."

The grip on her arse tightened. "You're right," said Olvir, "and you're cruel."

"I don't have to be," she said sincerely, wondering if she'd gone too far. "Just let me know and I'll contain myself."

He kissed her in answer, quick but thorough. "Never."

Chapter 15

"IT LOOKS VERY SMALL FROM HERE, DOESN'T IT?"

Two days' journey from the edge of the forest, the path wound up around the foot of the Serpentspine. The land was starting to fall away sharply in angles of dark-green grass and blue stone, but Olvir hadn't realized how high they were or how far they'd gotten until they rounded a twisting bend that brought them practically in a circle.

The world below was fuzzier than it would have been on a map, where trees were neat clumps of circles if they were so abundant as to show up at all and nobody bothered adding stones or animal tracks, but the outlines were quite clear. The scrubland stretched pale brown between the forest and the mountains, and the woods beyond it were almost black in the morning light. At the edge of those woods, near the horizon, Olvir could barely spot a trail of smoke rising into the air. That was the camp: the palisade of bare wood and stone that had been his entire life for six months. He almost believed he could smell the cooking fires or hear the soldiers calling to one another.

Vivian glanced where he pointed. "Extremely," she said, with a quiet, wry laugh. "There's a moral lesson of some sort there, I'm certain. The insignificance of humanity, maybe. Of Thyran and his creatures too. Except that the storms would blight all the forest and its creatures pretty thoroughly, too, as they did when Thyran first summoned them."

"Not forever," said Olvir, following her as they picked their way along the rocky trail. "At least, those storms didn't last. Now…"

"Now," Vivian agreed, sounding grim.

"I want to imagine," said Olvir, feeling something stuck within his mind begin to turn, though he couldn't have said what, "that at the worst, part of the world would survive. Or the gods would remake it. If what Thyran does damages creation worse than their presence would, they'll step in—but I'll grant that's not a line I'd ever want to cross!"

Vivian's shoulders, which had begun to stiffen, relaxed when Olvir added the last statement. "That's logical enough," she said slowly, "though I admit I'd never given it very much consideration."

"There hasn't been space for the long view, these past few months. It probably wouldn't have occurred to me either, but places like this can help take me out of myself."

"Riding does that for me," Vivian said. "Even when I was headed to a mission, the ride would leave me calmer, clear my thinking. Paying attention to another creature keeps my thoughts from turning inward too much."

"No wonder you commanded aptly."

"Flattery is a wonderful quality. And…hmm." She walked a short distance onward before continuing, her feet making methodical crunching sounds on the rock.

Those sounds didn't matter anymore, just as their talking didn't. The path wound, but without turns that any foe could have used for an ambush, the view below them was clear, and the mountain face was too stark for most things to come straight down. Both Olvir and Vivian glanced up regularly regardless—Thyran did have flying creatures, he could have beasts that could climb like insects, and stories did say there'd been dragons on the other side of the mountains—but silence was no longer essential.

They did keep watches at night, much to their mutual frustration. Given the circumstances, it would have been foolishness—perhaps lethal foolishness—to be distracted for a quick tumble.

Olvir kept reminding himself of that, especially when he was walking behind Vivian.

"I think that probably did help," she said. "Not that I'd say I always made the best decisions, but having to make them, and new ones each day, and be aware of how my Sentinels were bearing up... I suspect I did reason better, in general, than I would have if I'd been on my own."

"My mother favored singing for that. The last I heard, she was still leading the choir in her temple." Olvir gazed over the edge again, thinking about the land beyond the horizon and a large gray-haired woman in blue, with a grip like iron and a talent with bread. The two went together, Edda'd said once: a life of swordplay translated well to kneading dough. "I used to joke that she'd taken me in in the hopes of getting a baritone one day."

"Foresightful woman, unless your singing voice is higher than your speaking."

"Oh, no. Until the war, she had me come back for the spring festival so I could take Poram's part, despite my knighthood. She said there was nobody else in the village who could do it without invoking the god's wrath."

Vivian's head tilted back a little when she laughed again, her dark, curly hair brushing the collar of her shirt. "I'm sure Tinival doesn't mind you giving his father a bit of assistance now and then," she said. "Family, eh?"

"Family," he agreed and then remembered who he was speaking to. Sentinels were generally drawn from foundlings, bastards, and other unwanted children. He and Vivian had never gotten around to speaking much about their childhoods when they'd worked together before the war: they'd talked about their travel or the people they were dealing with and swapped jokes or stories. They'd never consciously avoided the past—or Olvir hadn't—but it had never come up. "If it's a sore spot," he added, "I'm happy to change the subject."

"Not at all. Even the Sentinels who don't know theirs are usually all right with it by my age."

"And," he asked, cautious but encouraged by the fact that she'd mentioned the subject, "you do?"

"Mm-hmm." Vivian took a swig of water from her flask, then slipped it back onto her belt. "I didn't enter the Order until I was nine. The crops failed that year, in spite of all Sitha's priests could do, and I was the fourth child. Sending me to the Sentinels meant we all survived."

Olvir nodded. There'd been years of that sort in his own village. Children were a gamble. Grown, they were a blessing in old age, but too many young ones could be an unlucky family's undoing. "You must've caught up with the training quickly."

"Fairly. Some of the others have better reflexes than I do, but"— she shrugged—"I can see how normal people work, at times, in ways they can't. It evens out."

The trail bent again as they went upward, carrying them away from the view of the forest and the camp. Vivian could see flashing glints in the distance. Memory, as well as maps, told her that they came from the sun shining off the edge of the western ocean, dancing and shifting as the waves rippled. Between her and the sea were flat plains, pale green with spring, where the broad Natarian River wound across the land. Small red forms moved over it in bunches: herds of the volqui that both grazed and hunted there.

She'd wanted one of them when she was a girl, inspired by stories about the stonekin riding them into battle. Her oldest sister had stopped her attempt to use their mother's red dye on their patient brown draft horse. Vivian herself had reconsidered her idea to add horns to the incongruously named Cricket: even that placid brick of a mare had seemed likely to object.

That had been long ago, in days she rarely thought of any longer except when she visited.

Funny that talking to Olvir had brought it up. He'd been the only person outside the Order to ask if she minded the subject. Sentinels didn't generally get the impulse to talk of family, since most didn't have them. Other people generally chattered blithely about theirs, though Amris, in the few weeks she'd known him, had been reticent.

Home is a vanished place for him too, said Ulamir.

"Home becomes a vanished place for everyone, in time," she said. "That just happens earlier for some of us than others. And more comprehensively."

Olvir, behind her, made an affirmative noise. "Nobody can go back to what they had as children," he said, "but I have a person and a place at least. I realize I'm very lucky."

"So am I," said Vivian. In the ensuing silence, she felt his search for the most polite form of the question and elaborated. "My mother went beyond the Veil a few years ago. My sibling Calyn went into the army—not posted with us, thank the gods; I don't want to fight alongside a person who remembers me in diapers— but my father's alive, and my brother runs most of the farm now, with his...let's say 'supervision.' My sister's a blacksmith in the village. I visit every so often, when I have the leisure between missions."

"I always wanted siblings," said Olvir. "The knighthood helped a little in that regard, but it wasn't like what I saw from the village families. It wasn't worse, but...not the same. Maybe it was that we all were half-grown already when we joined."

"It could be, but the Order takes us young mostly, and it's not the same. With siblings, there's more, oh..." She considered the best phrasing for it while the plains grew remote below them and the view expanded. The blue rim of the ocean was starting to be visible now. "Working out your place by wanting different things or being good at different things. Significant differences, not just your blessings or whether you're better with a bow than a spear."

"A shirt can be red or blue, but it's still a shirt, not a cloak."

"Right. Which I suppose makes the knighthood and the Order clothes chests." Vivian grinned into the thinning air of the mountain.

"Or tailors."

Calling the Reforging the Hemming would meet with little approval, I suspect.

That made Vivian snicker. Olvir laughed, too, when she explained it. Even though he was quiet, the sound rang merrily in the heights.

"But," he said afterward, "the Order does seem different. It takes you younger, it shapes you more. A priesthood's a vocation, but it's one you choose as a youth, as you'd choose an apprenticeship."

Vivian had heard similar sentiments in different tones. Then she'd taken the speaker apart, verbally, with icy precision or kept surly silence in the name of duty. Olvir didn't demand answers or insist that she justify the Order. He just sounded as if he was thinking things through.

She liked that. When he added, "I know I speak from the outside. I probably get half of it wrong," she liked it even more.

"No," she replied, "no, not completely. We do choose, in the end." Ties remained—the Order had members across the known lands who'd declined the Reforging but sent reports or waited for orders—but there was volition, as much as there could be in those raised to a task. "But there's a reason it's Reforging with us, not... What is it you have?"

"The ceremony's merely a dedication. Well, I say 'merely'..." Vivian could imagine Olvir's smile. "I doubt there's any among us who couldn't remember every detail of theirs. It does give Tinival permission to use us as he wills. There's some training for that too. For how to handle it."

"Right. You survive if you haven't done anything egregiously wrong. It's not a matter of what you can physically or mentally endure."

Vivian had fallen through fire during hers, or that was how she recalled it. Fire, then ice, with great eyes watching from places she couldn't quite focus on. She'd known every inch of herself, each bruise or scratch she'd ever taken, before the ordeal had concluded. The Adeptas had said she'd spent four days in the chamber. It hadn't been a record.

"We trust that the trainees know their limits," she said, "or that the Adeptas will spot the ones who don't long before the choice comes up. You have to let people take on their own pain."

"How can you be sure that they make the choice freely?"

"We try as best we can. It's probably not sufficient always, especially not for the foundlings." Vivian watched the path ahead of her, the gray scree that could turn an ankle. "A few of them do turn away at the end, if that proves a point. Otherwise…we need to exist, we need to be the creatures we are, so we make compromises. Gods willing, they're not the wrong ones."

Chapter 16

NEAR SUNSET OF THAT DAY, VIVIAN BEGAN TO FEEL HER secondary gift.

It was faint, as she'd expected so far from her goal and with the path mostly clear, but she could feel the pressure: she imagined it was like the rein against a horse's neck, not pulling but guiding. The sensation urged her broadly forward and a touch to the left, which was nothing that she hadn't known already. Still, it was good to know her gift was working. Vivian suspected they'd need it badly on the other side of the mountains, since there were no maps to the Battlefield or of the ground within it.

One thought led to another. She glanced backward at Olvir.

He was striding along steadily behind her, a light sheen of sweat on his face, although the air was cool. They were halfway up the mountain, nearly to the point where the maps they *did* have said they should find a pass. The angle was sharp, hard work even for the two of them.

Vivian could comfortably manage speech without effort however. "So," she ventured, reluctant to speak every word but trying to keep that to herself, "I suppose we're properly in the mountains, aren't we?"

"That we are," Olvir agreed, with as little emotion as he'd displayed in Magarteach's yurt—less, when Vivian considered the matter, because surprise didn't enter into it. "I'll have to ask you to stand guard for more than your share of the night. I doubt I'll be of much use when I…make the attempt."

"That won't be a problem," she said, leaving out the reasons she'd have been watching anyhow. "Do you know how you'll do it?"

Olvir shrugged. "Not in detail, no. I'll start by meditating."

All priests were trained in that: a form of contact with their gods stronger than prayer but not as dramatic as a full invocation. Vivian had seen Olvir do it in the past, when he'd needed Tinival's insight on the truth of a matter or, once, to translate a coded inscription.

"Seems like a good beginning," she said and hoped that was all it took.

Invocations were hard on the priest, which would be a problem in itself with days of hard travel ahead. Even worse, they opened the world.

After Letar and Gizath had fought, the gods had imprisoned Gizath and retreated from their creation. Sitha had drawn the Veil of Fire between them and mortals. Prayer parted it, making a path to the realm where the gods dwelled.

Given Olvir's burden, Vivian didn't know what other places he might reach by accident if he drew the Veil aside.

She didn't want to find out.

That night, they had a fire.

It was a small one, made of dry branches from the stunted pines that grew on the mountain ledge. Vivian and Olvir built it up against the stone face and behind a few large rocks, which, gods willing, would shield it from any prying eyes.

Olvir sat tailor-style with the flame at his back, telling himself that he'd meditated since he'd become a squire, meditated specifically on his strange powers after Oakford, and nothing had happened. It didn't help: the situation had changed, or he wouldn't be trying.

"Silver Wind, in your wisdom, guide my path," he said quietly, doing his best to adapt a prayer he'd learned in his youth. "Clear my eyes and let me see what I must. Clear my mind and let me know wisdom, truth, and justice. Clear my heart and give me courage to face what's before me. If all goes wrong, lend your strength to my comrade, Vivian Bathari."

Olvir couldn't see Vivian's reaction. She stood at the side of the circle, watching him and the path at once, as much as she could manage.

His sword was across the campfire from him. It had seemed the best course of action.

Calmness settled onto him, not nearly the complete detachment he felt ahead of battle, nowhere near the serenity he was sometimes granted at prayers, but the necessary tranquility to go forward. Olvir closed his eyes, placed his open hands on his knees with their palms up, and inhaled deeply four times.

He sank into himself and found, at first, familiar ground. There was his body, its strength and its weariness, the desire for Vivian woven with the longing for warmth, sleep, and hot food, the scar on his middle back that ached in advance of the spring rains, his weakness for wine although he had a good head for ale, all the small physical notes that he'd grown accustomed to. Next came his mind: memories of home and Edda, of the knighthood and his missions, scraps of songs and stories, names of people he'd met a few times and likely would never see again, admiration of Vivian, attempts to plan for the future, and the realization that it was probably futile.

Olvir noted it all and put it all aside, sifting patiently. He'd know what he sought, or he hoped he would.

The turning point came after his sorrow about those who'd died beside him, the ones he hadn't been able to save, and the melancholy of walking the ancient road. He sorted through his humor when he and Vivian had been speaking, his pleasure at the beauty of the view, and most of all his fears—that he'd die, that it wouldn't be enough, that he would fail and *not* die. Ruin was lurking in the future, and death on a scale he couldn't fully understand. He knew he'd be responsible for both.

He was sweating and half-sick by the time he got through that layer. Olvir had sat in contemplation once every four days since he'd started his training, but the sorrow never quite vanished, and the previous practice had only taken a little of the edge off the fear. The abandoned road and the long journey by night had honed it again, as was so frequently the case.

As he'd done since before his dedication, he broke through those doubts, that sorrow, and found his bond to Tinival. That ran through every part of his life and every aspect of the world surrounding him. Nahon had once described it as a light that shone wherever he looked closely, Morgan as a thread in fabric, but to Olvir, the tie to his god had always been harmony that gave structure to a complicated song.

That harmony was part of everything, but it was also, unmistakably, itself. Olvir had never been unable to hear it, never confused it for anything else, never found a pattern that even slightly resembled it.

Now he heard another. It wasn't part of Tinival, but it was so close in nature that Olvir perceived it in the same fashion, at the same time.

Olvir couldn't get nearly as clear a sense of that other as he had of his god. Simply noticing it took a curious mental or spiritual squinting. The edges kept going fuzzy and unclear even then—or maybe bits of those edges were missing. Olvir couldn't tell.

He reached out for it, cautious but not tentative.

For a moment, he made contact. A series of mixed images and feelings flashed through Olvir's mind, the best he could do to interpret an entity beyond the mortal world. He saw a vase smashing into large pieces. Sunset colors, orange and violet, flickered, formless. He felt the urge to grab whoever was nearest and didn't know whether he meant to embrace or strangle. Vines. Chains. A tree with many branches. A starving dog tied to a stake. A gleaming metal and crystal bridge. A coin lying in a street, gleaming gold. Shifting, dizzying images, not quite resolving into any coherent pattern. An insect, not dead, with others eating their way out of its body. A dagger, shining red in the sunset.

He didn't decide to stop. The power inside him didn't throw him off either. Olvir sensed it reaching back with desperate curiosity. Then whatever part was doing the reaching fell away, too weak to cross the distance between them—as was he.

All outside the ring of firelight was still. The night was windless. Any creatures abroad in it were either too small for Vivian to see or utterly uninterested in the little camp.

Vivian still watched the stark landscape, mindful of what magic or simply human meat could attract, but she kept a keen eye on Olvir.

He sat as motionless as the mountainside itself, except for the regular rise and fall of his chest. At first, that was all. The fire crackled, the stars glittered overhead, and Olvir held his place, becoming part of the night itself.

It would have been easy to miss the beads of sweat that sprang to his forehead or the sudden ragged inhalation of a man who'd just had a shock. Vivian noticed both. She crossed the distance between them quickly, not standing directly at his back but close enough to catch him if he passed out.

Ulamir's gem shone blue in the unsteady light. Shadows danced along the naked blade.

Nothing approaches, he said, *and I sense no change in the knight.*

Vivian asked whether he would, not daring to speak aloud.

I might. I can't be certain.

The soulsword had picked up the trail of magical creatures in the past, but human wizards generally didn't stand out. Where did the incarnation of a god, or part of a god, fall? It probably depended on how incarnate it became.

She sent Ulamir understanding. Then she stood and waited.

Olvir's lips parted. His closed eyes moved rapidly beneath his lids. On his lap, his open hands strained suddenly, fingers splayed and stretching outward, then snapped closed with such force that even Vivian winced at the idea of being in that grip.

His mouth moved but formed no recognizable words.

Vivian swore silently. She wouldn't interfere unless she decided that irreparable harm was about to happen, she'd said. She thought she'd do a decent job of judging that where the body was concerned. The mind and the soul were dicier.

Her awareness began to center itself around her stance, her arms, and the mild strain Ulamir's weight was placing on her muscles. The world was resolving into forces: push and pull, up and down, thrust and parry. It was the same way she saw the world before a battle.

Wait, she told herself.

A shift has taken place. How great it is, I cannot say, but there is power now where there was none before.

Ulamir couldn't tell her the nature of that power, or he would have done so already. In death, he retained his people's awareness of magic, but nobody could read minds.

So Vivian stayed as she was, braced to strike or to save. She watched Olvir's fists unclench. His shoulders abruptly slumped, his face relaxed, and his eyes opened. The pupils were very large, color only a narrow rim around the black.

Vivian wanted to be relieved but didn't let herself. "Name?" she asked.

"Sir Olvir Yoralth, knight of Tinival." His voice was rough.

Clearly he wasn't going to topple over, so Vivian dug the weeping sculpture out of her pouch. "Touch this and proclaim your faith," she said, holding it out.

"I look to Tinival for wisdom, justice, and truth," Olvir said, cupping the woman's chin with fingers that shook slightly. "I revere Sitha and the works she inspires from mortal hands and minds. I celebrate and protect Poram's creation. I praise Letar for her healing, for her passion, for being the flame that burns bright against corruption."

The wood stayed cool to Vivian's touch. She took the statue back, then handed Olvir the waterskin from her belt. "You deserve stronger."

"And we both deserve hot baths and a bed that's not the ground," he said with a smile that was probably his. He drank eagerly but not too quickly.

"So?" Vivian resheathed Ulamir.

"It was a good idea, I'd say. Not an easy one, but likely wise." Olvir wiped his mouth, then his forehead. "I touched the fragment or spoke to it—whichever metaphor you want to use—and I think I can do it again. Maybe I can manage more as we get closer or with practice. I'm not sure."

Vivian thought of the statue, which would *probably* have burned Olvir if the fragment had completely taken him over but might not have responded to partial control or subtle influence. She remembered the strength of his grip and how his lips had formed phrases of silent gibberish.

"I suspect," she said, "that we may have to give up on being sure of many things."

Chapter 17

FROM THE GROUND, ONE OF THE DIPS BETWEEN THE Serpentspine's peaks was notably lower than the others. That was the Vadar, the Cattle-Running Pass in the old barbarian language, and Vivian and Olvir's best chance of getting across the mountains, assuming the old stories held true. It was also the source of a stream that ran briskly down to join the Natarian. So early in the spring, it was a vigorous cascade, thick and turbulent with snowmelt.

Olvir first heard it in the early afternoon, and the sound made him lick his lips. He'd been drinking regularly but never indulgently, always careful of their supplies, and the water itself had gone stale several days since. It did its job, but the taste of leather pervaded it. The thought of refilling their skins with a new supply, clear and cold even with the necessary purifying wine, was sufficient good news to break through his gloomy mood.

For three nights running, he'd been reaching for the fragment, never quite succeeding. He thought he was getting closer with every attempt, but the difference was subtle enough to easily have been wishful thinking.

That had almost been worse than complete failure. If Olvir had reached for the fragment and gotten no response, he wouldn't have been left wondering if he could have found some practical application or discovered more about the thing had he just been a bit stronger or smarter.

He wouldn't have been fearing what else he could almost have done either.

It never felt bad. Oh, the dagger looked sinister, the scene with the insects was revolting, but the sunset was beautiful and the bridge fascinating. In addition to that, the impression he'd gotten beneath the images hadn't been malice.

As much as he'd gotten any impression from the fragment, it had been loss, in many senses: of being broken, abandoned, cast off, but also of being *lost*, unable to get its bearings on a world so fundamentally alien to what it had known.

The gods didn't often manifest directly through people. Priests had very specific powers, which were generally all that mortal flesh and minds could channel without permanent effect, though there were occasional stories about exceptions. Even more occasionally, some of those exceptions survived with all their wits. Those few had described presences that they couldn't quite put into words, perspectives completely different from that of any human or elder folk.

"Do you think," he asked Vivian as he led them up the ridge toward the Vadar, approaching the highest point they'd have to reach in the mountains, "that a god would find us as disorienting as we find them?"

She gave it some consideration. At any rate, she was silent. Olvir liked to assume that she was contemplating the question rather than trying to contain her impatience with him or evaluating whether or not he was showing symptoms of possession and should be stabbed in the kidneys.

"I don't see why not," Vivian eventually said. "And it could depend on the god. Poram, for example, doesn't deal with mortals as regularly as the other three."

"Animals are mortal."

"Fair point. But I don't get the impression that they contact him much. Is this about the fragment?"

"It is. I wonder if one problem may be that we need to learn to speak each other's language, as it were—that it's not just strength of mind separating us but the need to find common ground, or at least common terms."

"That's more your area of expertise," she said, "but I can't find any argument against it as a course of action. None that wouldn't also argue against us being here"—Vivian gestured at the mountain trail—"to begin with, at least. Do you have any notion of how to start translating?"

"Nothing firm yet. Understanding languages is one of our gifts, though, at need. Maybe I can find a method that'll let me use that. Or maybe it'll come as we get to know each other."

"You talk as if the fragment is its own person." Vivian's voice drifted forward to Olvir, carefully pitched to carry no judgment, no question, simply observation.

Nonetheless, the first words that occurred to him were defensive: *It surely isn't me,* and then *What are you suggesting?* Irritation tightened Olvir's neck and shoulders. The fragment *wasn't* him, and he was trying to handle it, and—

And Vivian wasn't wrong. He stared at the dark line of rock ahead of them and kept silent until he'd given her words a chance to sink in. "I do. I'm not sure if that's right or not. It's on the same, oh, level of my spirit as my bond with the Silver Wind, and I'd never presume that He and I were the same person, but…it is a different situation, isn't it?"

"I think so," said Vivian. "I'm not going to claim to be an authority. And—" She tilted her head a little and waited as Ulamir spoke. "There's a reasonable chance keeping a distance, in your mind, is wise. Then again, there's a reasonable chance it isn't. I just figured that being aware is likely a good thing, and gods know it's as much as we can manage."

Olvir nodded. "We're on unfamiliar ground," he said, consciously throwing his bad temper to the winds. "In many ways."

At the highest point of the pass, the road joined with the stream, which rushed past in a torrent of white foam and curved away down in the opposite direction from the trail Vivian and Olvir had followed. Small trees, more like shrubs, had grown up on its banks, and moss coated the ground nearby. The current was too fast for them to fish, and they didn't have time, but Vivian filled her waterskins, adding a bit of wine to each, then stood watching the path while Olvir did the same.

The trail wound too much to give her a straight view of the road they should take. She could see down the slope of the mountain below them, though: sheer blue-gray stone, striped with irregular ridges and dotted with patches of green.

Below that, the land ran flat and rust-red—Vivian thought it was covered with a sort of grass, but it was too far away to tell—for what looked to be five or ten miles. Then it…stopped.

She recognized the Battlefield, because it couldn't be anything else. Vivian was very far from her youth, but a child's instinctive shudder worked its way up her spine at her first sight of the place.

The…"surface," she decided, because her mind tried to connect what she saw with the word *land* and gave it up as a bad job, was glossy, nearly transparent. At first, it seemed black. Then, as Vivian watched, it rippled. Parts rose and fell in no discernable pattern. Vivian thought it had a green tinge, or maybe lightning-flash blue. Beyond the spot, she saw a thin trail of red, probably the place where the world grew normal again, but her gaze immediately went back to the shifting colors.

It is stone, of a sort, said Ulamir, but he sounded as thunderstruck as she felt.

"The stories said it was like a scar," said Vivian, knowing that she sounded faintly, foolishly betrayed.

"It might be," said Olvir. "That… Scars aren't regular flesh, are they? Why should a scar on the world, one the gods made, be regular…" He spread his hands, grasping for the right word and not finding it. "A regular part of creation?"

"Ugh," said Vivian, not disagreeing.

If Thyran did more harm to the world than the gods' presence would, Olvir had said, then presumably the Four would step in. Once they breached the Veil of Fire, though, Gizath could too—and just a few minutes of his fight with Letar had created the Battlefield. Vivian had always known divine intervention was nothing to hope for, but watching that land-scar flex and shimmer in the sun, she felt it on a bone-deep level.

Humanity might survive a new round of storms, even one that Thyran had let build to full power. The waterfolk and the stonekin had a better chance. At the very worst, there would likely be creatures that survived and reclaimed the world once the storms had run their course—and not even Thyran's power could last forever. Vivian had that faith.

That long view didn't change her duty, or Olvir's. Their loyalty was to those who lived now and who would be lost in the storms. Their lives were small things weighed against that butcher's bill. Vivian would pay her price gladly when the moment came—but there were other balances.

"I understand Them now," she said. "Or at any rate, I understand the Veil. There's almost nothing worth risking another instance of that."

Vivian didn't point. She didn't need to.

―――――――

For the first time since he'd known Vivian, Olvir had the urge to comfort her.

He didn't enjoy the sight of the Battlefield. He doubted any mortal could. For a good hour or so, it lay in front of them as they descended the narrow, twisting trail, rippling in the distance as though it didn't want to let them forget they'd have to face it before too long. At times, it looked completely smooth, at other times scaled, or like grains of sand moving with the wind. It shone black and green, blue and almost white from different angles. Watching it made Olvir's eyes hurt.

But that was the way of the gods. Even the Four, meaning the best and trying to restrain themselves, were too great for the average person. Only a very few knights, at rare intervals, called on Tinival in major ways. Sitha's most powerful priests tended to have the same ethereal air as Gwarill, standing always a touch separate from the world and the present moment—and she, with her elder son, made up the gentler half of the Four.

The gods reshaped the Sentinels, blessed them, but didn't live in them the way they did their priests. Vivian had spent her life in harder and more deadly fights than Olvir at times, he suspected, but she hadn't spent it side by side with power she knew she could never comprehend or even face fully.

Olvir couldn't give Vivian his experience. He certainly couldn't reassure her. They were walking into the Battlefield, trying to find its heart. If their reason for doing so hadn't been likely to end in both their deaths, the journey still would've been horribly dangerous. Vivian understood that as thoroughly as he did, maybe better. Besides, he'd taken a number of oaths against lying.

Tinival ruled words. Olvir took a few and flung them out, hoping they'd be a handhold. "Do you sing?"

"Wha—now?"

"No," he said, "no, that'd be a bit risky even now that we've left the forest. And we could get avalanches. In a general sense, I meant."

"I've been known to. I wouldn't say it's one of my most stunning talents, but I've never had any complaints about how I carry a tune." He heard her voice softening, losing some of its wire-strung tension. "I'd say that melancholy ballads in the bath are my specialty."

"'*The Violet Banner*'?"

"It's very suitable for scrubbing your back. 'And they met below the staaars on the riversiiide,' and so forth—a very repetitive chorus, nothing too distracting."

"Important not to miss a spot," Olvir agreed, "especially if—Ah."

He'd rounded a blind corner, his view blocked by a stand of pines, his sword half-drawn as was his usual practice in such cases. At once, he'd seen that the blade would be neither necessary or, unfortunately, helpful.

The trail *had* continued from that point. In the past, though, the mountains had shaken, or the winter snows had loosened rock. Now a boulder stood in their path: twice Olvir's height, so wide that it blocked the path on either side, and far too massive for both of them to lift.

Chapter 18

THIS, SAID ULAMIR, *WAS OLD BEFORE THE STORMS.*

"I can't say I'm surprised." Discouraged, yes. Annoyed, entirely. Surprised, no, not at all. The boulder, blue-gray like the rest of the mountain, was polished so smooth that it nearly shone, and so were the mountain walls to either side. Vivian hadn't studied stonework to any great extent, despite partnering with Ulamir, but she had the idea that a surface like that was the result of wind, water, and, most of all, time.

It also limited their options considerably. Climbing the boulder would take either hands and feet like a lizard's or a method of making holes in stone, neither of which she or Olvir had. "I can't see a crack in the godsdamned thing," she said. "Can you?"

Olvir stepped forward from her side and peered at the boulder, craning his neck to see as far up as he could before shaking his head. "If there is one, it's too far for us to reach, much less drive a spike into."

"I can't see any on the sides either," said Vivian. She took a careful look around, alert for details she might have missed in her first, exasperated inspection.

The pass was narrow and winding. Below, the stone plunged straight down, ending in red grass—as a small blessing, the Battlefield was no longer visible from where they stood—and trees so far away that they resembled thistles. The mountain's face was sheer directly above them and for a distance beyond. Two pines grew a few yards away, where the trail was a little wider, but they were short and wind-twisted, no good for climbing.

"The stone predates Thyran, Ulamir said. The nomads must have had another route across, but I don't see it. I don't sense it, either, or not nearby," Vivian added after a quick internal check. Her blessing felt as it had for the last day: a sense of general direction and the now-frustrating conviction that the path ahead of her was right.

"They might have stopped crossing before he went to war with them," Olvir replied. He put a hand on the boulder, rubbed his thumb against the shiny surface, and frowned. "The histories aren't exact."

"Of course not. Why would they be?" Vivian fought the urge to kick the boulder. A broken foot wouldn't help. History, it seemed, wouldn't either. It was possible that the tribes had asked for rides from dragons, for that matter, or had the winged horses of legend. Neither were available. "I think we'll have to go back and up. There's a rougher patch near those trees, and then…with luck, we'll find another ridge. Otherwise, sideways and then down."

She didn't bother trying to sound hopeful. *Sideways and down* meant crab-climbing between one forced handhold and another, trusting their fingers, the pitons, and the rock to all hold, with a drop waiting that even a Sentinel's healing likely wouldn't let her survive. Vivian had learned the basics of mountain climbing in her training. She'd never used them since.

Odds were that she'd blend well into the red grass when she fell. That was convenient.

"This is a strange question, I realize," said Olvir, the thoughtful frown still crinkling his brow, "but can Ulamir tell what kind of rock this is?"

A wise question, I would say, though I know not where he wants it to lead. It lived, once. It is the bones of small swimming creatures from a great gulf of years. Limestone, I deem it, in your language, he added, with the air of one forced to speak in small words and short sentences.

"Probably limestone, in essence," she translated. "Why?"

"I have an idea. How much wine do we have left?"

Flames roared against the base of the rock, licking up from the pine branches placed around it. The air was fragrant with the smoke. Now and again, the fire would pop as the flame hit a pocket of sap, or a pinecone would explode.

"It's getting there," Vivian said. She stood in a small bare spot on the left side of the boulder, one hand resting on its surface. The sight made Olvir's own palms ache, but Vivian didn't seem at all disturbed, merely alert both to the boulder's temperature and to any stray sparks that could set her clothing ablaze.

Sentinels were unnerving that way, even to him.

Vivian was more than unnerving. Surrounded by smoke, with her eyes and the tears on her cheeks glowing, she could have been a spirit of the fire itself or modeled for an icon of Letar, whose element it was. Watching, Olvir was torn between worry for her safety, concern that his plan wouldn't work, and the impulse simply to engrave every detail of the image into his memory.

"Where did you learn about this?" she asked.

They'd been too busy earlier to talk, first cutting limbs from the trees and then building the fire, but now they had leisure while they waited for the rock to heat.

"One of the grooms for Lord Farren—the first knight I served—was the son of a copper miner. He was an old man. He liked to tell stories, as old men do, especially on the winter evenings when he was teaching me how to mend saddles. They do this to open veins, he said."

"We can only hope it doesn't end up opening ours," Vivian joked.

Olvir made a face at her. He knew there was no use in volunteering for the next step. Vivian would have said it was nonsensical.

Given her blessing and the Sentinels' rapid healing, she'd have been right, so Olvir kept the offer to himself.

"We've likely done all we can with this fire," Vivian said after consulting with Ulamir. "Next step, please."

Promptly, if reluctantly, Olvir handed her an open wineskin.

Vivian turned her head away and upended the leather flask over the rock.

Cold wine, nearly vinegar, met heated limestone. A froth of white bubbles foamed up. As they died down, they revealed a web-work of cracks and pits.

"One more," said Vivian, and Olvir complied.

Another wave of fluid hissed and bubbled down, sending up more steam from the fire. This time, the cracking sound that followed was far larger. Vivian and Olvir both sprang back just before part of the rock's face sheared completely off.

Stone fell into fire with a crash that shook the trail, and sparks flew upward. So did a flaming branch, which flipped end over end in the sky, then landed in front of Vivian. She stamped it out without looking down: her attention was fixed on the remaining boulder and the mountains on either side.

Finally, she spoke. "No avalanche, Ulamir says." Vivian's voice was hoarse from the smoke, and the rapid rise and fall of her breasts beneath the tunic showed her exertion, as well as drawing Olvir's eyes. "And we've made enough cracks to give ourselves plenty of hand- and footholds. Are you all right?"

"Me? I'm perfectly fine. You were standing closer. Are you hurt at all?"

"Not significantly." A thin red line ran down Vivian's jaw, probably the result of a flying chip of stone, and a series of scratches laddered her wrists from the same source.

Nothing else had touched her. The heated stone, which would've blistered the skin of any normal person, hadn't so much as reddened hers from what Olvir could tell.

"I'm very glad you're the one who came along," he said and, when he noticed the slight upward tilt of her lips, added, "and this is only the latest reason."

———————————

They scooped dirt over the remaining fire, not a particularly hard task given the amount of debris that they'd shaken loose from the boulder. Vivian watched gray dust stream down from her cupped hands, smothering the flames on a small branch, and felt her heartbeat returning to normal.

It quickened again when Olvir knelt in front of her, the top of his chestnut head bent level with her breasts, and slipped the rope around her in a rough harness. There were many enjoyable ways that matters could have proceeded from there. Vivian imagined them and thrilled both to the ideas and to Olvir's nearness.

"It does seem a waste," he said, looking up at her with gleaming dark eyes. His hands lingered, warm on the sides of her waist, then stroked upward to the undersides of her breasts. They tingled in response, the nipples going hard. Vivian wished the layers of leather and wool were gone so that Olvir could see how she reacted to his touch.

But the rock waited, and the rest of their mission after that.

Olvir rose and caught hold of Vivian's hands. He only drew her to him for a few moments, just long enough for his lips to settle over hers, soft and warm and seeking. "A tragic waste," he repeated when he stepped away.

"Or," said Vivian, "a reminder for when we have more time."

She felt his attention on her as she turned and began to climb. Most of it, Vivian knew, came from concern, and she wouldn't have had it any other way. That made him valuable as a companion and marked him as a good knight. Now, however, she was sure that there was a healthy amount of lust mixed in with his regard, lingering from the kiss and enhanced by the view she offered him while she was climbing. She was glad of that too.

No gladness, Ulamir reminded her, frustrating but useful. *No fear. No hope. Only the stone, and you.*

Chapter 19

IT WASN'T A LONG CLIMB, AND THE HEIGHT ITSELF WASN'T overpowering, especially since a fair amount of the stone had broken off. Falling from ten or twelve feet had killed people, though. Bringing down the full weight of a rock on top of that would be very unpleasant, even for a Sentinel and certainly for Olvir.

He didn't want to dwell on the possibility. He had to be aware of it. The trick, Lord Farren had told his squires, essential in all matters of life and death, was to let the gravity of the situation inform the mind without letting the mind dwell on that gravity.

As Emeth would have put it, it was a hell of a trick.

The view while Vivian was climbing helped a good deal. She rose without haste, cautiously seeking out niches for her hands and feet, alert for any detail that could be significant, but she moved lithely, and her clothes showed off the flexing of her muscles.

She met Olvir's gaze from the crumbled top of the rock before she began hammering in a spike with a rope tied to it. Her grin was apparent across the distance between them, as was the teasing lift of her eyebrows. She'd guessed where at least some of his mind was, and she clearly approved.

Knowing that gave extra strength to Olvir's arms as he started on his own journey up, though they were aching nonetheless when he hauled himself over the top. He barely saved his dignity by getting to his feet rather than collapsing beside Vivian. It was some consolation that she was also rubbing at her biceps.

"Darya was right," she said, pulling a wry face. "Fighting is less preparation than you might think. Perhaps I should've taken more missions that involved running around in the wilderness or ruins."

"You preferred to stay on the ground?"

"On or under. Ulamir's a greater help in subterranean places, by and large, and I'm more comfortable there myself."

"I helped get a family out of a wine cellar once." Olvir tugged on the rope to make sure he hadn't pulled the spike loose, then dropped it over the other side of the boulder. "That was the closest I've come to underground work. Morgan once had to track a kidnapper and her victim through the sewers of Abhlien."

"Wine sounds considerably more pleasant."

"To me too." He stretched one last time, then gripped the rope and began climbing down, easing his feet into cracks as he found them to once again avoid putting too much strain on any single spot. "It was a few weeks until I could really enjoy a glass, I'll grant."

"How did it happen? I can't imagine people lock themselves in wine cellars often, temptation to the contrary."

"There'd been a bad windstorm. They'd taken shelter, which was wise, even given what happened. My squadron had to dig through the house first." The memory was still vivid, one of the less grisly images in an unfortunate collage. "Nobody would've survived staying there."

"They probably wouldn't have survived the cellar either. It was fortunate that you were there."

Olvir stared at the rock. Climbing meant he didn't have to squirm at the compliment. "I had good people with me," he said. "Morgan was alone. She had the harder mission in general too. Wine is better than sewage, as you say. And it was a tough fight—close quarters, you know, with a sword. As it was in the tent."

"Never my favorite," said Vivian, "but I'm fonder of closeup work than I am having to try and get at your foe from a distance, or when they have reach and you don't. That was the problem with the geisbar."

"In all truth, there were more than a few problems with the geisbar."

Olvir heard her laugh as he reached the bottom of the boulder, making sure his footing was solid before he let go of the rope. He watched once again as Vivian followed, reflecting with gratitude this time in addition to lust. This was not her favored terrain, but she'd offered to come—insisted on coming—regardless.

He would have expected it from her. They were both creatures of duty, raised to it from long before they'd been man and woman. All the same, Olvir wasn't so jaded or his priorities so misplaced that he could overlook the value of carrying out that duty. Heroism, Tinival taught, was worth no less for being steadfast— worth all the more, in fact, than a flashy and surprising act from someone you couldn't depend on normally.

———

Vivian made the sign of the Four once she was on solid ground— relatively solid, that was, given the winding mountain trail. She'd never minded danger, but trying to balance her weight while she groped for holes was a different matter.

Olvir's smile when she landed made the earth feel steadier beneath her.

Take care, my Sentinel, Ulamir said. *You are as well aware as I am that you walk a narrow path with him.*

She knew. She did her best to remember. Vivian still clasped Olvir on the shoulder before turning back to the rope, stretching up to cut it off as high as she could. There was no way to get the spike out of the rock, but they had most of the coil, and it would be that much harder for pursuers to follow them.

There was no particularly dramatic difference in the trail on the other side of the boulder. A low drift of smaller stones made a gentler hill for Vivian and Olvir to pick their way over before they could continue, but the path forward was essentially clear. Vivian glanced down and saw the same mountain face below them, the same red grass below that. Now she could spot trees on the plain, sprawling dark and spiderlike over small pools of water.

She averted her gaze before she could look too far into the distance.

The sun was high overhead and beginning to slip into the west. By Vivian's estimation, though, they had at least one day left to them until they reached the mountains' feet. It was considerably less than if they'd tried to go up and over to avoid the boulder, assuming they'd survived that route.

"Good idea," she said. The path was wide enough for a while that they could walk two abreast, so she didn't have to turn her head to glance at Olvir when she spoke.

"Unexpected memory," he replied.

"Effective, either way."

"I'll be sure to tell Lord Farren." Vivian heard the empty space where all the caveats would've gone. If they got back alive, if Lord Farren himself survived the battle, if the storms didn't break. Olvir filled the silence not by changing the subject exactly but by going down a side trail. "I've found, at times, that what I pick up from others, in our idle moments, has been almost as useful as the temple's official training. Stories, names... You must have similar experiences."

"I work alone more often, or I did, and people don't talk to Sentinels as freely. But once in a while." The trail narrowed to single file again. Vivian took the lead, contemplating haylofts and taverns, flashes of insight while saddling horses, snatches of conversation that stayed in her head. "Half the time, I think we pass on what we don't mean to more reliably than what we do."

"I've seen that with families too. It can be a good thing, in some cases. Much less so in others." That wasn't her gentle companion of the road who spoke but the instrument of Tinival's justice, a man who'd seen the face of mortal evil as often as Vivian had seen the monstrous sort.

"It was in yours," she said, flattening herself close to the mountain wall. The trail was older here. If the nomads had ever traveled the path, it had been long before Thyran's first rise. "Not just your training. I can't imagine all Edda taught you was deliberate on her part."

"There's a compliment implied there, unless I'm wrong."

"You're not."

"Then I thank you."

"Only one of the many ways I try to be of assistance. I'm sure all the knights you work with are as helpful."

"We're all trained to exhibit courtesy."

"Good manners and nicely polished armor, among other appealing traits."

"Should I test my luck by asking further?" Olvir's voice developed a teasing lilt.

"About Tinival's servants in general or you in particular?"

"Am I only allowed a single question?"

Vivian chuckled. "The oracle is feeling generous, but I'd wager you have a fair idea of the answers to the second."

She walked with caution, alert to noises that might signal avalanche or ambush, but without some of the knotted-rope tension that had been forming between her shoulders and in her stomach when they'd begun descending the trail. Talking with Olvir almost allowed her to ignore what waited for them—what she could make out the edge of if she looked a little farther into the distance.

Chapter 20

ANOTHER NIGHT IN THE WILDERNESS. ANOTHER NIGHT WHERE Vivian stood by the fire, Ulamir bare in her grip, and watched Olvir sit cross-legged and pray before he took the journey into his own soul. Another hour of waiting, dry-throated and cold-minded, for signs she could only hope she recognized before it was too late.

There were a few changes. Olvir had come up with the idea of pillowing their cloaks behind him, giving Vivian both hands free even if he collapsed. There was a waterfall in front of them, its roar a counterpoint to the flames, the spray shining in firelight and moonlight. At dawn, they'd take the path behind it.

Of course, they'd both have to live through the night for that to happen.

Vivian didn't feel any more optimistic about this bit of meditation than she'd been about the last ones. Granted, Olvir had gone through it so far with no apparent bad results, but poking a bear didn't become any safer the more often you did it. The fragment was likely to be more alert each time. It might have been able to realize the situation it was in, to come to resent it, and to plan.

And they were nearer to the Battlefield every night.

Vivian could make out the edge of it, off on the side of her vision that Olvir's head didn't block. It bubbled, shone, swirled. Parts rose as she looked, others fell. Vivian would have felt impractical and ungrateful if she'd ever really regretted being able to see in the dark, but right then, she came closer than ever to wishing away the Reforging's effects on her vision.

It's no surprise that my people left, said Ulamir. *The company of your kind is quite tolerable in comparison.*

Vivian snorted in response to his joke, but silently. Olvir's calm, steady praying was going on, and she badly wanted to let him concentrate without any interruptions. The more Tinival could help him, the better off they'd all be.

Should we add a third god to what's before us, Naviallanth is likely the best choice.

He sounded doubtful. Vivian asked him why.

Two gods were responsible for that aberration. Will a third, even one as orderly as the Silver Wind, be a blessing when we're in it? The Traitor governed harmony once.

It was a sobering notion, which was a bit unfair when she was quite sober already. Vivian drew her attention back from the scar on the world. They wouldn't be entering it tomorrow, she reminded herself; there was the rest of the mountain to get down, and then the plains.

Thinking of those, she asked Ulamir if all the elder peoples had left that side of the Serpentspine.

As with so much, I can give you no certain answer, Death-Touched. Those who left were three generations older than mine. They kept no records. They told few stories of that time, save for what seemed necessary in warning. Some few may have remained. The land isn't all the scar, and the scar isn't poison, as such. People could live.

She wondered why they'd all, or almost all, left if the land could support them.

It was where their world shattered. Nothing could rebuild what was, what they remembered. Staying in such a place would be beyond my imagination.

Vivian let that sink in.

The ruins Thyran had left could be reclaimed. The problem was generally a shortage of people to clear them out and settle them again. His forces had killed many, his storms more. He'd spawned horror to haunt dreams and stories for generations—but people did die, in their time, and their cities might have fallen. Thyran had broken the world, but it could heal, even if many of its inhabitants didn't.

Gizath had not only killed Veryon, one of the greatest among a mostly immortal race, but he'd also set in motion the events that led to the Veil of Fire. He had forever set a barrier between the gods and their creation. In no more than an hour, the world had become unrecognizable to those who'd lived there.

Most shun the places that remind them of pain, said Ulamir.

It was a concept foreign to Vivian's life, if not her knowledge exactly. Sentinels saw sudden grief at times but rarely the aftermath when those hurt began to restructure their lives. Almost all the sorrow they themselves felt was expected—mourning for those who'd willingly gone into danger all their lives, by comrades who did the same, all of them walking side by side with the Dark Lady for years.

Veryon's murder had been not only sudden pain but pain that nobody, not even the gods, had known *could* exist: the first betrayal. Vivian could barely get her mind under the weight of it.

She forced herself to peer out onto the edge of the Battlefield again, taking gulps of the night air and smelling smoke while she watched the world ripple. The place itself would never seem right to her, but its existence, in a way, did. What had happened *should* leave a scar. It shouldn't ever look entirely normal.

———

Journeying inward, like any task, became easier with practice. Facing his fears and his sorrows didn't banish them—and others always arose to take the places of those that faded—but their claws were a little blunter, Olvir slightly better prepared for them. He could anticipate roughly how they'd hurt. He knew how long it would take for him to wait and feel the pains until he could gently move them aside.

Tinival's song washed over him again. It was complex, with subtle layers and parts spiraling off into tangents, but all of it came back, connected in a great pattern that was clear in Olvir's soul even if his mind couldn't pull it together.

He thought of the Battlefield and wondered what would have happened if Tinival had been among the combatants. Would the damage to the land have been as great? Would the nature of the god of justice itself have prevented such a fight?

Olvir's vows hadn't given him nearly the sort of divine connection that would grant those answers. That would have been the province of the Lord of Justice, Tinival's greatest living servant, and maybe one or two of his high captains, and that very rarely. Those people were similar to Gwarill, barely living in the world as it was.

Olvir turned his attention elsewhere, to the less predictable, more opaque power of the fragment.

This time, he sent rather than reaching. First he tried an image of himself: he'd intended one from temple duty, with armor shining, but what came to mind was the man he'd seen in the mirror when he last had the chance to shave, all drawn lines and shadows beneath the eyes. *Olvir*, he thought. *Me*. He paused, remembering what Vivian had said about him and the fragment. *Us*.

The fragment waited, quiescent.

Next he pictured Tinival. That image *did* come from the temple, specifically from the painted screen in the one where Olvir had grown up. A tall man, fair-haired and blue-eyed, with a tinge of blue about his skin, stood at the walls of an anonymous city gate. He raised a shield on one arm and held a glowing silver sword. Olvir sent thoughts of his first vigil, his prayers, and, as much as he could manage, the shining presence within him.

He waited. A hum, a shift, gradually ran through the fragment, subtle enough that Olvir almost missed it.

Was it a response? An invitation? He had no means of knowing, but he'd previously emerged safe and himself from every contact. Slowly, he extended a part of his mind.

Vision overcame him again, but now it was more coherent.

He was the fragment, and he was Olvir. At once he was a tall, tired man and flashing sunset colors, broken and just, abandoned by all and comrade in arms. He struggled to sort the two out without losing either perspective. Sense began to emerge—not precisely a story but a series of experiences.

He was lost in a place that was at once shining and dark. He was drawn through space from there and funneled into a mold of flesh, into a vessel already occupied, into a room full of pale people in dark clothing whose faces shone with the fanatic's odd mixture of lust and gluttony and pride.

That was long ago. Now was now. Now was the body, larger by far, older by far, the man trained in honor and bloodletting both. Now was the rock beneath him, the fire at his back, the Sentinel who waited with sword shining before her. Now was the mountain. Now was the vast expanse of sky above him.

The sky.

Now was elsewhere, too, a person who was not Olvir and not yet the fragment but was connected to what the fragment had been. Under the rules of old and lost magic, they were bound to it as well. Now was a person who'd stopped being a person long ago, who'd cast personhood aside as his patron had once cast off the fragment, because neither suited the demands of pride and greed, of mine and *mine* and *MINE*.

That used-to-be person was watching the sky, and more than watching.

Patterns filled the night, lines of force and vortices of strength. Olvir, who couldn't make sense of them at first glance, began to feel meanings creeping into his awareness but had no chance to come to a full understanding. The being whose vision he was sharing—he knew the name but didn't want to think it with their minds so close—gripped one of those lines with an outgrowth of his power, wrenched it ninety degrees, then moved on to twist its neighbor.

Winds collided and circled, shrieking. Olvir saw darkness, ice, water whipped into a froth of white above thrashing black waves. For a hellish second, he had a glimpse into the other consciousness and understood it as a mirror of the storm: howling fury, rampaging cold. There was no tranquility in that winter, only a hunger for destruction.

Then the link vanished. He was united with the fragment for just a moment longer, then that connection was gone too. He was only Olvir, seated on the rock and snapping his eyes open.

"My name is Sir Olvir Yoralth," he said to Vivian. "I'm a knight of Tinival. I'll gladly swear my vows on Letar's token, and I think there's another storm coming."

Part III

Gizath still has influence over his old dominion, which is bonds and links. This doesn't cover only sentiment or even only flesh and bone. All living beings are made of many connections. Storms are air interacting with air: Thyran was the first among Gizath's servants to discover how to pervert that.

Really, we should be glad he hasn't yet figured out how to twist the connections governing the land itself.

—Gerant, via the Sentinel Darya,
Theories of an Apocalypse

But the most notable distinction, I would say, is in the way we regard them. We respect them, yes. We serve them, certainly—as you've seen in this city, we have priests, even as you do. Yet they are not so strange to us, nor so unreachable.

I cannot speak for Lycellias, but I would suspect that he, speaking as honestly as any of the knights, would say he regards his knighthood as you do service to a very loved and respected patron. None of us, even those who did remember the gods, would claim to understand them—and yet they walked with *our forebears once, not so many generations ago. It makes a difference.*

—*Gods as the Elder Peoples Know Them:*
A Lecture by Altiensarn of Heliodar

Chapter 21

As usual with bad news, Vivian's thoughts condensed down to *oh*. Even *oh damn* or *oh shit* were too much, lest the additional syllable overwhelm her mind. She just became a numb *oh* without any emotional overtones at all.

She still functioned. She held out the statue and listened to Olvir's vows, careful to hear every word correctly and alert for every potential change in the relic. If Olvir *wasn't* himself, the announcement he'd delivered would have been a terrific tactic to throw off her focus.

As far as the statue could discern, he hadn't changed.

He stood in front of her after the vows, all horror and honor and muscle, explaining. "I couldn't say how quickly it's coming, I'm afraid, or where it's supposed to hit—I don't get the impression that Thyran can actually aim these things very precisely—but it felt strong. And imminent. We should probably assume the worst."

"That we should. Lucky we're still mostly packed up, and it's too dark for us to need bonemasks."

Putting out the fire was harder than it would've been if they'd let it burn until morning or if they'd been in a place with more loose soil. Vivian and Olvir made dust suffice, digging when they had to, small stones cutting at their hands and dust in their throats. It kept them from talking.

Still, they were less thorough than they'd have been in the forest. *Little here will burn, and that will be slow,* Ulamir confirmed when Vivian asked him, *and a storm that does strike here will kill any flames, of course.*

Vivian didn't grumble this time, even inwardly, about having to walk again rather than sleep. There might or might not be shelter lower down, the Serpentspine itself might or might not keep the storm on the other side, but if there wasn't and if it didn't, lower was still better. High up, the air would get so cold that it'd harm her and possibly kill Olvir. The wind would play hell with the narrow trails there, too, and both wind and snow could spawn avalanches.

Descent was no guarantee of safety, but altitude would almost certainly make matters worse.

Olvir, thank the gods, packed and walked without questions or comments. It was only when they'd found the trail again that Vivian focused on *how* they'd learned about the storm.

She didn't turn to speak. The trail was narrow and crumbled in places, so any division in her focus could've gotten her a broken leg or worse. But she spoke and made the first thing she said an apology, regretting not that she'd done wrong but that the situation hadn't let her do more. "I'm sorry. We were in such a hurry that it didn't occur to me to ask. Are you all right?"

The answer was slow in coming, slow enough that Vivian began to wonder if Olvir resented her and to worry about the possibility for tactical and other reasons. To her relief, he mostly sounded uncertain when he did speak. "I believe that I am, thank you. It was unsettling, but if it's left me marred in any lasting sense, I can't tell."

"I'm glad to hear it. Not glad that it was unsettling, of course."

A section of trail turned half-sized, a thin ridge with a broken edge. Vivian crept with one foot directly in front of the other, hands on the mountain face to support her weight. On the ground, she'd never really thought of wind as a force, but here she could feel it pushing at her, almost making her sway toward the void at her side.

Talking was the last thing on her mind, and presumably on Olvir's, for a long stretch.

Gradually, the ground broadened, though the wind kept up. Vivian dared a glance upward: clouds were filling the once-clear sky, streaming like dark banners.

"You should know," came Olvir's voice, "that I was in Thyran's mind. Lord of Justice be praised, it was brief and I don't believe he sensed me. But I can't be certain."

Certainty about anything now would be unnatural and alarming, said Ulamir.

"There isn't much we can do about it if he did, but it's better to be informed." Vivian considered the matter as best she could while she picked her way along. "I don't know if there's much *he* can do about it, if he did, except perhaps putting up better inner walls."

"Unless the link works both ways."

"Could he take over your body?" The heartless nature of her training prompted another question. "Could you take over his?"

"No. Or probably not. Tinival guards us against possession. I'm sure of *that*, and Gizath doesn't let go of what's his. Neither does Thyran, for that matter." Vivian heard leather creak as Olvir shuddered. "There's too much in there for me to subdue."

A pity, said Ulamir. *Not a bad work of sapping, if it could be done.*

"Probably best not to try," she said.

"With respect, Sentinel, I wouldn't do so unless my commander or my god ordered me to. One's leagues away by now, and the other doesn't instruct me directly."

"I'm only glad he protects you as well as he does. I'd rather not wake and… Never mind." Even joking, the idea of Thyran's clutching will behind Olvir's kind, handsome face was too painful to think about while they walked in the night wind. "So the most either of you can do is figure out what the other one's up to. He may not be able to do that much, since you weren't trying any magic. Did you get any idea of his thoughts or where he was?"

"No. We didn't share vision. I…" He swallowed audibly. "I felt what he was like, what he wanted in a very broad sense, but otherwise, no, no thoughts."

"So the reverse wouldn't be wonderful," said Vivian, "but probably wouldn't give him information he doesn't already have. And we have a decent head start."

"For the moment," said Olvir as the clouds above them grew thicker.

───────────

He didn't know how long they'd been walking when the snow started. With the sky overcast, it was harder to tell time, and the shifting schedule of the journey had played havoc with his internal sense. Olvir knew that he and Vivian had covered a fair bit of ground when the first flakes hit his face. He also knew that those flakes shouldn't have appeared nearly so soon, not when the sky had been clear earlier.

Of course, *should* didn't come into Thyran's storms.

It was a dangerous word anyhow. That had been part of Olvir's training. Gizath, and Thyran later, had committed themselves to their paths out of the conviction that they knew the way the world should be—a goddess *should* be above love with a mortal, a wife *should* never think about seeking another, a lowly scholar *should* stay far from the territory of a lord of impeccable bloodlines—and that they were justified in destroying lives when it wasn't. Gizath's cultists worshipped him not as the Traitor God but as the Lord of the Great Chain, the one who decreed the rightful place of every creature in the world.

For servants of Tinival, whose realm was justice, the border between their mission and Gizath's will was often unnervingly close. Olvir suspected it was likewise for Letar's Blades, who embodied the Dark Lady's vengeance, though he'd never asked.

Speak of who an act harmed, Olvir's superiors had taught him, what recourse they'd had before the knights intervened, and how it could be mended or atoned for. *Should* was a tantrum, a blind beating at the walls of the world. At best, it identified a circumstance as abnormal and did no other good.

He did his best to remember that while he followed Vivian down narrow paths that began to grow slick with snow. Every step became its own world, a sequence of actions that took more deliberation than Olvir had put into walking during the last twenty-odd years: know the ground, test the friction, shift weight slowly forward, then repeat.

The voice of the country lad he'd been, who'd picked berries in summer and trapped rabbits in fall, kept whispering in his head, aghast: *This shouldn't be happening, this is wrong, this isn't how seasons work.*

The storm at camp had been bad, but he hadn't known for sure. He hadn't been present as Thyran warped the winds until they did what he wanted, going against every aspect of their natures for that time and place. Watching the snow fall faster, feeling the wind stream icily past his face, was like looking at an arm and knowing from the angles that it was shattered in a half-dozen places.

Olvir watched Vivian instead. She was steady ahead of him, a tall, dark pillar in the middle of white chaos.

The mountain was solid to his left. To his right, the ground dropped away to nothing. The snow kept him from seeing how high they were before long, and that was probably good.

Olvir's feet began to hurt, then stopped. His face stung, then it went numb. He didn't mention either phenomenon. He knew what they meant, but there was nothing to do about it. He and Vivian would just have to walk until they didn't have to, or until they couldn't.

Vivian didn't think even she could take more.

A few hours of watch at ground level, with hot drinks before and after, stable footing, and walls to block the worst of the wind, came easily within the realm of her blessing. The mountain wind was significantly colder than the storms had been on flat land, she'd been traveling for days on nothing but rations and water with a drop or two of wine, and the snow did horrific things to her footing.

She kept going, naturally. It wasn't a particularly heroic act: the alternatives were throwing herself off the mountain or sitting down to freeze, which would take about ten times as long as it would for a normal human. Even if she hadn't been on a mission, she wasn't nearly so cold that either struck her as a good idea.

Olvir was following along too. Vivian heard his boots crunching on the snow and saw his shape on the few occasions when she took a second to look behind her. Both of them were upright, both moving forward.

Still, it was only a matter of time until that changed. The cold would probably get to Olvir first. Vivian thought she could keep him from taking off all his clothes and crawling into a snowbank, as people often tried to do in the worst stages of freezing, but even that would only do so much good. Alternatively, one of them would take a wrong step when the snow got too treacherous or their own reflexes too blunted.

It was still a long way down.

She was walking blind now. The blizzard hid all but the mountainside itself, making the world into a formless white mass full of screaming. Nobody with sense, or a choice, would try to walk a yard over flat ground in such a storm, much less feel their way along on a ledge the width of their shoulders.

Ulamir had gone silent. Vivian wasn't sure why and was too preoccupied to wonder, so when she heard his mental voice, it damned nearly startled her off the mountain.

My people lived here once. I can feel their echoes in the rock.

That was good, she thought. When she died, at least he'd be left near familiar territory.

Shelter *will be near, Sentinel Bathari,* he snapped. *Is near! The entrance is at hand. Get your mind out of your feet and seek it.*

Chapter 22

"CAVES!" A WOMAN CALLED TO HIM OUT OF THE WIND. "NEAR here!"

The figure in front of Olvir turned sideways, put her palms against the mountainside, and began slowly shuffling forward.

Vivian, he thought, putting a name to the shape and the voice. Memory was a stone he had to lift now, heavier with every step. That was a bad sign. Olvir recognized that but didn't have the strength to worry. All existence was the shape in front of him, the rise of a single foot, then the fall of the other. They got heavier too. The snow sticking to his boots was only a small part of that weight.

"Here!" Vivian called in triumph, cutting through the fog in Olvir's mind. All the same, he nearly ran into her: his legs were slow getting the message that she'd stopped.

She stood with her chin tilted up, peering at a hole a few feet above her. "You go first."

Olvir didn't argue. First of all, he doubted his lips could move. He simply grasped the edge of the opening, the stone sharp in spite of his gloves. *Up*, he told himself. *Up*.

On a normal day, entering the passage would have been a trifling effort. Olvir's arms were shaking before he got his head and shoulders inside. When he finally pulled his whole body up, only the knowledge that Vivian needed to get in behind him kept him from simply flopping onto the stone like a dying fish.

The tunnel rose high above him, glowing with bright colors, but he was only really conscious of the entrance. He turned, reached down, and grabbed Vivian's upper arms.

Helping her into the hole wasn't as difficult as Olvir had feared. She was no featherweight, but she was strong and had long ago learned how to move most helpfully in such circumstances. He provided leverage more than anything else and a more comfortable grip than the ledge.

They collapsed together when she'd gotten inside. The storm shrieked only a few inches away. Soon they'd feel the cold again, but right then, they were each content to slump against the wall, their vision slowly clearing until they could take in the details of their shelter.

A series of rings led off down the tunnel. Olvir and Vivian half lay in the first, ten feet or so of milky moonstone that wrapped around them from the smooth floor to the equally smooth ceiling. The ring became pale opal at the inner edge, then a sapphire hue not quite as dark as that in Ulamir's hilt. After it turned a deeper blue, the tunnel widened to become the entrance of a room.

All the stone glowed from within, not quite as bright as the sun but better than moonlight. The patch of floor against Olvir's cheek was faintly warm. He stripped off a glove and laid his palm against the wall: it, too, was heated.

"Ulamir says the old enchantments are still here," Vivian said, a heavy breath between each two or three words. "He had no relations from the enclave that lived here, so the mountain wouldn't unfold for us, whatever *that* means, but the magic inside kept going."

"Defenses?" Olvir managed the wit to ask.

She paused for the answer, then shook her head. "Built in more innocent times. The stonekin, or these stonekin, abandoned it when those times ended. They didn't consider attackers. Bless them."

"They have my thanks, wherever they are."

Olvir dragged himself to his feet, using the wall for balance at first. When Vivian had done the same, they began walking side by side down the tunnel. Moving told his legs that they *could* move and his spine that it could hold him vertical. Bit by bit, the worst of his exhaustion eased.

Besides, every inch they moved was an inch away from the snow and wind, which was a significant compensation for the effort.

He started feeling a warm breeze when they reached the opal ring. It might have been there all along, only drowned out by the cold near the entrance. It was unmistakable farther in. The air smelled pleasantly of hot metal.

"Your people do wonderful work," said Vivian to her sword.

"I'll second that. I've never had the honor of visiting their homes before." Very few people did, particularly since Thyran's first war. After Gizath's first treachery, many stonekin had moved not merely over the mountains but halfway into another realm, one Olvir had never understood. When Thyran's storms had struck, most had retreated farther.

"Neither have I. Clearly I've been missing out." She waited, then passed along Ulamir's reply. "He says the welcome would be better where they actually live but not the scenery: some of the arts that built this place are lost. The stonekin called the bands here to the surface; they didn't mine them or carve them."

Olvir studied the seamless rock, gleaming with multicolored light. "That would explain why it's so smooth. They can't do that any longer?"

"Talk rocks into position or shape? Not as deftly. Or Ulamir's enclave couldn't. People scatter among the stonekin, as we do, and knowledge slips through the cracks. Things vanish."

"Not entirely," said Olvir. "This place lasted long enough to save us."

Past the sapphire-rimmed archway, a great blue-green room opened, its walls shining with their own light. Flowers formed of jewels bloomed there: roses of black opal climbed over one opening, little four-petaled white flowers twined up another, and irises with lapis blossoms flanked a third.

The beauty of it stopped Vivian in her tracks, despite her exhaustion.

Great celebrations would have been held here, said Ulamir. *Holy days, births, deaths. They would have danced in patterns we can only try to imitate these days.*

"It's lovely," said Vivian, putting a hand on the gemmed hilt of her sword. "Are you all right?"

Awed, touched, but not sorrowing, he said in return as Olvir glanced sideways, registered that Vivian hadn't been asking him, and kept a respectful silence. *Not truly. Listening, too, for there are…echoes here.*

"Echoes," she said aloud.

No ghosts. Any who died here would have gone to their rest long ago. Say, rather, tracks with personalities. I would learn more, if I can.

"Sounds wise," said Vivian and summarized for Olvir.

Roses mark the gate to rest. In that, I'm sure there's been no change. Food for us would lie through the iris door. It will do you no good, but near there, you'll find a chute for waste as well.

"What do the white flowers lead to?" Vivian asked after additional translation.

Knowledge. The tales of these people were kept there once, their scholarship, too, and although I'm certain they've taken what they could, some remnant may yet lie within the room. He hesitated. *Fireforged, I must leave you for a time and seek knowledge elsewhere.*

"The echoes?"

Yes. Nothing here will harm you in my absence, I swear it.

"You don't need to swear. I believe you. How long will you be gone?"

Two days, perhaps. No more. Most likely I'll return long before the storm ends.

"I wish I didn't know you were right. Farewell for now."

She felt the sword-spirit depart. It was a slightly different mental sensation than the one Vivian got when he'd expended his strength or when he left so that she could pursue a liaison. The Veil of Fire didn't stand between them on this occasion, but she still knew Ulamir's attention was gone.

"Is all well?" Olvir asked after a moment.

"It should be. He'll be back in a day or two."

"Then I wish him joy. We have plenty to occupy us here." For a moment, Olvir's gaze passed over Vivian, making her heart start pounding. Then he cleared his throat. "We'd best start with finding a place to dry our clothes."

———————

"They all slept in groups?" Olvir asked, surveying the circular amethyst room they'd entered.

A dozen hollows were carved in the floor. Each would fit two or three of him, and he was both taller and broader-shouldered than the average stonekin. Most enclaves had ten members or fewer, so there was plenty of room, but the lack of walls or screens was startling.

"Privacy is less of a concern for them, from what Ulamir's told me." Vivian chuckled, beginning to unpack her belongings. "He said it made matters awkward when he was first joined with a Sentinel. He's learned odd human customs since."

"That's a relief for me," said Olvir. Admittedly, he'd never bothered worrying about Ulamir the last few times he'd embraced Vivian: he'd assumed the two of them had worked out their own arrangement years ago, and he'd been very focused on other matters.

Remembering those made him fumble as he lifted his bedroll out of his pack. *Business first*, he reminded himself and spread it out in one of the hollows. The stone was warmer there. He arranged the rest of his belongings to take advantage of it.

"I'll sing the stonekin's praises for the rest of my life," he said when he finally had tended to his gear and could sit down to tug off his boots. Freedom from wet leather briefly overtook lust as his dominant sensation. From Vivian's gusty sigh while she did likewise, Olvir suspected she'd understand very well.

"Gods, yes… Oh." Vivian made the most girlish noise Olvir had ever heard from her and pointed to a pearl archway on the wall. It was too narrow to provide a good view of the room beyond, but above it sat a rose-quartz flower with many points. "Am I right about what that is?"

"A water lily," Olvir confirmed, "and I think you're right about what it means."

Chapter 23

THE JADE CHAMBER BEYOND THE PEARL ARCHWAY HELD THREE pools, all with abundant room to fit a score of people at once. The one nearest to the door was shaped like a crescent moon, the one in the center like a star, and the one on the far side, from which steam gently rose, like a sun.

All three contained fresh water, as Vivian and Olvir found by dipping their little fingers in each. The moon pool was ice cold, the sun pool not quite boiling—Vivian tested that one, taking her cue from the rising steam—but the star-shaped pool was pleasantly, if a bit intensely, warm.

That was all she needed to know.

They left their weapons carefully outside the door so that the moisture in the air wouldn't damage the blades. It was the last careful action Vivian took for a while.

She was the first through the door, and as Olvir came in behind her, she turned, caught him by the shoulders, and kissed him hard. For a moment, he was stiff with surprise. Then his lips parted and he pulled Vivian close so that her breasts pressed against his broad chest.

Despite haste and hunger, Olvir's lips were deft. His hands wandered after that first urgent grip on her waist, sliding up to cup the back of her head. Vivian did the same to him, and his wet hair twined like silk around her fingers.

He rapidly grew stiff for reasons other than surprise and in more pleasant ways. Vivian felt that pressure against her, its size a pleasant promise of the future.

For a moment, she considered taking him then and there, not bothering with undressing any more than was necessary—but it would probably be almost as much trouble to get damp trousers down without taking off the rest as it would be to disrobe fully.

And they did have time now. Later, they might not.

"Pool," she said, pulling her mouth from his with a distinct effort of will.

"Hmm?" Olvir's eyes were dark and dazed. The sight sent its own thrill through Vivian, as did the half-drunk huskiness of his voice. "Oh. Yes. Should undress, too, I shouldn't wonder."

"Mm-hmm."

Vivian let him take care of his own armor—chain mail was difficult to remove at the best of times and the Sentinels not generally accustomed to it. She slipped off to the star-shaped pool. Standing beside it, she got herself out of her jerkin, moving as fast as she could without snapping the laces.

The shirt was easier. The trousers were not. Leather had many good qualities, but the way it clung when it was the slightest bit wet wasn't among them. Vivian had wriggled the waistband down past her hips when she heard Olvir's sharp intake of breath from the doorway behind her.

"You're not making my task any easier, you realize," he said, speaking low and unevenly.

"No?"

She didn't turn to face him but glanced over her shoulder as she worked one leg free of the leather. Olvir, unlacing his breeches, was staring up at her, his eyes gleaming. Vivian couldn't see lower than his waist from her position, but the hunger in his expression was quite clear.

Giddy joy, the sort she hadn't felt in years, shimmered through her all of a sudden. The cave was its own little world and duty as far away as the end of the storm. She could think of nothing they could do until the blizzard ended, so there was nothing they needed to do.

Vivian grinned, then slipped into the pool.

Hot water closed over her head, cushioned her sore feet, and began stripping away the grime that days of travel had left. If Vivian hadn't been underwater, she'd have moaned again, in sensual delight different from what she'd felt when kissing Olvir but equally as powerful in its own way.

The water wasn't still but flowing slowly, draining into some space below that Vivian couldn't see and constantly replenished with clean, hot water from an equally invisible source. She felt the currents move past her, gently tugging at her hair.

Another form sliding into the water made the waves briefly more dramatic. When Vivian surfaced to breathe, Olvir was behind her. He grasped her hips and pulled her back against him, until his cock slid just slightly between the cleft of her buttocks. "Mmm," he said and bent to kiss her neck. "You're the loveliest woman... My imagination wasn't anywhere near adequate."

"And did you imagine a lot?" she asked, closing her eyes to better feel the motion of his lips.

Olvir chuckled, and his breath on her wet skin made Vivian shiver. "Enough that I probably should've felt guilty. You can slap me for it someday if you'd like."

"Only if that's how your tastes run."

She didn't dwell on *someday*. It was easy not to, because Olvir moved his hands up to her breasts, and the sure, gentle strokes of his fingers rapidly took Vivian's mind off any sort of abstract thought. The water lapped around her like an echo of his touch, rising to her shoulders as she stood with her feet brushing the bottom. Vivian leaned back, letting the pool and Olvir take most of her weight.

From all she could tell, he didn't mind that in the slightest. His cock rose against her arse, a solid source of heat in the middle of a liquid world. When the welcome pressure between Vivian's legs grew and she began to rock her hips, Olvir thrust against her with a low moan. The pool rippled with their rhythm.

Time drew out. There was no outward need to hurry. The only urgency was the rising of their own needs, and that was a welcome edge to ride. Vivian sank into desire, into the way Olvir's breathing quickened with hers, into the coiled tension in his hands while he caressed her and the throaty noises he made when she wiggled. She couldn't reach him from her current position, wanted to touch him, was content to let that happen later.

Need was a pleasant sort of drowning.

Olvir went slowly, too, slipping his hands down her sides only to draw them back up and circle her nipples until Vivian groaned. He kissed the straining arch of her neck, nibbled the edge of her ear, and then took her mouth deeply when she turned her head toward him. His arms were tense around her, and she could hear the rapid pounding of his heart. Still he showed no haste, working his way gradually from her breasts down the wet surface of her body to run his fingers through the hair between her legs.

At first, his fingers only brushed the wet folds of her sex and the hard pearl between them. That was enough to make Vivian gasp.

Almost as soon as the sound left her lips, his fingers were gone, trailing across the plane of her stomach, brushing the undercurve of her breasts, then down.

All she wanted was that moment, that touch, the warm clean smell of Olvir and the sound of his breathing. At the same time, she ached for more.

Vivian had opened her legs even before Olvir slid a large finger inside her, at the brush of his hand between her thighs. The sound she made at that first moment of penetration drew a strained chuckle from him. Her own hands clenched, finding only water and nothing to grip as Olvir stroked her from the inside, gradually slipping another finger into her, building her desire.

"Now," she gasped when she couldn't take any more. She bent forward a little, inviting, urging.

He obliged—eagerly, from the way he sighed as he slipped the thick tip of his cock inside her entrance—but was leisurely about that too. It was a long, maddeningly blissful moment until Vivian felt him completely within her. The fullness of it made her swear, or maybe pray. She wasn't sure.

The gods probably understood, whichever it was.

She looked over her shoulder at Olvir in that moment, when both of them otherwise held still and the water swirled warm around them. It blurred her vision, but not too greatly for her to see and appreciate the man she was there with.

Olvir's chest and stomach were flat and hard beneath mats of wet dark hair, and the muscles in his arms and shoulders were taut as he struggled to maintain control. His neck was tense, too, his head thrown back. The line of his jaw was sharp in contrast. Vivian couldn't see any lower, between their position and the water, but her view alone made her tighten around Olvir, who caught his breath in response.

Because of the water, because of the long journey, because of the lingering warmth and safety of the moment, neither of them moved vigorously, and neither of them needed to. Vivian felt every slight flex of Olvir's hips, each pulse of his cock inside her, and each slight withdrawal and thrust. The water, or the moment, magnified each, and every one built on the last, until she was all sensation, potential, momentum, needing no dramatic action but merely a final whisper.

He gave it to her with another brush of his fingers over her sex, a small circle that sent the waves of her climax breaking over her, so powerful that Vivian screamed over and over again into the empty, echoing room. She felt his cock jerking and thrusting within her, his hands firm on her hips. They were the only solid things in the world, all she felt other than her own pleasure, as she heard his final groan mingled with her cries.

For a few moments, she was content not to be aware of anything else.

Chapter 24

OLVIR RETURNED TO HIMSELF GRADUALLY, WITH VIVIAN languid in his arms and the water bearing both of them up. He doubted he'd have been able to hold her if it hadn't. All his muscles felt loose bordering on insubstantial, which was pleasant but an obstacle to feats of strength.

Drained contentment was familiar, but Olvir didn't remember it being so intense in the past. Granted, it had been a while since he'd had a partner, and he'd been pushing himself to the limit in other ways, but he was largely inclined to credit the woman herself.

He spent a moment simply looking at her, appreciating the smooth muscle of shoulder and bicep, the way that her full breasts bobbed in the hot pool, the angle of her jawline, and the dark fans of her eyelashes. She looked no weaker in repose than fully alert, but there was an air of peace about her. Olvir was honored to have been responsible, even if only partly so.

Sleep threatened, as alluring as the water surrounding them. The two made a poor combination, however, so Olvir gently nudged Vivian. "I'd love to stay here, but I can't breathe water."

"It's one of my flaws too," she admitted.

They slid apart as Vivian shifted to take her own weight. Olvir watched her climb out of the pool. As tired as he was, the sight was worth the delay. She lingered on the edge herself, and her own gaze was as frankly admiring as Olvir suspected his had been. The implied praise made Olvir blush, though they'd gone too far for conventional modesty.

"My imagination wasn't adequate for the task either," Vivian said and grinned. "And I can usually imagine quite a bit."

"Thank you. I'm glad I didn't let you down."

"Oh, no." This smile came with half-lidded eyes. "But I expect you know that already."

The memory of her screaming out her climax hit not just his mind but his whole being. "When we've rested, you may need to make it clear again. I'm very slow to catch on in certain matters."

"I like to think I'm a tolerably patient instructor. And gods know we have time, in all likelihood."

"There's that." Olvir, picking up the items of their clothing that weren't made of leather, felt a cold trace of guilt intrude on his satisfaction. "Though I'd certainly be happier if the storm ends quickly, and I hope we have the worst of it here."

"Of course. I assumed that went without saying."

"It should. But—" Olvir shrugged and dumped the clothing into the cold pool. "I thought it would do me good to say it, I suppose."

Vivian slipped an arm around his waist, her touch comforting now rather than seductive. "It probably did me good too."

They collected armor and Vivian's trousers, picked up their weapons from outside the door, and, naked, walked back to the sleeping chamber. The air was cooler than the water had been, but after the pool and their activity, it was a refreshing change.

"I don't believe," Vivian said, stretching out beside him in the combination of bedding that had been both clean and dry, "that I've ever fully appreciated lying down before."

"Mm-hmm. One of the great unsung pleasures of life." Olvir found a secure place on her waist for his hand. Her head tucked neatly beside his, and her breath was pleasant against his neck. "Of course, until now, I'd only done it once with you."

"Flatterer."

"Sworn to truth."

"A convenient quality in a lover. Mostly." Vivian pulled a blanket up to cover them, yawned, and closed her eyes.

Sleep descended quickly: the walk from the bathing chamber had been a very small interruption to set against not only warmth and satiation but the previous days of fear and fighting and simple exertion. Olvir held it off for a few minutes, though, while he whispered prayers to Tinival.

The first part was as familiar to him as his own name, the usual litany for knights in the field. *Guide my arm, clear my eyes, and give me courage,* he finished, hearing the faint harmony in his soul. Then he went on.

Thank you for this refuge, Lord. Thank you for Vivian. And— There were some in the temples who believed it a sacrilege to ask the gods for favors. A just cause would already have the Four's attention. No mortal could know better than they did. There'd been times when Olvir could see their point, but right then, the words seemed important—not to tell Tinival what was important but to let Him know that Olvir appreciated it. *I pray that we've gotten the worst of this storm, that the people we left behind are all right. They're valiant soldiers. Some of them are good friends. All of them deserve better than what we went through outside.*

The world was what it was. Many people suffered in ways that they didn't deserve. Olvir had seen plenty of that in only the last few months and more in the years he'd been a knight, much as he'd tried to carry out his duty to avert it. He knew *deserve* was a treacherous word and that hope rarely prevented disaster.

He hoped nonetheless.

The music that was his bond with Tinival remained as it always had, giving no answer but its presence. Olvir received no guarantees, no prophecies of victory or visions of his friends' safety. He knew that his god was in his soul, and Vivian was next to him, and he himself was whole and strong, capable of taking up his task again when the storm permitted.

Olvir surrendered to sleep.

———————

Time meant nothing under the mountain, so Vivian had no idea how long it was before she woke up. When she did, her limbs felt lighter than they had at any point since she'd left the camp—maybe before that, since she hadn't precisely been in the habit of rising late there. Using her well-being as evidence, she estimated that she and Olvir had been asleep for at least ten hours, maybe twelve.

A silence in her mind meant that Ulamir hadn't returned. That was all right: he'd said he might be gone for two days. Besides, very little could hurt the sword-spirits themselves.

She and Olvir had shifted during the night so that he was curled around her from behind, one arm draped loosely across her chest. Each breath Vivian took shifted his hand back and forth minutely against her stomach, a sensation that became increasingly noticeable as sleep faded.

It had been quite a while, too, since she'd woken up naked at all, let alone with another person in her bed. Vivian hadn't realized that she'd missed it—or maybe she hadn't missed it until that moment. Partners as pleasant as Olvir had been few and far between.

As a matter of fact, she couldn't remember any partner she'd had that was as generally pleasant as Olvir had been, in bed and out.

Vivian retreated quickly from that line of logic. Even her fatalism was finite.

It was better to focus on the present, to be aware of little but the hair on Olvir's chest brushing softly against her back, the low, steady sound of his breathing, and the solid weight of his arm across her side. The places where they touched began to tingle, a feeling that spread through her body as her drowsiness started giving ground to arousal.

When she felt Olvir's cock swelling against her, arousal took a solid lead.

His breathing suggested that he was still asleep. When Vivian turned her head, she saw that his eyes were closed and his face relaxed, unaware. She bit her lip.

It would be unkind to wake him and unethical to gratify herself with the man while he was in no state to agree to it, whatever his body was doing. The situation called for patience. Vivian was good at patience, most of the time.

On the other hand, there was nothing wrong with enjoying herself while she was patient.

She did her best to turn over slowly and gradually, shifting her weight while keeping Olvir's arm in roughly the same place and their legs entwined with each other. She didn't make any sound louder than a sigh when she was finally facing him, the hair on his chest brushing against her nipples and his erection, full and large now, nudging her stomach.

It was the sort of discipline the Adeptas wanted from their trainees, Vivian thought, not that she'd ever be inclined to boast about that particular manifestation at the chapter house. She slid an arm across Olvir instead, underneath his, and nestled closer to him, content to torment herself.

He woke to desire.

That was fairly common in itself: he was a young man by any standard other than that of war, and such things happened in the morning. The feeling got considerably stronger with Vivian next to him, though. That had been the case even when they'd been in the wilderness, waking early after two straight days of walking.

In the stonekin's caves, Olvir woke with his prick as stiff and throbbing as it had ever been since the first embarrassing mornings of his youth.

He couldn't say he was surprised, not with Vivian lying against him, all smooth skin and soft hair, toned muscles and full breasts. It didn't take him long, either, to feel how hard her nipples had gotten or to catch the scent of her arousal.

When he opened his eyes, she was watching him, a slight smile on her parted lips.

"Oh," he said, because there were a number of reasons that words were difficult just then. "Vivian—"

"Good morning, or whatever it actually is out there." She slid the tip of her tongue across her lower lip. "Are you feeling well rested?"

"I'm feeling many things. That's one."

"Really?" Vivian ran her fingers downward, across his chest, circling one of his nipples. She stroked her free hand along the outside of his thigh as well, a long, steady sweep that ended precisely at his hip bone. Olvir's cock jerked against her stomach, and he drew a ragged breath at that motion too. "How complicated of you."

"Everybody has—" She set her mouth against his neck and drew the hand at his hip inward. Olvir tried to remember how to talk. "Facets."

Vivian laughed against his neck, then licked a long trail up to his ear. "I don't know," she murmured. The words, low and sensual, wrapped themselves around Olvir, adding to the overwhelming feelings of her tongue at his throat and her hands lower down. "I feel remarkably single-minded at present."

No witty reply came to Olvir's mind or to the increasingly small functioning amount of it left. Desperately, he reached for her in turn. Her thighs opened readily to his touch. He found her sex already slick, its wet heat surrounding his fingers as intoxicating as the moment that she finally grasped his erection.

He had no warning before Vivian rolled them over. It was a gentle, fluid motion, not at all jarring, but one moment Olvir was thrusting eagerly into her grip, and then he was on his back.

Vivian rose above him, a sight to inspire as much reverence as any temple window. He'd become familiar with her body the night before, but the sight of her sleek thighs and the shadowy patch of hair where they joined, with the hint of dusky rose beneath it, left him as breathless as when he'd seen her peeling off her trousers. Her breasts swayed as she moved, dark nipples stiff and tempting.

It was her face that enthralled Olvir most. Bent over her in the pool, he'd not been able to watch the ways that desire blended with focus, need with will, becoming storm light in her gray eyes. When she guided his cock to her entrance, her neck arched back, and when she sank down, taking him fully inside her, the raw pleasure on her face hit Olvir as hard as the feeling of her body.

Needing to touch her, he settled his hands on her waist but made no effort to control her as she started to move. Vivian knew what she was about. The rhythm she settled into had him gasping and arching upward into her almost from the first circle of her hips.

Still he wanted more—not more control, not more speed, simply more of Vivian. He leaned upward, took one of her nipples into his mouth, and delighted in the way she cried out and tightened around him. Her fingers clenched on his shoulders, causing pressure just short of pain. That, too, heightened Olvir's arousal, until he could no longer reason in terms of want and will but simply acted on half-blind impulse.

Lust was a storm, far more pleasant than the one raging outside but equally as easy to get lost in. Olvir went with it gladly.

Vivian's movements on top of him sped up. Her moans turned to cries, desperate and then triumphant. Olvir felt every second of her climax, as her hips jerked and her body rippled, and the mind-shattering pleasure of his own.

He couldn't have separated one moment from another. He didn't want to. All was one, all was ecstasy, and he never wanted it to end.

Chapter 25

BODIES WERE ANNOYINGLY COMPLICATED.

Vivian would, in part, have been content to have lain with Olvir for hours longer, resting on top of him and relaxing, satiated, with occasional talk and the sound of his heartbeat to keep her attention. She'd been thinking, planning, *doing* for months. Stillness, particularly with Olvir, was damned appealing.

On the other hand...

She sighed, stretched, and slipped to the side. "My stomach, as they say, thinks my throat's been cut."

Olvir laughed. "I didn't want to be the first to say it."

Their packs were just far enough away to be out of reach from the bed, which Vivian now considered one of her worse decisions. Once she stood up, she remembered that they'd left their clothes to soak. "And one of us should check what the storm's doing," she added aloud. Movement spurred awareness, awareness spurred memory, and memory held many tasks. Damn. "Probably me, considering. Mind laying the clothes out to dry while I'm about it?"

"Oh, I mind us not having the day to ourselves and an army of servants," he joked, getting to his feet. Vivian, who was wrapping herself in a blanket, paused to watch. He was quite the sight in motion—quite the sight lying still, for that matter.

He was new, she told herself. Familiarity would wear the shine off the view, if...but that led to thoughts of the time they didn't have and the sneaking suspicion that her own advice might not be entirely true, neither of which would be helpful to dwell on.

"I'd take one or two. Or a single laundress," she said, jammed her bare feet into boots, and headed toward the outer passage.

The good news was that Vivian didn't need to go all the way down the tunnel and stick her head out into the blizzard to know it was continuing. She could tell that perfectly well from the sound of the howling wind, which she could hear from the entrance room.

The bad news was that the wind was still strong enough to hear from the entrance room.

She did go a little farther than that, down the length of the passage until she could see the hole where they'd entered, just in case the noise of the wind had all been due to the tunnel and the storm was really over. No such good fortune: there was only a cloud of whirling white beyond the cave opening.

Olvir was in the sleeping chamber when Vivian returned. He'd found a set of clean linen in his pack—despite the heated stone, the air was too chilly for most people to walk around naked, sadly—and it looked as if he'd taken another dip in the pool before he'd put them on. The rations were spread out on the stone in front of him: dried meat and fruit, bread, and their waterskins.

He'd been waiting for her to return before he started eating. Vivian felt a foolish smile work its way across her face, one that was too much trouble to try to hold off.

"Thank you," she said. "You didn't have to hold off."

"It isn't as though we've reason to hurry, do we?"

"I'm afraid not."

"Well," he said, picking up a piece of bread as Vivian sat down across from him, "the company's good, at least, even if the food is nothing spectacular."

She bowed, in as courtly a style as she could manage while wearing a blanket and sitting cross-legged. "I certainly can't think of anybody I'd prefer to be with in this particular situation—unless perhaps a wizard who could turn stones into honey cakes and water into wine."

"I'll try and make up for my flaws there."

The food was *food*, so Vivian had no real complaints, except that she had to remind herself to leave adequate supplies both for Olvir and for the future. She thoroughly enjoyed every speck of the dry bread, and the tough meat and fruit were likewise a pleasure, which made her laugh.

"It's a common joke for us," she said in response to Olvir's questioning expression. "Trail rations tasting good is a known sign of starvation. I'm fairly certain the Mourners would back us up on it."

"I wouldn't be at all surprised." When they finished, Olvir got to his feet. "Shall we take a look at the other rooms?" he asked, offering Vivian a hand.

"I admit I'm curious," she said, letting her gaze linger on the hard muscle of his thighs. "But I also don't know that I'll get a better view than what I have now."

Laughing, she let him help her up, and they went exploring.

━━━━━━━━━━

As flattering—and as arousing, even with his strength not yet quite back—as Vivian's comment had been, Olvir knew that it wasn't true. He would have suspected that without Tinival's gift, given their surroundings, and the first room they entered proved him right.

It was spun out of tiger's-eye and emerald, woven together in twisting patterns without a seam or a lump. Slim stone trees grew in stately groves. Hanging from them, glowing, was fruit made of jewels: dark garnet cherries, topaz citrons, grapes in a darker shade of amethyst than had gone into the walls of the sleeping room. The stonekin had only paid vague attention to nature, for ruby apples grew on the same tree as jade pears, but it was a sight to make Olvir stop and wonder nonetheless.

Vivian plucked a peach, which came off easily in her hand.

"They're stones, all right," she said, trying and failing to squeeze it. "But smell."

The fragrance, when Olvir leaned closer, brought long summer days to mind. His mouth watered.

"If Ulamir believes it's all right," he said, "I'd like to stop here again on the journey home."

They both ignored all the other *ifs* involved in that. It wasn't the moment for realism. "They'd make wonderful souvenirs," Vivian said.

"Or gifts for other stonekin."

"Do you know any?"

"No, not personally, but you never can tell what might happen. Unless you think that'd be rude," he added, suddenly considering that possibility.

Vivian walked up to him and kissed him lightly. "I'd have to ask Ulamir," she said, "but I'd bet it would be fine."

The archway with white flowers led to a long room, slightly too wide to be a tunnel, with fire opal walls. A small dais rose at one end, with niches scattered near it in different shapes and depths. Many were strung with silver or gold wire, others filled with hollow stone pipes.

The stonekin had carved words into the other parts of the walls. Each subject was a shape: mostly they formed abstract curves or ladders, but a tree spread its branches near the exit. Over the dais rose a star larger than Olvir.

"Knowledge," he said. Tinival's gift allowed him to understand the writing. The star was praise to the gods, who went by different names with the stonekin but whose roles were obvious. One of the ladders was a poem about the darkness under the mountain. It sang to the writer. A human would have found that unnerving, but the verses made Olvir's heart ache with the beauty of hearing the unknown. "Gods, if this is what they left, I can't imagine what was here when this was still their home—"

"They handed some of it down, I'd imagine," said Vivian, staring. "Some has even found its way into human hands by now. Just not this."

Perhaps they'd remembered the poems on the wall or recorded them elsewhere. Perhaps they'd crafted spaces for music in their new homes that were almost as fine.

"I'd like to stay in here for a while," said Olvir.

Vivian gave him an understanding smile. "Only if you read the walls to me."

It was a day of busy contentment such as Vivian hadn't had in a year.

Sitting in the ancient stonekin's music hall, she listened to Olvir read her the poems of a vanished people while both of them took care of the many small chores they hadn't had time for until then. She basked in the poems, laughing at one, then wiping away a tear at another, marveling all the while at the rich resonance of Olvir's voice, even over words he'd never spoken until then.

They lingered when the poems ran out. There were still tasks to do, and from what Ulamir had told her of his people, Vivian doubted they'd mind human art in the place they'd once devoted to their own.

While she and Olvir sharpened their swords, they sang "The Violet Banner" and then went on to a drinking song Vivian had learned in Myrias, one that described the increasingly unlikely visions of the several-sheets-to-the-wind speaker. It had the sort of chorus that anyone could learn by the second verse and that stood up to being sung by people who had difficulty pronouncing entire words:

> *The wine down in Silane will make you see double.*
> *The ale up in Criwath will make you go blind.*

And though saying it may be asking for trouble,
The beer in this place is the best you will find.

One could substitute "worst," depending on one's opinions on the city, country, tavern, or army in question.

Olvir had a healthy supply of material to offer too. Apparently the knights, or some portion of them, had a good ten verses or so on appropriate actions regarding drunken squires. Vivian had heard a few applied to sailors or soldiers in the same condition, but some of the ones Olvir knew were damned inventive. She found herself with new respect for Tinival's servants.

Their goal waited, success as uncertain as ever and the path every bit as unclear. Outside, the storm kept raging, a sign of what was to come if they failed and likely a danger to those they'd left behind. Vivian never quite forgot any of that, and she would've sworn before Olvir's patron god that he didn't either. It was easier to sit with that knowledge when they were talking or singing or even just working with each other close at hand, though. What was to come and what might happen shrank down, providing space for lighter thoughts.

Vivian had known such moments in the past. *I could die tomorrow* was, in fact, a fairly constant tenant in every Sentinel's head as far as she was aware. Each member of the Order found methods of living around it, bringing it out for extra alertness on missions and then trying to send it away again. Drink often worked. So did lust, or violence of a less lethal sort.

Being able to live with *The world may end in a few days, and we have to stop it*, and still genuinely laugh at a tale of irascible superiors or contentedly grumble about the laces on her armor was a step or two beyond what Vivian would have expected.

She doubted she would've been able to manage it with many other companions—maybe Emeth or Katrine, possibly Bran, who she'd trained with. The idea of going to bed with any of those people held all the allure that trailbread did when she was well fed.

Denial had never been one of her skills. Holding off realization was exhausting.

Gods damn me, Vivian thought, watching as Olvir held up his shirt of mail and gave it an endearingly serious inspection, *I'm well and truly in for it at the end of this.*

She didn't let herself consider that she might not be. In theory, they could succeed. In theory, Olvir might come back unchanged, and she wouldn't need to do anything but serve as an extra body with a weapon. Those were theories, goals, impossible until she'd succeeded at them.

If she couldn't keep herself from falling for the man, she at least wouldn't let herself start hoping.

―――――

Until he spent a day inside the mountain, Olvir hadn't realized how silent the wilderness never was. There was always some sound outside, whether the movement of small animals through the underbrush or the creaking of trees or the wind itself. Inside the caves, he and Vivian were the only sources of any noises at all.

It was comforting in a sense. There was a certain security in sitting indoors, relatively warm and comfortable, while outside the wind howled and the snow fell sideways. The guilt of knowing that many others didn't have their shelter preyed on Olvir more than once in a while, but he could do no more about that than he was doing already.

He had a daunting task ahead of him. He'd be all the better for warmth, food, and rest—for a bit of amusement too. And he'd been understating his case when he called Vivian good company.

He'd known he loved her in the moment when she'd slipped

laughing from their shared bed, and he'd thought, *I could wake like this as long as I can imagine and never tire of it.*

Telling her would be cruelty. He was certain of that as well.

Vivian glowed in the light from the cave walls. She looked up occasionally from the sole of her boot, which had started threatening to come unstitched, and smiled at Olvir. He couldn't tell if she loved him or not.

It didn't matter.

There was another reason she'd come with him, one that was more specific than simply being a companion to face off the hazards of travel and less specific than her powers. She hadn't mentioned it. Olvir hadn't asked. He hadn't even let himself name it inside his mind.

He wished he could have spoken it aloud, if only to reassure Vivian that he understood—that, if the last extremity occurred, he was glad that she was by his side to meet it as she'd faced every other danger they'd encountered. But to be too conscious of what might happen, let alone speak it aloud, could deprive her of any advantage she had if the moment came.

Acceptance and the need for surprise made an odd balance.

Give her peace, please, he prayed silently, *if my wishes can sway the matter at all. If this ends badly, let Vivian do what needs doing without undue pain, and let her know, somehow, that I thank her for it.*

His bond with Tinival remained as it ever had, its rhythm constant. It neither strengthened in acceptance nor weakened in rebuff.

The Silver Wind was just and kind. Olvir would have to trust to that.

"Think it'll suffice?" Vivian asked, glancing over at the mail shirt that lay, recently oiled and rewrapped, in Olvir's lap.

"Ah." Realizing she meant the armor, he had to pause for a moment to find an answer and to face what came next. "As well as any mending can without a blacksmith handy. And if you don't mind watching me for a little while, I suppose I should meditate again."

Chapter 26

Olvir went into his own soul cautiously this time, braced for the sudden onslaught of memories and more for the proximity to Thyran's hideous consciousness. He was surprised to find neither.

The fragment wasn't quite a fragment any longer. It wasn't fully Olvir, either, or not in the same way as his day-to-day experience of himself. The memories it carried and the images it sent were still separate from his normal awareness, and he still had to reach for them—but now the effort was less like speech in an unknown language and more like trying to remember events from long ago, maybe with a bottle or two of wine to further blur his recollections.

He saw a grizzled man in brown and gold livery bending over him, his face haggard and his lips raw where he'd bitten them. A forest rose, all shades of green and brown, and he ran laughing through it with two others, beings who shimmered too brightly for Olvir to see clearly, even through memory. A knife rose, and he fell when it did, the ground cracking and shifting around him. Fire roared through a dark room full of robed figures.

Tinival's song ran through it all now, becoming the steady harmony beneath the variations. The memories spread themselves out accordingly. Olvir doubted that he could control which ones arose and when, but he had a little space apart from them, a bit of room to think, and the sense that the ability was within his grasp. It would only take practice.

Warily, ready to retreat at any moment, he thought of Thyran. The connection was there when Olvir focused on it, but fainter, blurred, whether because Olvir had gained some control or because Thyran wasn't using Gizath's power just then. Olvir was glad of it, whatever the reason, and glad to let go once he had found it out. Pressing further would be far too risky, especially since they couldn't do much about Thyran's plans if they did discover any surprising information, and he had no desire for additional contact. At a distance and veiled, the possessive rage that was Thyran's nature nonetheless scraped against Olvir's soul, cold and slimy and sharp.

He turned his attention away from Gizath's messenger and in the retreat became aware of the world around him at that moment. Olvir felt the mountains in which he sheltered, the solid shape of rocks and the pathways that wound through them. Atop them in the caves, or within them, were the echoes Vivian had said Ulamir was talking to. Olvir had no part in that conversation, but he knew it was happening and felt a trace of the ties that had once joined the stonekin: parents to children, lovers to lovers, priests to people, friends to friends.

His bonds with Vivian, and hers to Ulamir, stood out among those echoes, the only ties recent enough to be clear and well defined. The connections between them hummed, clear notes occasionally rising to the surface. Olvir suspected that he might be able to turn those into a song, but he veered away. Vivian was her own woman, no target for his power, especially when he didn't fully understand it.

He went outward instead, beyond the mountain.

The storm was there, of course, and Olvir wouldn't have liked anybody's chances if they'd tried to travel in it, but it was no longer quite the howling fury it had been. The spiraling patterns of wind that had formed it were loosening, strands drifting off from the main body. The blizzard was unraveling like an old garment.

Olvir thought that he could help it do so.

Thyran's example showed him the method. The knowledge felt

as if it had always been his, simply rusty with disuse. He reached out with his spirit and found the wind pattern closest to unwinding from the main body of the storm.

Easing it out was a slow, tiring process. There were many places where that wind was tangled with the others, and the simple task of moving it left him wearier than an hour of hard riding would've done. Wind had no weight, and it didn't actually fight him, but the pattern of what it had been doing had a strong hold.

All the same, he uncoiled it from the others, bit by bit, until the last loop straightened out. Freed, it whisked off westward. The circling center of the storm expanded in its absence, still going but becoming looser, calmer. Olvir caught a glimpse of more wind shapes separating from one another.

He fell back into himself then, but the change was less significant than it had been after his previous attempts at contact. All his limbs felt heavy, his brain numb with weariness, but there was no feeling of losing a separate connection, only of shifting his awareness away from what he'd been doing.

"Forgive me saying so," Vivian said after he'd duly sworn on Letar's statue that he was himself and followed the gods, "but you look utterly wretched. In a handsome sort of way, of course."

"I think a child could knock me over right now." Moving his lips to speak wasn't precisely taxing, but Olvir was aware of the motion, as a well-rested man wouldn't have been. "But I also think I may have made the storm end a touch quicker."

"That bodes well," Vivian said.

Putting the statue away, she handed Olvir a waterskin and sought the rations once again. She doled out slices of the mushrooms he'd found to each of them, in addition to their normal bread and dried cherries. If the fungi helped people go without water, Vivian reasoned, they must be generally good for somebody recovering from exertion, physical or otherwise—and they made a change.

He ate ravenously, too well mannered and well trained to simply bolt the food but clearly holding off the impulse only by will. Vivian, taking her time over her own dinner—or whatever meal it was—didn't interrupt him with conversation.

"I'm sorry," he said, mostly through, with a sheepish smile. "That was uncouth of me."

"Just hungry. I've had a few moments of the sort myself. The first meal after my Reforging, I recall stuffing myself like a snake with an egg. Magic will do that. Even my greater blessing did, when I was new to invoking it."

"Tinival's gifts—" He paused and considered, the waterskin in one hand. "The greater ones, maybe. The rituals when a traitor trades information to be spared the worst of Letar's punishments, for instance, but I haven't led those. Hearing an oath or understanding languages never leave me worse off than usual." Olvir chuckled. "Of course, I was sixteen when I started using those powers, and that's an age when young men can eat their way through most of the world at a sitting anyhow, so it could be that I simply didn't notice."

"That hit me about when I started training," Vivian said. "When I visited at feast days for a couple years, Calyn used to say our parents timed it nicely by getting me off their hands before my growth started, and the Order never would've taken me on if they'd known how much I'd cost in bread and meat. I told them they were just jealous because I'd end up taller than they were."

"And did you?"

"Only by a finger's breadth or two in the end. But I had most of my height before I was twelve, and they hadn't particularly started growing at fifteen, so I had a weapon for a few years."

Olvir swallowed a mouthful of water. "Weapon, hmm?"

"You're always at war with your siblings a little, until you grow up and have your own lives. Even if you're fond of each other in principle, you know each other too well, the others are always nearby, and one of you is always the reason why another can't do or have exactly the thing they want. Mostly, you get over it when you hit eighteen or twenty."

"The things I've missed." He looked thoughtful as he finished off his piece of bread. "I wonder, was it similar for the gods? The three younger, that is?"

"I've never thought of that." All the stories, all the books, all the liturgies and paintings and songs spoke of Letar, Gizath, and Tinival as siblings, but Vivian had never before considered what that actually might have meant. It had simply been a fact of the world. "I can't imagine them being children, though."

"No, nor Sitha or Poram being parents. They can be people-shaped when they want, but they're not people, not really. I know that. But I'd think it must have taken a while to learn how the world works and what they could do with it or with each other."

Vivian studied him. Sitting cross-legged on the rock floor, hands folded in his lap now that he'd finished eating, Olvir appeared weary but otherwise the same as he had as long as he and Vivian had been acquainted. His eyes were grave and serious, his expression purely curious. She didn't suspect he was trying to argue any particular point.

All the same, she was careful to sound neutral when she replied. "It's possible. Some aspects of it were probably more obvious than others, but I suppose it depends how quickly they learned and how much knowledge they entered with. And I have no idea about either."

"I can't think of anybody who could say. Maybe the high priests, if the knowledge hasn't been lost. Or the elder peoples, the ones who lived then, but I've never heard of anybody that old coming into human lands."

"Neither have I." Most of the waterfolk and the stonekin had retreated to their own domains during the first round of Thyran's storms, a century back. From what little Vivian had learned about the years before Thyran, the ancients among them had kept largely to their realms even then, and humans generally had struggled to reach those places.

Olvir stretched and got to his feet. "And I'm probably just being philosophical because I'd give my right eye for an archpriest of Poram to tell me what I was doing half an hour ago," he said, adding quickly, "not that I would trade your company, you understand."

"I have many uses," Vivian said easily, "but weather magic isn't one of them, and neither is communing with the gods. What you say makes it sound as though you figured matters out well enough."

"I hope so. I saw what happened with the storm here but not what that may have done if another's happening back on the lines, for instance, or whether I've given Thyran more to use in the future."

"I wish I could set your mind at ease." She rose, put an arm around Olvir, and leaned her head against his shoulder. It was no definite reassurance, no guarantee that his actions wouldn't harm them or others, but it was within her power. "I've been there myself a few times in the last year or so. Nothing I've done has been as cosmic as your tasks, but with command…it seems like we're always going forward half-blind in this war, and it's never only our necks on the line."

"That's generally been how it works when I've led." Olvir sounded as if the recollection cheered him, or at least steadied him. "There's never any means of being sure, just doing what you can and trusting that the people you command know their business. It's easier to trust the ones in charge of you. Or it was for me."

"Simpler, certainly. Like working alone. We don't even really get orders most of the time. The Adeptas send us notifications: there's a monster here, probably, go do the needful. Or people seek us out directly if they're sufficiently desperate."

"I'm surprised you adapted so quickly."

"Thank you," she said and actually felt her cheeks heating a touch. "It comes down to trust again. In theory, I suppose I commanded the other Sentinels at the camp, but actually I just told them the situation for the most part. Occasionally I suggested that a particular blessing could be particularly handy midway through a battle or noticed when one of us had been on duty for too long at a stretch. Mostly I trusted them, as you say, and hoped like hell I didn't get it wrong."

Olvir nodded, the silky ends of his hair brushing against Vivian's forehead. "Sleep helps with that, if you can manage it." He was talking as much to himself as to her. "And thank the gods, that's one thing I can definitely do at the moment."

Chapter 27

Sleep was a deep, soft darkness, as it usually was after Olvir had been doing any sort of hard labor he wasn't used to. He didn't pass out the moment his head hit the pile of blankets, but he'd barely embraced Vivian when his eyelids dropped shut.

If he had any thought, it was vague regret that he was in no shape to take further advantage of the caves.

Later, as he drifted toward wakefulness, the idea came back to him. Rest had done him good, and having Vivian tucked against him, the curve of her hip under one of his palms and his other hand lying temptingly close to the upswell of her breasts, had an unsurprising effect. He believed she was awake: her breathing wasn't as slow or deep as it would've been otherwise, nor was she as relaxed.

Olvir was sleepily bending to nuzzle her neck when she slid away. Concern broke through most of his drowsiness immediately. Had he assumed too much? Was she uninterested? He pulled back, waiting to learn more and trying to wake up further.

Then he knew there was somebody else with them.

As methods of killing arousal went, that was fairly effective. Concern turned to alarm in a second. Olvir had bolted upward before a few details entered his mind.

First, the presence was *in* his mind. The room was physically empty except for Olvir and Vivian.

Second, something was flowing between that being and Vivian. It resembled conversation in a different room, too muffled to make out distinct words. She was communicating, and the other was responding, in a give-and-take that became clearer the further Olvir got from sleep.

Third, although Olvir couldn't sense the new arrival in any great detail, they seemed familiar.

Pieces of information snapped together into an understanding as awkward, in several ways, as it was surprising.

"Ah," he said.

Vivian turned toward him, frowning. "I didn't mean to wake you," she said, putting a hand on his shoulder. "We're in no danger."

"No, I… That's all right. You didn't." He rubbed the back of his neck, feeling worse than he would've if he'd walked in on her undressing. Even if they hadn't been lovers, *that* sort of mishap was reasonably common in camp, but the situation now was miles from normal. "I think," Olvir went on, "that I can sense Ulamir now. He's back, isn't he?"

It was far too early in the morning for surprises.

It's not morning.

Vivian couldn't contradict Ulamir. She prodded her consciousness upright, forcing herself to address the topic of most immediate concern. "He is," she told Olvir. "How much are you… overhearing?"

"Not very. I just know that he's here, and I can tell when the two of you speak."

If he was lying or possessed, Vivian couldn't tell it. Olvir looked as earnest as he ever had. Sitting up half-naked, gradually beginning to lose the first strung-wire alertness of a warrior surprised from sleep, he also looked as appealing as he ever had, not that she could do a damned thing about it.

The world, and its need for saving, needed a good kicking.

The last two days have let you gratify yourself. Greed is unbecoming.

"It's so lovely that you're back," said Vivian. "Are you any more aware of Olvir than you were before?"

No. He stands out no more than any other mortal who isn't you.

"Ah." Vivian stood up and began to dress. Figuring out what to say about Olvir's newfound ability required figuring out what she thought about it. "He can't sense you," she finally said as her head emerged from the neck of her shirt. "And it's probably a good sign that you pick up on his presence. The more you can perceive, the more you can affect, or some theory along those lines."

"Not that I would, in this case," Olvir said quickly.

"No, I'd really rather you didn't." In another situation, Vivian might have wanted him to try and see if he could let Ulamir talk to both of them. Translating was unwieldy at times. The circumstances that made it a possibility, however, meant it was one of the last things she wanted Olvir to do.

Guilt over her secrecy, or its potential cause, wasn't really the right word for what she felt. Her possible task was vital. Secrecy could be crucial to accomplishing it if the need did arise. Vivian had no doubt of that. She still wished that neither had been the case, for as much good as wishing ever did.

"Perhaps best just to write it off as an interesting symptom. I'll try to pretend it isn't happening." He gave her a sweet, rueful smile, the acceptance in it like a needle in Vivian's heart. "I hope he fared well with the spirits he was talking to."

They were echoes, not spirits, but we were well met all the same. He asks kindly.

"Ulamir says thank you," Vivian relayed. "He also said that the storm has basically ended. It's chilly, but nothing that should be dangerous for either of us to walk in. I was going to mention that earlier."

"I assumed you likely had a reason for getting dressed," Olvir said, fastening his belt over his own shirt and tunic. "And that was the only one that seemed likely. It's good that we can be on our way again."

He didn't, Vivian noticed, say that he was happy about it. It was a small distinction, but the knights, barred from lying, could be very exact in their phrasing.

"I'd be glad to hear what you don't mind telling," she said to Ulamir.

Even if there were words for most of it, you would find no sense in them. As usual, unless he was teasing her, there was no feeling that he was boasting, only acknowledging the difference—whether between humans and stonekin or the living and the dead. *I can speak of three things I found. One is a story, which may interest you. One is a spell for gathering food in the outside world, which is unlikely to be useful unless you develop the ability to eat stone.*

"And the third?" she asked, after relaying the information.

Vivian felt Ulamir's satisfaction before he responded. *The third,* he said, *is a passage from here to the bottom of the mountain.*

Chapter 28

Behind the dais in the music room, a wall opened at Vivian's command.

More or less.

It was really at Ulamir's command, but he gave Vivian the word for it, which took her three attempts to say correctly. Stonekin syllables could be as slippery as cut gems or as rough as shattered rock. Magic, like this command, was often both.

She did get her tongue around it eventually, though. The wall in front of her folded back, and Vivian walked through the narrow archway it formed. Olvir followed her into a narrow passage constructed of glowing jet, where shallow stairs led steadily down. Rock brushed against his shoulders with every step, but he remembered the storm and had no complaints.

"I wouldn't mind hearing the story, if you're in the mood to tell it," Vivian told Ulamir after they'd been descending for half an hour or so. "It'd pass the time."

Ulamir replied, which Olvir sensed as a steady stream of information that paused only briefly.

"Once—" Vivian herself stopped and glanced over her shoulder, eyes shining gold in the darkness. "Let me know if you'd rather I shut up, hmm?"

"No. Or I will if that ever happens, but I'd like to hear the story."

"This is a tale of Kanrath," said Vivian, her voice becoming slower, echoing the rhythm that Olvir perceived from Ulamir, "who led the circle that lived here when the gods walked the world. He traveled over the land many times but always came back to his people, bringing word and goods from the lands beyond."

Olvir tried to imagine being one of the people who'd talked to Ulamir—not Kanrath himself but one of the stonekin who'd spent all their life within the mountain, knowing nothing of the outside but what a few adventurous souls brought back.

Was it so different from the thousands of people who lived and died without going farther than a day's journey from the villages where they were born? Olvir had known plenty of those, in his childhood and his duties both. Never seeing the outdoors sounded more restrictive, granted, but perhaps the stonekin viewed other mortals as deprived, spending their lives so far from the heart of the earth.

Vivian continued.

"Once, when Kanrath was young and hadn't gone very far from the tunnels of his birth," she said, "he met an old man planting trees. They were all kinds of trees…" Vivian fell silent, and for a while, the only sounds were their footsteps on the rock. The passageway spiraled down, dark and close. "Pine, apple, plum, oak. As soon as the old man put a seed in the ground and stepped back, the tree would grow right up. The ones that were supposed to have fruit bore that fruit immediately. All of them became very large all at once. Kanrath had only a passing familiarity with plants, but he knew that wasn't precisely usual. He was extremely courteous when he wished the old man a good day."

"Wise."

"Very. When the old man greeted him in return, he used Kanrath's name, although they'd never met. Kanrath saw that the man's eyes were bright green, with gold centers that danced, so he knew he was talking to Poram."

Olvir walked on, listening, picturing the world as it had been in the days when a traveler could come upon a god unaware.

"Kanrath, being stonekin, had no food fit to offer the god in the form he'd taken, but he volunteered to help dig holes for the seeds. Poram thanked him.

"Now, there was a custom in those days that a mortal who encountered a god could get a favor and true answers to two questions if they were willing to answer the god's questions honestly in return." Vivian paused, then laughed. "Kanrath, like most of us would, found his mind blank when faced with just that situation, however he might have thought about it beforehand. He asked Poram what he was planting. The god told him about the trees, their names and natures, and he asked Kanrath where he'd been going.

"'I'm not sure,' Kanrath said. 'Wide is the world, with many places to see, and I don't know where to start. Why, lord, do you create these? They don't last nearly so long as stones.'

"'But they'll spread far in their seeds and farther in the lives of those they feed or shelter,' said Poram. "'All things end, and all go on. What wisdom can you give me that I don't know already, child of the mountains?'"

If they hadn't been under miles of rock, Olvir would've whistled. The Lord of the Wild, like his daughter, Letar, was one of the dark gods, the ones hardest for mortals to understand or meet on their own terms. Tinival was demanding—few knew that better than Olvir—and Sitha's priests bore their own burdens, particularly when fate began to get involved, but both of those two had a gentleness about them, a forgiving nature that Poram and Letar didn't share.

He would've panicked in Kanrath's place.

"A reasonably intimidating question," Vivian said, sounding as though she'd been thinking along similar lines. "Kanrath froze for a moment, the story says, then took a bit of rock from nearby. It was just granite, but it sparkled in the sunlight. He worked it the way the stonekin can do barehanded. In a few minutes, he'd formed the shape of a star. 'I never saw these in the sky until recently,' he said. 'Perhaps you never saw them on the earth until now.'

"The god beamed at him. 'The seed I plant bears fruit I hadn't expected,' he said. 'You will understand such things in the years to come.'

"He vanished in green light. As Kanrath was gaping at the space where he'd gone, one of the trees that had just grown up spoke to him—but that, Ulamir says, is a story he hasn't managed to put into human words yet."

———

I would have brought you to the echoes if I could have, my Sentinel. They would have enjoyed your company.

"I'd have liked that too," said Vivian, though she wouldn't have given up her days with Olvir. Mostly, she wished that she'd had the capacity for one activity and the leisure for both.

"At least you can tell me some of what you heard," she went on, "and maybe more after a while. Or when I'm not so encumbered by being alive."

There is freedom in death, though I would not wish it on you so soon. It seems that you were happy, too, in my absence, and I'm glad of that.

Vivian felt what Ulamir was restraining himself from saying. She didn't press him. Partnership—any friendship, in truth—was built at least in part on what either party could have said and didn't. She and Ulamir had worked together for years. They knew the job they'd taken on, and there was no need for either to remind the other.

She peered down the endless staircase. No ornament adorned those walls, no shifts in stone marked different sections. All was blank. It was quiet, too, with the soft slide of her footsteps and Olvir's and their paired breathing all the sound that traveled up and down the long passage. The world felt very far away and yet closer than it had when they'd been in the caves.

There was open sky on the other side. She trusted Ulamir on that point. Beyond that were plains and the Battlefield—and behind them was the forest and eventually the cities of the south and west, though those had stopped seeming real to Vivian months earlier.

Her thoughts turned to the camp, which nobody had ever tried to give a proper name, although she'd stayed there longer than she'd ever remained in one place since she'd been sixteen. Naming the fortifications would've made them seem too permanent, or maybe too important. Week by week, month by month, everybody at the camp had behaved—save for logistics—as though they'd be packing up the next day and heading back to their normal lives.

Had even that changed with the new assaults?

Katrine would be leading the Sentinels adeptly. She was level-headed, she lacked only a few years of experience compared to Vivian, and if her decisions weren't always what Vivian's would've been, they worked out as well on average and better sometimes. Vivian could've left the camp in no better hands.

Nonetheless, she wondered, and she worried. Had the animals Emeth used to scout received proper food and shelter, particularly if the storm had hit the camp? Were the soldiers and the knights working smoothly with Katrine? Magarteach and Nahon were good, reasonable sorts, but there were always differences in personality and command style, and those could widen under pressure.

Were all the front's leaders still alive? Were any of them?

Vivian had been too tired through most of the journey to truly consider what might be happening behind her. Safety and rest had their drawbacks, especially when she followed them with travel through a monotonous tunnel. Another geisbar might actually have been a welcome change.

What had she said to Olvir? That she had to trust the ones she led and hope to hell she was justified in doing so. It wasn't being wrong that worried her, though, but the possibilities where there was no *right*—and she couldn't do a damn thing about them regardless.

Be easy, said Ulamir. *You take a weight your shoulders were never meant for.*

Everyone had done that lately.

Vivian listened to her sword-spirit, though, and then to the steady sound of Olvir's breath behind her. She kept walking, head bent, leaning slightly forward, because that was the thing that did lie within her power just then.

And after a while, there was cold air against her face. After a few steps more, there was light, pale and dim but unmistakably present.

The mountain opened in front of them.

Chapter 29

THE LIGHT WAS DAZZLING. VIVIAN BLINKED SEVERAL TIMES—
for the same reason that she could see in the dark, she weathered
the transition from dark to light faster than normal mortals did,
but it still took a moment—and began to make out the landscape
in front of her.

We have come to an exceedingly flat place, observed Ulamir.

They certainly had. The ground stretched off with no hill in
sight, broken by occasional dark plants somewhere between
shrubs and trees in height and as wide as they were tall. Snow covered their tops and the ground, but it was already melting as the
weather escaped Thyran's constraints and nudged on toward late
spring.

The last storm had been more than a week before, and Vivian
and Olvir had come a long way from the border camp. Vivian
couldn't tell whether the air was taking longer to warm up than
it normally would. She supposed there was no point in trying to
figure it out. Thyran was sending the storms. Eventually, unless he
was stopped, they'd build up enough force to tip the larger balance
of the weather, and the endless winters would come again.

It would have been nice to figure out how long they had, all the
same.

"Well," said Olvir, who'd straightened up with an almost audi-
ble click of his spine, "it's a nice change to be on level ground."

Vivian turned her thoughts away from pointless melancholy,
letting the tall man beside her lead her toward cheer even if he
wasn't aware that he was doing so. "There's that," she agreed. "It'd

be wonderful land if I had a good horse. You could ride for hours out here, as fast as the beast would go. Assuming there are no rabbit holes."

Olvir laid a palm against his stomach. "Oh, I wouldn't mind a rabbit or two."

"For both of us? I could probably manage to eat two by myself at this point."

"It's a while to sunset." Olvir glanced up at the clear sky to confirm it. "We still have a chance of running into dinner."

"Your mouth to the gods' ears. All right." Vivian closed her eyes and brought forth her blessing. It was harder to manage with only words to give her the central target, but she thought *the Heart of the Battlefield* and pictured the Battlefield itself, that multicolored shifting mass that she was glad the horizon hid for a few hours longer.

All was calm for a couple breaths. Then one particular direction gained weight, pulling at her like a very gentle version of iron to a lodestone. She fixed the feeling in her mind, devoted a small portion of her awareness to sensing where it told her to go, and then opened her eyes.

"Ready?" Olvir asked, attentive but not impatient.

"That's debatable. But I can find our way there."

The first step Vivian took cleared away some of the snow. Red grass was bent beneath it, moisture darkening the former rust color to a shade that more closely resembled blood.

She could only hope that wasn't an omen.

―――――

For the first few miles, Olvir let go of his worries about what lay ahead and simply enjoyed being outside. He felt a little guilty about that, in truth. The stonekin's caverns were beautiful beyond anything he'd imagined, had saved their lives, and had been the setting for the most intense pleasure he'd experienced. The passage had gotten them down the mountain far more quickly and comfortably than an outside journey would've done.

Olvir was over six feet tall, though, he'd spent most of his early life in the open air, and he was human. *We're unreasonably fond of the sky*, he said in a silent apology to the vanished stonekin who'd built the cavern or perhaps to the gods who'd directed him and Vivian there. *But thank you for the shelter.*

It would've been enough to see the sky stretching above them even if it had been sullen gray or raining. Instead, the storm had cleared away, leaving bright blue that stretched from the peaks of the mountains to the eastern horizon. The snow was very white against it, the trees midnight-dark.

They'd come to a land of contrasts, Olvir thought as he and Vivian walked, leaving a bloodred trail behind them. Colors were simpler. The land was flat, the trees almost square, and all that he saw seemed less complex than any of the places he'd been before—more straightforward.

Cleaner, he thought, and then: *no*. Only a few miles away, the first betrayal in the world had happened. Even away from the Battlefield, there likely were the rabbit holes Vivian had mentioned or some equivalent. The trees appeared solid, with leaves and bark like normal plants, so they probably died in their time as others did, and things fed on them.

Life was complicated. If it wasn't complicated, it probably wasn't life.

He listened to his feet and Vivian's, crunching on the snow, and to the gentle wind blowing through the trees. As they walked on, the sun got warmer, and the snow began to melt away. A bird flew up from one of the trees, wings flashing bright gold against the peacock sky.

"It feels older here," said Vivian. "I know Poram created it at the same time as He did the rest of the world, but...that's not the sense I get."

"Unchanged, perhaps," Olvir said. "Or not changed in a long while. If this land's ever been plowed up for wheat or the trees have been cut down to make lumber, it was thousands of years before this." It would've still been unlikely that long ago. There would have been fewer people then, and the elder races didn't farm, as a rule. "One of the lessons of Poram I read was that everything in the world changes, but mortals and gods are the ones who change things on purpose. I'd think humans are the ones who hurry those changes along the most."

Vivian considered the point, then lifted her dark brows, curious about a new subject. "Are you supposed to read Poram's teachings as part of your training, or was that on your own initiative?"

"We're not required to study the other gods in depth, but... encouraged, yes, especially when the weather or our health means we can't go out and train." He laughed, remembering his youth. "I started with Poram because the fewest of His teachings are written down."

That drew laughter from Vivian too. Her light soprano echoed in the clear air. "Strategically sound of you."

"Thank you. Did the Order want you to do that sort of thing?"

"In a sense. They cared less about the gods themselves—the Four remake us, but we don't need to understand them—but the Adeptas did want us to improve our wits and our knowledge. Mostly it was collections of legends for us, and bestiaries. Or memory games if we had company."

"That sounds very practical."

"Practical depends on the aim. Your training was practical for you, I'd say—understanding the gods is what we have priests for."

Olvir held up his hands quickly, lest lightning smite him. "I don't think any of us would say we actually *do* understand them, not completely. We just try and try to help others to make the effort as well. I doubt any mortal can really comprehend the Four."

"No," said Vivian. "Honestly, I doubt that any being can

completely understand any other. There's always going to be some unknown part." She looked ahead of them at the ancient, foreign landscape. "That's the appeal of company, isn't it? Maybe even of the world. The unfamiliar."

A certain amount of the unfamiliar, Ulamir corrected. *Contentment lies in mystery of well-established shape and size, not to mention the certainty that it will never bring destruction to your doorstep.*

"Mostly, yes," said Vivian and translated for Olvir. "But there are plenty of people who aren't really content unless they're risking their necks at least once in a month."

"Darya," said Olvir with a quick grin that vanished as quickly. "Or that was true until Oakford. She mentioned, after the battle was over, that she was surprised to be hoping for a long stretch of safety. I'd bet even she and others who enjoy danger have had their fill of it for years by now."

"Possibly. And those who never liked it before may have developed a taste for it."

"I've seen that happen on occasion, yes. Some of them make good knights, but generally they're not so suited to working with others."

"It's a quality more suited to us. Or the Blades."

"Do you mind me asking if it's one of your qualities?"

Vivian shook her head. "Or, rather, no, I don't mind, but no, it's not. I like getting things done, having a mission. I don't mind danger. It's a part of my life, and that's all right. But it's not what I seek."

This holds true, said Ulamir, *until the moment you mount a horse.*

"Ulamir thinks otherwise," she said, "but he never understood how riding can be enjoyable. He could have a point, I suppose—"

Thank you.

"But I've never thought of speed as danger, exactly." She studied Olvir for a moment, watching the sun glint off his armor. "What about you?"

"No. When I was young, I believed I might, but—" He rubbed a hand across his square chin, with its half-day growth of dark stubble. "Danger means people are going to get hurt, and there's only ever so much I can do to prevent that. Knowing as much takes away from any thrill the risk might have had for me."

"There is that." The awareness of other lives in jeopardy and how little ability she had to keep them safe had been one of the largest changes Vivian had experienced when she'd taken command. "Usually, in normal times, there's already been a death or two before we get called in. There are rare occasions where we happen to be in the right place at the right time, or a wise villager reads the signs and summons a Sentinel before events turn fatal, but mostly it takes a body to summon us. Then the only further risk is if we fail, at which point we're probably too dead to worry about it."

Death prevents worry, does it?

"Unless we become soulswords," she added with a glance at Ulamir so Olvir would understand what had prompted her to speak. "Or otherwise feel inclined to remain and fret about the living, which I admit is rather kind, up to a point."

Olvir nodded. "There was a man who called on us for help because the ghost of his mother was holding him captive—barring the doors and windows whenever she suspected he was going to put himself in any sort of danger, right down to going outside when it was a little too cold. It sounds a bit funny in retrospect, but he was going out of his mind."

"I would be." Vivian squinted at the horizon, trying to decide whether the glints of light and motion there were the Battlefield's edge or water. Not wanting to raise either of their hopes prematurely by putting her speculation into words, she went on. "I don't

have children, of course"—the Reforging prevented it—"but I get
the impression bringing them up, once they reach a certain age, is
a lot like command. You give people a certain amount of guidance,
and then you have to let them do their jobs or live their lives, I suppose, even if you're sure it won't end pleasantly for them."

Yet commanding is a matter of what you cannot do yourself, Ulamir
said, *and raising young a matter of what you shouldn't.*

"Fair," said Vivian and explained.

"There's that. I should talk to Edda about it, perhaps, next
time…if I see her again," Olvir replied after a pause where he
clearly decided that putting uncertainty into words was better
than tempting fate. "Is that a stream, do you think?"

"I've been wondering." Shading her eyes against the sun, she
could see that the movement was all heading in a single direction, not the swirling chaos of the Battlefield. Trees screened that
motion in places, and they were taller and closer together than
elsewhere on the plains, some of them pearly-white rather than
the square black ones Vivian had started to get used to. "Looks
that way."

Neither of them spoke of fish or drinking. There was no guarantee that the water, or any living being in it, would be fit for
human consumption, and they were in no position to take risks.
All the same, there was a chance that there'd be fish in the stream
they'd recognize or familiar plants growing on the banks. Even
the change in the landscape would be welcome, a landmark in the
unending plains.

Vivian felt new life in her feet. She didn't hurry, she kept herself
alert, but eagerness rose up within her regardless, making the land
go by faster even though she and Olvir kept the same pace. Before
long, they were a few yards from what was clearly a small river.
Soon after, they'd closed that distance to a matter of feet.

That was when the horror stepped out from behind a tree.

Chapter 30

IT WAS FAMILIAR IN TYPE, IF NOT AS AN INDIVIDUAL. FEATURES on a hairless head had run like wax, leaving only pitted eye sockets full of squirming flesh and a narrow lipless hole below them. The shape below was roughly humanoid, save for too many fingers on each hand, and dressed in gray and orange robes. This was one of Thyran's wizards. Olvir had fought them on occasion and seen them once by their master's side.

He drew his sword in an instant.

Vivian was already in motion. The sun flashed off Ulamir's naked blade as his holder sprinted forward.

One of the wizard's hands drifted upward. The forest of fingers waved gently, and a beam of gray-orange fire flashed outward toward Vivian. She dodged sideways, letting a nearby tree take the brunt of the spell.

The substance of its trunk shifted before Olvir could blink. Bulges and tendrils sprouted from some bits. Other sections vanished entirely, holes appearing in the tree's middle. He saw it all while he charged at the wizard.

Vivian swerved directly back into her original path, then leapt in a strike that should have put Ulamir through the Twisted's heart.

An invisible force flung her backward. Olvir froze, hearing a steam-on-metal hiss fill the air, watching as Vivian fell sprawling on the ground.

"We had to have that demonstration, didn't we?" the mage asked, turning its head so that its twitching sockets were facing

Olvir. "I promise I can do the same to you. I offer conversation, not battle."

Valiant denial was the proper response. Half of Olvir's attention was occupied with watching to see if Vivian was still breathing, though, and so the first thing he said was a question. "How did you get here before us?"

It shrugged what weren't quite shoulders any longer. "I had no need to cower from the cold."

"Yes," Vivian grunted, pushing herself up on an elbow. "Stolen lives would keep you fairly warm, wouldn't they?"

Olvir's chest unlocked when he heard her voice. He doubted that his own sword, skillfully forged and blessed as it was, would get through the barrier that had stopped Ulamir, so he waited. He noticed a mound of dirt behind the wizard: had the creature brought its sources of power and sacrificed them while it waited for Vivian and Olvir to arrive? Or was another scheme in play?

"I claimed my rights. You couldn't understand," it said to Vivian, and then, to Olvir, "but I am sent to offer you the chance to do so."

"To understand?"

"To understand a great deal." The Twisted mage's mouth opened a little wider, lamprey-like. It seemed to be what passed for a grin. "Our Lord has many things to show you and many rewards for those who will work to bring the proper order to the world. You claim to serve justice. Through Our Lord and his high priest, you will be able to see its true form."

Communication was flowing quickly between Vivian and Ulamir. Olvir hoped one of them had an idea that hadn't occurred to him.

Vivian was on her feet. That gave Olvir a coherent plan: buy time.

"Forgive me," he said, "but what I've seen of how your lord treats his servants doesn't appeal to me. Would I be…reshaped… as you and your fellows were?"

It huffed in disgust, a phlegmy sound through its mouth. "Shallow, shallow. Appearance is nothing, a bauble for those who fail to respect true strength." The creature cocked its malformed head, thinking or listening to silent instructions. "Still, arrangements could be made."

"Would you—could you—guarantee that?" As Vivian reached Olvir's side, her gaze switched quickly between him and the mage, and she appeared equally dubious about both of them. Olvir saw her fingers tighten on Ulamir's hilt. "Would I have your oath, and Thyran's, that I would remain alive and in my current form if I gave him my loyalty?"

"You presume yourself clever in your corruption," the mage spat.

"Only cautious."

There was another of those silent moments, which were starting to make Olvir as wary as the thing's speech did. "I would swear it in his name, on the right hand of Gizath," it gurgled at last. "I can't break such vows without severe consequences, and those would fall, too, on any who broke them for me."

Agreeing, then maneuvering Thyran into a position where he broke his own oath, had a brief mad appeal. A Blade could have done it, maybe, or a wizard, or somebody raised in court politics and intrigue. Olvir had grown up with truth, justice, and goals. His talents lay along a more straightforward path.

"Then my terms are these," he said. "Thyran surrenders himself to the Order of the Dawn, to Letar's Blades, or to Tinival's Knights, whichever he can find first. He comes alone, wearing nothing but cloth with no magic about it, gagged and with his hands bound behind him. He submits to the judgment of those he has wronged and makes proper amends—by which I mean that he lays his head on the block so that the Dark Lady can give his wretched excuse for a soul some manner of its just deserts."

It might be his last speech, Olvir knew. He remembered the tree and the fire, and the idea made him sick, but that was all remote. The words were immediate. So was the power he felt pouring through him as he spoke, a steady and quickening beat, and the sword solid in his hand.

Anger on the Twisted mages looked no different from other emotion, but the wizard made another of the disgusted sounds again, only longer. "I expected no different," it said. "Be cleansed, then, as the world will be."

Sickly fire flew from its upraised fingers toward Olvir. He dodged to the side opposite Vivian's, knowing that he'd be too slow without a Sentinel's speed and that he had no soulsword to protect him.

A glow the color of the summer sky surrounded the writhing gray-orange shapes, then closed on them, snuffing the Traitor God's force out as if it had never been.

Olvir heard the mage snarl in anger, but that was of little concern. Awe gripped him instead, and gratitude.

Very distantly, he heard a great voice: *Fair is fair*, and realized that its owner wasn't talking to him.

She had her answer for the moment.

The ground was cold and damp beneath Vivian's stomach, and a rock had caught her just above the right hip. Still her mind was full of Olvir's speech and of the blue light that had shielded him from the wizard's power.

Tinival trusted His servant, it seemed.

With luck, that would let her do more than die relieved.

Ulamir was silent in her head, gathering power for the next time that he needed to protect her. The tree she'd sheltered behind provided temporary cover. Vivian sent it a quick mental apology given what had happened to the other, then peered past it while exposing as little of herself as she could manage.

Olvir had made it behind one of the other trees, a few yards from her cover. The wizard was pacing in front of the mound.

The size of the dirt-covered pile bothered her. Marching that many twistedmen over the mountains would have been a difficult job, whether or not stolen lives had kept them all safe from the storm. And why would a wizard bother bringing his sacrifices to the site? Generally speaking, from what Vivian had seen in the war, the Twisted mages could store their power for a while after they'd stolen it.

Vivian eyed the distorted figure as she'd done before. Her combat blessing might work on the wizard through its shield, but the protection would probably keep her or Olvir from finishing Thyran's creature off, even if it had suffered a near-fatal wound in the past.

She surveyed the terrain: trees, mound of dirt and probably bodies, river behind them. The cover was passable, but there wasn't much else she could use. Olvir had set a good example, though: keep talking until the situation changes.

"Well," Vivian said. She raised her voice so that the robed figure could hear but threw it a trifle, one of the tricks that the Order had taught her in her youth. Deceit was a weapon too. "I don't guess any of us want to do this, mmm?"

The wizard spun and unleashed another bolt. This one went wide of any trees, thank the gods, and dissipated in midair, still closer than Vivian ever wanted to be to such power. Leaves rustled in its passing, as though in reprimand.

She moved her voice. "You can keep doing that. We can keep evading. We have protection. Soon, if I understand your kind, you'll wear out your reserves—and if we don't both outlast you, there are two of us."

"I only need the knight's death."

That was very possibly true. Vivian estimated the distance between herself and the monster. If she told Olvir to run and triggered the combat blessing...maybe. It was too uncertain to be a first resort. She bluffed instead.

"Really? Do you imagine that to be the case here, over the mountains and so close to the Battlefield? Do you really think your...master"—she put as much disdain as possible into the word—"can draw what he seeks if it escapes here? I suspect it may become unsuited to a physical frame again, and he'd have to redo whatever tiresome ritual Gizath's little worshippers in Heliodar performed in the first place."

For all Vivian knew, she could have been completely correct about every word she spoke. She hoped that helped her sound convincing.

A strangeness lies in that pile of earth, Ulamir said faintly in her mind. *Protecting you, I can't sense it completely, but I'm trying to feel more.*

She sent acknowledgment and thanks, then dared another glance at the wizard. It had stopped pacing and was considering, or maybe communicating, again.

"You may be honored to die for your lord and his god, completing their mission," she added, "but will you be as honored to die in vain? Or even making matters harder for him? I assure you, two of us against one of you won't end happily. And if you slay Olvir"—she hated to speak the words, but there they were—"and I live, I assure you I can put considerable force between Thyran and retrieving the Heart. Your talents may be best needed elsewhere."

The wizard turned. Vivian wondered, briefly, if she might have gotten through to it.

No, no, it's not earth, not entirely.

The wizard raised its hands again.

Vivian sprang to her feet.

Beyond the wizard, the mound shuddered, then split. Earth fell away around parts that wriggled themselves together: six legs ending in paws, a huge body, a great rotting head.

The geisbar lumbered forward once more.

Chapter 31

DEATH HADN'T TREATED THE BEAST KINDLY. OLVIR COULD SEE bones clearly through great gaps where scavengers had been at its meat, only magic and a scrap of flesh held its head to its body, and all four of its eyes were gone. Gizath's power flickered in the sockets, the same gray-orange as the force that the wizard had thrown at him and Vivian, but Olvir didn't think the geisbar had sight: it swung its head back and forth constantly as it headed toward them.

The undead sensed life. Vision wasn't necessary.

The wizard was watching, hands half-raised. However much power it had expended on raising the beast, it clearly had some left.

The ground shook beneath the bear's paws. It came on slower than it had in life, another gift of the Dark Lady.

Olvir noted that, combined the information with what he'd seen of the wizard's power, and came to a quick decision—one he didn't dare shout. They needed every advantage they could get. He bolted back the way they'd come from and hoped Vivian realized what he was trying to do.

He ran at as wide an angle as he could away from where she'd taken cover, zigging and zagging while he went. Behind him, the monster's feet thudded on. The Twisted wizard had too much control to shout in rage or lacked the parts to do so, but Gizath's power slashed a wound in the air far to Olvir's left. Darting a glance in that direction, he saw an amber light flare around Vivian, deflecting the attack. She was running, too, as opposite to Olvir's direction as she could manage without heading back toward the wizard.

As Olvir had half hoped, the geisbar hesitated as his path and Vivian's diverged.

When the creature began shambling after Vivian, it was the better part of tactics to let it. Vivian was lighter, less armored, and, in the coldest thinking, the less essential. Olvir still felt a sickness in the pit of his stomach, distant only because of the battle.

Now the geisbar was between the wizard and one of its targets, though. The Twisted must have worked that out or be running short of power, because the gray fire stopped.

That was when Olvir spun around to face the lumbering undead. He charged, sword flashing in the sunlight and battle cry on his lips: "Tinival and Justice!"

The undead geisbar would have no notion what he was saying, the wizard wouldn't care, and there were no others to inspire. None of that mattered. The cry drove Olvir's feet forward, then, as he came to the geisbar's hind leg, lent power to his arms, his hips, and his blade. He swung hard at a spot he'd noticed from a distance, where the flesh had fallen off and exposed the bone behind its knee completely.

Bone that had been lying in the wilderness for a few days, even geisbar bone, quickly gave way under two hundred pounds, the force of an all-out charge, and keen-edged steel. The leg cracked in two. The geisbar rocked, suddenly off-balance.

Olvir let himself keep going past the creature. The wizard was on the move now and not at all indecisive any longer. A last-second leap sideways brought Olvir barely out of the way of another strike. The light writhed a few inches from the side of his neck, cold and slimy even when it didn't touch him.

The Twisted had adjusted to them running away. It was a good moment to catch it off guard again—and to see if its shield still held. Olvir spun in a tight half circle and rushed it, head down, pushing himself to go faster when he glimpsed Vivian dodging a swipe of the geisbar's claws.

It almost worked. The wizard stumbled backward, not nearly fast enough. Olvir started to sweep his sword down from his shoulder, a blow that had left plenty of Twisted with cleft skulls in the past. He braced himself for the backlash if the shield held.

No force struck him. He felt the air beneath his blade resist, then start to give way. His stroke would be slower for it, but Olvir was a large man and a determined one. He thought the blow would do the job.

The wizard clenched one fist. Deep within the horror's sunken sockets, patterns squirmed across dull gray eyes.

Olvir's armor clamped down on every side of his chest, then wrenched. Metal links cut through his shirt and bit deep into the skin beneath it, but that sharp pain was the least of his problems. His sword fell as his arm went limp and bloodless. The pressure on his ribs equaled his weight or more. He fell, wheezing, to his knees.

The wizard was too smart to gloat. Its maw wouldn't smile anyhow. Olvir had no notion what it was thinking. He didn't know, either, what the oncoming blow would do to him—whether it would be death or unconsciousness so that he could be given to Thyran for a leisurely dismantling.

He knew only that he could do nothing to prevent his fate, whatever it was.

———————

Hand-length teeth snapped together on the back of Vivian's doublet. She lunged, then finally shot forward as the leather parted, leaving half her armor in the geisbar's jaws.

She whipped around as soon as she'd gotten a little distance. The geisbar turned clumsily at best, especially missing a leg, and undead senses were sluggish. While it was trying to work out the change, Vivian dashed back the way she'd come, passing within a few inches of the geisbar's side.

The thing reeked. She'd smelled decay before, from open graves to untended battlefields, but the geisbar was different. Behind the natural rot lurked a scent like burning hair. Vivian wished she could hold her breath. She needed all the air she could get, though, stinking or not; her lungs were already faintly aching.

She shot past the monster's dirt-covered flank, caught sight of Olvir and the wizard, and almost did stop breathing.

Training took over and kept her moving even as she saw Olvir's sword fall to the ground and shrieked internal protest.

She didn't have time to draw her bow and nock an arrow. The wizard was out of knife's range. Still running, Vivian recognized futility, thought of the lone move that could have any effect, and started to gasp out the command. "Lethal—"

Lend me your voice first, said Ulamir, urgent. *Will you?*

Vivian didn't know what he meant, but they'd been partners for decades. He had a plan. "Yes," she replied at once.

The geisbar thudded across the ground behind her. Olvir fell to his knees. The wizard stepped forward and placed both its palms on Olvir's forehead.

Olvir slumped over, then toppled to one side. He went silently, with a strange dignity even when clearly unconscious. Vivian opened her mouth to scream.

The series of sounds that came forth was so deep that they almost burst her throat. Her body shook with the force of them. They moved her jaw at angles that Vivian would never have been able to consciously manage, agonizing contortions that she welcomed.

The sounds sank into the earth, and the earth answered.

Rocks burst up through the ground near the wizard. Most were the size of Vivian's fist or larger, and the force of their ascent sent up explosions of dirt—dirt now absent from the ground beneath the Twisted's feet.

Caught by surprise, the mage stumbled back. One of the stones slammed into what passed for its ankle. It fell, clutching at the earth with its distorted hands.

Vivian could almost have felt sorry for the thing. Except, looking at Olvir, she couldn't.

"Good," she rasped to Ulamir when she could talk. She hadn't stopped running while the rocks erupted, and her legs no longer felt like they belonged to her, but that was fine. "Now."

Now, he agreed, and the lethal blessing surged through them both.

As always, Vivian saw what she was doing for a split second. The wizard had a scar on its chest from an old fight for dominance. Human soldiers had burned one of its legs badly when it had helped attack Oakford. When it had been human itself, before it had gone over to Thyran and been changed to its current form, it had broken its wrist.

None of those wounds were fatal. Even together, they wouldn't necessarily kill the thing. But when the fault lines made the injuries fresh again, the wizard couldn't so much as try to get back on its feet.

When Vivian reached its side, the creature was only writhing in pain. Dark blood pooled on the ground beneath it. Vivian lifted Ulamir and thrust him down into its chest, once and then again, then swung him down to decapitate the monster entirely.

That was more than enough for her.

Chapter 32

A NONE-TOO-FEELING ENTITY HAD OPENED UP OLVIR'S HEAD, briskly rearranged the contents into tidy piles, and slammed it shut again. It was not pleasant. It was one of the least pleasant experiences he'd ever had, in fact, and he'd once taken a large club to his right kneecap.

Slowly, he recognized sensations beyond the pain: cool moisture moving lightly over his skin and a voice saying his name. It was quiet, that voice. Gentle. The pain in his head got worse when Olvir tried to listen, but he thought—oh, he could think again—that was because listening was effort, movement away from stillness and darkness.

The voice was worried.

Olvir put a name to it: Vivian. Her face came back, guiding him away from the darkness, reminding him of the reasons he needed to get through the pain. He forced his eyes to open a crack. Needle-sharp light poured into his brain. It was still midday or so.

"Not long then," he said, or assumed he said. His throat and mouth both were slow following his commands.

Vivian made the sign of the Four, not bothering to put the damp rag she was holding down first. "You gave me a horrible moment or three there," she said.

"Sorry," Olvir managed.

"Hush." She helped him sit up, then handed him a waterskin. "When you feel ready for it, tell me: do you know who you are?"

The water was impossibly sweet. He could taste the faint flavor of wine in it and the hint of leather, and he loved every second. Discipline kept him from gulping—that and consideration for Vivian, who was sitting beside him with her arm around his shoulders, trying not to openly show any signs of worry.

Pieces of the world kept resolving themselves and taking on meaning: the feel of Vivian's shoulder and side, for instance, absent her leather armor. The remains had been under Olvir's head when he woke. There wasn't much to them any longer. He took another, hasty look at Vivian but saw no serious wounds.

"I'm Olvir Yoralth," he said, keeping his speech short. His throat hurt. That could have been related to what the wizard had done or to how loudly he'd been yelling beforehand. "I serve Tinival and justice."

"So you said." A few of the strain lines on Vivian's face eased. "It was quite impressive."

"You're Vivian. A Sentinel. We're saving the world. I bear the Heart of Gizath." He'd been going to ask about the wizard and the geisbar, but his sight was coming back. The nearby landscape told him all he needed to understand.

The geisbar was a small mountain off at the edge of his vision. A bit nearer lay the wizard, or, really, the wizard's component parts. Vivian had been very thorough. She'd cleaned her arms to the elbow before touching Olvir, he saw now, but her legs were spattered with purple-black blood.

"Smart," Olvir said and gestured to the Twisted mage's remains.

"Angry," Vivian admitted, with a rueful smile that went straight to Olvir's heart. The pain in his head was still very present. It mattered less at that moment.

He put an arm around her in return, moving carefully in case either of them was more damaged than was obvious. For the most part, Olvir found, his body seemed to be in decent working order, though his muscles were going to have some complaints and his chest felt downright sanded.

"I'm not completely sure why it didn't kill me," he said. "Whether it meant to and didn't have as much force left as it wanted, or the Heart gave me a little resistance to Gizath's power, or it meant to take me alive if it could."

"There was no sign one way or another. It touched your forehead, you collapsed—no lights or noises. No expression on the damned thing to read either," Vivian said flatly. Feeling the communication between her and Ulamir, Olvir suspected she was thinking of the third option, as he was, and of what that would've likely meant for him as well as the world. "I wish I'd gotten there sooner."

She spoke with a matter-of-factness and a lack of self-recrimination that they both were familiar with from other battles. The world was what it was. It would've been better in another form. That was nobody's fault, and nobody could change it.

"We both survived, thank the gods. Very specifically." As reality became sharper, awe rose up within Olvir again. He looked upward, into the cloudless turquoise sky. "Lord Tinival, you have honored me far above what I deserve today and far beyond what I ever could have expected. I vow to be as worthy of your grace as mortal flesh and will permit." He paused. "And I vow to praise you more formally as soon as my circumstances allow."

Once he was capable of kneeling, after all, he'd be capable of walking. At that point, he rather suspected that the god of justice would prefer them to be about their mission, saving the lengthy devotions for when evening brought them to a stop.

"I'm in no position to say anybody's earned divine favor," said Vivian, "but your speech did Him credit, in my opinion."

That was an understatement. She'd crept to Olvir's side while he asked the wizard questions, trying to determine whether he was being sincere, feeling Ulamir holding himself in check for whatever was to come. It had been a profound relief when Olvir had finally answered, and then much more than simple relief.

He'd shone. The tall, handsome, wholesome farm boy, the earnest companion of her journey and the diligent servant of the gods, had blazed with starlight and glory for a few moments, even before the Silver Wind had made Himself manifest for Olvir's protection. The actual divine radiance had seemed almost redundant.

And now he was actually blushing. It was also a relief to see that: his skin had looked nearly bloodless when Vivian had found him.

"Thank you," he said. "I'm not so vain that I'd say you're right, but I tried. Besides, I wanted to…to make it clear where I stood, I suppose. I never really had the chance until then. That doesn't mean I'm glad any of that…" He hesitated, trying to choose a word. Vivian would've expected various forms of profanity from others. She didn't think Olvir was avoiding it as such. It just didn't come to his tongue as readily as it did most people's. "…situation happened. I suppose I'm thankful that I found the words when the moment arrived."

"And I'm glad I was there for it. The questions were good too. Unnerving, but good."

"I wish I could've warned you."

"It was more convincing without any advance notice." She hesitated, then looked straight into his hazel eyes. "I know you'd never willingly sign on with Thyran."

Ulamir was absent. Likely he'd stay that way for longer than usual, given the combined effort of channeling the lethal blessing and summoning the rocks. Everybody else Vivian knew was far away. The land stretched off alien and empty beyond where she and Olvir sat. In all of it, there was no anchor for her except Olvir himself, and she couldn't let him serve that role.

All she could allow herself was the brief interlude while they sat with their arms around each other and the slight emphasis she'd placed on *you*. If not for the speech and Tinival's grace, she very likely wouldn't have dared that.

For a little while, Olvir was silent. Vivian could hear the river running past them in the distance. They hadn't run so far, or perhaps they'd come back farther than she'd realized. She hadn't paid any attention to the geography.

"*I* wouldn't," Olvir said slowly, meeting her gaze steadily. "But I'm honored by your faith. You don't owe it to me. I know that you have your duty, and I wouldn't want you to swerve from it for a second. Not for my sake."

Vivian knew one fact in that moment, heart-deep, and figured out another.

From the way Olvir regarded her, the thoughtful precision of what he said, and all the empty space where he kept silent, she was fairly sure of what he was telling her: that he knew, as much as he could let himself know, the mission she hadn't told him about. He might not be able to put it into words, even in his head, for fear of revealing too much to his other self. Still, if their quest didn't end well, it would be no shock to Olvir when Ulamir came down.

He was saying, as clearly as he believed it was safe to say, that it was all right.

That was the conclusion Vivian figured out. She nodded, said "Thank you," and knew the other fact with every breath.

If worst came to almost worst, if Vivian had to kill Olvir to keep Gizath from returning fully to the world, she would do it. She wouldn't hesitate. There was a larger world at stake, full of people who loved each other as deeply as she'd come to love her knight. For their sake, she would strike without flinching if it had to be done.

She knew, as she sat with Olvir on the edge of the river, that the act would break her.

Part IV

Now Veryon knew how little regard Gizath had for him. The god had made that plain. Still, he had no suspicion. None then living would have thought of treachery—none but Gizath himself.

"Who is that coming toward us?" asked the Traitor. Veryon turned, all amiability, to greet whatever new arrival Gizath might have sighted.

The tragedy is, in part, that murder was so easily accomplished.

—*The First Betrayal*

The Dark Lady weeps forever, for a love she'll see no more,
And the gods say nothing of the cause.
To this day, the world winds on in shadow and in pain…

—Lines from "Shapes of Wind and
Night," by the poet Elyan

Chapter 33

There wasn't time for pain: not for Olvir's, which was obvious, or for Vivian's, which she hoped she hid.

Neither of them had broken bones, all their bruises would heal, none of their cuts needed binding, and Olvir's pupils were both the same size. That would have to suffice.

"My armor," Vivian said as they got to their feet, "is probably a loss."

"Mending it would take a day or two, from what I can tell, and a fair bit of a cow," Olvir agreed. Carefully, he stretched his arms, put weight on his legs in one stance and then another, and rotated his head. The last motion made him grimace but not cry out.

"A deer would probably be enough," Vivian said, "but I haven't seen one nearby. The only things with suitable skin to do the job are you, me, and our foes."

Olvir wrinkled his nose. "I'm all for being practical, but…"

"But. Besides, we don't have time, even if I was willing to make the rest of this trip in part of an undead bearskin. I don't think I actually left enough whole on the wizard."

"Now that you mention it, no." He picked up his sword from where it had fallen beside the Twisted, cleaned the blade, and sheathed it again. "The skin wouldn't be undead."

"I really doubt either of us can be sure of that."

"Horrifyingly, a good point."

"I do my best."

"I'm usually very glad of it. Back on the horse, then?"

"Oh, don't mention horses. I'd give my left hand for a good steady-paced gelding right now," Vivian said.

"Your Order needs to give better lessons in bargaining," Olvir joked as they started making their way toward the river again.

Vivian laughed. She didn't have to force it, which rendered the whole fucking mess better and worse at once.

It was still easy to talk to him. That was the heart of the matter. He made her laugh, he made her think, he made her feel able to say whatever came to her mind—except on one topic. That subject meant every laugh came with a shadow of pain.

Possibility wasn't certainty. But Vivian couldn't let herself dwell on that either. *No fear,* Ulamir had said before. *No hope. Only you and the stone.*

Vivian strode down the trail beside Olvir and tried for that balance.

———

Olvir approached the riverbank with his sword drawn, and Vivian had Ulamir out and ready, but no shape came from beneath the trees to confront them. A few shining birds took off from the treetops, and an emerald-green squirrel with three tails ran a short distance away and stared at them reprovingly. That was all.

"If I had a hawk," Vivian said, "or was a better aim with a stone…"

She didn't sound too disappointed, though. Olvir didn't feel much desire to hunt the little creature himself, as good as the notion of fresh meat sounded in the abstract. It was the first thing with a face they'd seen since they'd left the mountains. Given a couple of days, he was sure sentiment would have surrendered to hunger—it did easily with rabbits and deer—but when an animal was novel, he'd rather admire than hunt.

"Besides," he said aloud, "I don't know that what lives here is still safe for us to eat. Or ever was, come to think of that. It was the elder peoples who dwelled here, and at least the stonekin are harder to poison than we are."

"And waterfolk can eat fish that'd make us turn purple and stop breathing," Vivian replied. "We can't afford to take chances, either. Not while we're going toward the center."

Her expression hardened as she spoke the last sentence. Olvir had a rough idea of her thoughts, a better one of her sorrow.

Ulamir spoke to her, though Olvir couldn't hear the words themselves. The essence of what Vivian sent back was a resigned shrug.

"It's too bad," he said aloud. "Not about the little green beast—I don't have the heart to kill that right now—but if there are creatures like it, there are probably nuts and fruit."

In fact, silver apples, or silver fruit that resembled apples, grew on the white trees. Olvir's mouth literally watered when he saw them. He remembered the crispest, ripest apple he'd ever bitten into, on an afternoon in high fall after a long session of sparring. Nothing but his mission could have kept him from stretching up and taking a few of the shining silver globes that hung close above his head.

He satisfied himself with washing in the river. That didn't give him complete satisfaction either, since Olvir felt both horribly exposed without his armor, damaged as it was, and guilty about getting undead geisbar blood in the clear water. He still couldn't deny the physical relief of getting that blood off his skin. It eased his spirit slightly, too, taking him a step further away from the darkness where the wizard had sent him.

Poram, he hoped, would understand, especially since they were at least trying to save His creation.

Not much human blood went into the water. Olvir was going to have some livid bruises on his arms and neck in a few hours, Vivian's right side was already going dark red, but nothing had broken their bones, and very little had pierced their skin. The exception was Olvir's chest, where his armor had twisted to cut him.

"It looks," Vivian said, inspecting the wounds with a gentle thoroughness that would have been arousing if Olvir hadn't been one large mass of aches, "as if somebody took a cheese grater to you."

"Do you know how that looks?"

"I admit that I'm guessing. But it's a reasonably educated guess."

"I wouldn't expect any less."

The cuts, though they stung, were small, shallow, and no cause for bandages. Vivian applied ointment from the jar Olvir had packed, which stung in a more cleansing fashion. The sharp orange scent of it cut right to his memories: dressing wounds in camp after a battle, and before that, the herbalist who'd served the knights in Affiran, wispy and calm.

"I wish I could do more for you," he said, gesturing to Vivian's side. Olvir had kept watch while Vivian bathed, as she'd done for him, but nobody except the Mourners could heal bruises, and they usually wouldn't.

"Mine will heal faster. It evens out."

Olvir pulled his tunic on, ignoring the aches in his arms. He considered asking if he should have run again toward the end, tried to get away while Vivian distracted the wizard and its creature. Even leaving aside emotion, the answer could have been "no." The Twisted might have simply turned and blasted Olvir or hunted him down later when it and its creature would have been two against one.

There had been sound tactical reasons not to bolt. Olvir couldn't tell himself he'd been thinking of them, though, not when the mere idea felt like pressure on a broken bone.

He'd never liked abandoning his comrades. Nothing in his training had encouraged it. But it happened—part of honor was self-sacrifice, and part of justice was seeing the larger picture—and Olvir had lived with it. He hadn't felt nearly so soiled in the aftermath.

Strapping his sword on at his waist, he wondered if the change was because of what Vivian was to him. It was an unnerving possibility.

The other conclusion Olvir could come to was worse.

———————

After they crossed the river, Vivian's gift got stronger.

She didn't know yet whether it was useful. From the mountains, the Battlefield had looked as if it spread across the entire middle of the land. Any route should logically take them to it.

Some paths are better than others, Ulamir said. *Only some points of entry will let you reach the center alive, perhaps. The power knows your whole desire.*

"Nice to feel like I'm of some use," she whispered when she was reasonably sure Olvir wouldn't hear and try to reassure her.

You have been as is, and you will be again. Not necessarily by killing him.

Vivian didn't wince to hear the possibility put into words. She walked in silence, staring ahead of her at the stretch of red plain.

You will have done enough, said the sword-spirit, his mental voice subdued. *If you have to kill him, and if we survive, that would be sufficient for any mortal, let alone one whose life has been so dedicated to service as yours. You'll have earned the right to collapse. None would say different. I would speak of you with honor to my next bearer.*

If she had to kill Olvir, Vivian mused, the world might not be able to let her collapse. Still, hearing Ulamir calmed a portion of her churning heart. She would break, she knew, past all healing, but at least she wouldn't disgrace herself or the Order by doing so. The notion was a surprising balm to her spirit.

"Thank you," she whispered and touched the hilt of the sword.

That was approximately the moment when the horizon started to shift, or the moment when Vivian, staring ahead so that she didn't see Olvir too often, noticed the far edge of the landscape wavering. This time, the movement was no river, no ocean. She could tell that much just from her blessing at first, but it quickly became obvious as she and Olvir walked on.

Ahead, the ground shifted colors. It rose to reach the sky, then fell, taking bits of the sky with it so that blue turned to green or black in eye-hurtingly specific spots. The world surged back and forth without any of the rhythm of waves.

There was the wound in the world, the place where everything had shattered before.

Vivian shifted closer to Olvir. He'd likely splinter her heart soon, but he was real. He was steady. Nothing in front of them was either.

They'd come to the edge of the Battlefield.

Chapter 34

"Do we just walk in?"

"As far as I can tell," Vivian said. "You're not getting any... insights?"

Olvir closed his eyes briefly, searching out the fragment. It was a shorter process than it had ever been, but he got no guidance, no sense of a specific path to take or a necessary ritual to perform. "No," he said and added as he figured out more, "but I wouldn't, would I? The Heart's only known this place from its center."

"Hmm," said Vivian. Obviously, that complication hadn't occurred to her either, which kept Olvir from feeling too sheepish. "Well. If prophecy says we need to go to the center, it's...not *very* likely that we'll disintegrate as soon as we step over the border."

"Then," Olvir said, gripping his sword tighter, "I should go first."

"Really? Between the two of us, you're the less expendable one."

"I'm also the one who can—" Every word he could say sounded like bragging. "Who might have some control over parts of all this." Olvir gestured to the Battlefield, which shifted from green to white in the spot where he pointed, though he mostly thought that was only chance. "Which one of us is expendable won't matter if neither of us can get through. Besides, if I disintegrate or explode as soon as I take a step inside, you won't have to go the rest of the way."

Ulamir spoke: troubled agreement.

"You're both right, damn you," said Vivian. Despite the

profanity, her tone held no anger, only resignation. "Go ahead. Let's get this over with quickly, whatever the consequences."

It was his parting from Nahon again, with all the inadequacy of words to cover Olvir's possible fate and how much he cared for those he might leave behind, but the worst case could be far more immediate. He and Vivian had no time for ritual goodbyes, either, as they stood on the Battlefield's edge: Thyran clearly had some notion of where they were and what they were trying to accomplish. The wizard might well have been in direct contact with him, and if not, he would likely be aware of its death before long and draw the appropriate conclusions.

Olvir reached out and stroked Vivian's hair, trailing his fingers down through the short, crisp curls. He could only let the touch last a few heartbeats before he turned away.

Then he braced himself, took as deep a breath as he could manage, and walked into the shining scar on the world.

He only took a few steps, venturing no greater distance than he could retreat if trouble started. Olvir had gone half that far before he truly believed that he still existed.

There'd been no explosion, no lightning bolt. The ground beneath his feet was unsteady, less yielding than sand but with an odd upward bounce that followed each step, but it was ground and it held. Olvir didn't catch fire, he didn't start dissolving from the toes up, and the air didn't turn to vitriol against his skin.

His lungs ached, but that was to be expected. As slowly as he could, he exhaled, then inhaled just a little. The air smelled metallic, but it was air nonetheless.

Olvir, at least, could survive. He couldn't sense the land shifting around him any more purposefully than it had been or any effort from the fragment to keep him alive where another person might have perished.

Conclusion, if a tentative one: the Battlefield wasn't directly deadly to mortals.

He turned. Distance blurred and waved, but he could see light shining off Ulamir's blade and make out the crouched tension of Vivian's posture. She was ready to spring at a moment's notice, Olvir could tell, whether to drag him back to safety or strike him down for the world's sake.

He would have kissed her for both, had time allowed.

"I believe it's all right," he called.

It seemed necessary *to* call, rather than speak at his normal volume, although he hadn't gone far at all. Space was odd. Olvir's voice came out oddly, too, catching crosswise echoes that faded some words while doubling the volume of others. *All* was longer than it should have been, *right* completely disappeared.

Vivian heard him or guessed what he was saying. She crossed the few steps to his side, alert but swifter than he'd been.

"Well," she said, "this...isn't quite as awful as I'd feared. So far."

"Disorienting, and it smells like a forge at noon, but if that's the worst of it, the gods will have been very good," Olvir agreed. "Can Ulamir sense aspects that we can't?"

Vivian tilted a hand back and forth in the air. "He says it's not really stone, which isn't surprising. He believes it might have been actual stone before"—the gesturing hand swept across the scene in front of them—"all this, but it's been reshaped in a number of different ways."

"The Traitor again," said Olvir. Peasant superstition overwhelmed knightly training as he stood with the world squirming in front of him. He had no wish to speak Gizath's name aloud.

The sudden lengthy flow of communication from Ulamir to Vivian surprised him, as did her careful answer when it came. "Partly. But death is transformation too. So is healing, if the wound's very bad. Love as well, I suppose." She was staring off into the distance when she spoke. Olvir didn't let himself try to read her expression. "And vengeance, for both the avenging party and the target."

"This really is both of the gods' handiwork, then."

"Yes, as far as either Ulamir or I can tell without having actually spoken to them, and I'd really rather we not. In Letar's defense, she probably didn't do any of it deliberately." A mound of…surface, Olvir supposed, as it wasn't earth by any stretch of the imagination…rose in a scintillating bubble, then fell down. Vivian sighed. "And in complete fairness that he doesn't ever deserve, I doubt the Traitor intended these particular consequences either."

"No," said Olvir. "Do you have any sense of which direction we should go? As far as there are directions here, that is." He didn't bother getting out his compass; he suspected it wouldn't work. The sun was directly overhead, which corresponded roughly with the day, but he couldn't count on it to move predictably from that position.

Vivian shut her eyes, grimaced, and pointed. "This way, and the quicker, the better. Ugh."

They traveled as fast as safety allowed, balancing and rebalancing on ground that shifted with each step. It kept the odd buoyancy Olvir had initially felt for a few yards, then switched to dragging them down, so that simply raising a foot and putting it in front of another made Olvir's legs ache. To the eye, the ground just in front of him and Vivian always remained flat, just as the place always smelled of heated metal, and the sun kept its position in the writhing sky.

All of it had been an accident. Olvir kept coming back to that.

That wasn't new information—the Blades themselves had never blamed Gizath for willfully creating the Battlefield, and no story had ever faulted Letar for it—but it was unnerving to consider so close to the results. One god had acted, unthinking, in grief and rage. The other had knowingly given himself over to spite, pride, and his notion of what should be—but Olvir doubted he'd predicted what would happen after Veryon's death.

He wondered how long the fight had lasted. No amount of time seemed long enough to mar the world forever.

That was, in Olvir's experience, generally how scars worked.

—————

The knight sends no influence forth to this place that I can sense, Ulamir said, *but that may only mean I can't sense it. I have my limitations, and I would believe them strongest here. Existence may shape itself readily to his will or may resist his presence even more strongly than it does ours.*

He was right. As he'd reminded Vivian earlier, two gods had created the Battlefield. The remnants of Letar's power could be decidedly hostile to any contact from Her brother. For that matter, the echoes of Gizath once he'd turned traitor might not feel very pleasant about a reminder of the piece of himself he'd cast aside.

Whichever was the case, Vivian couldn't tell from their journey.

The footing of the Battlefield was never certain, the smell was unusual—not bad, exactly, where Vivian was concerned, but she liked the scent of a forge—and the sight sickening, though not in the typical sense that people used the term.

There were no entrail-draped trees or rivers of bodily fluids littering the landscape. In the abstract, the colors were actually quite pretty. They never stayed still, though, and they never moved along predictable routes. Usually their motion wasn't even sensical—if Vivian had tried to describe it, she would've ended up using phrases such as "left, but a little north" or "down, and sort of outward."

She'd never been seasick, but after an hour treading cautiously through the swirling hues of the Battlefield, she'd completely stopped regretting their lack of fresh food.

Vivian's blessing didn't help either. It was *useful*, no doubt—the sense of destination never wavered, and gods knew she and Olvir wouldn't have had consistent landmarks to go by—but the conflict between it and the terrain made her stomach churn. Before long, a band of pressure was tightening from Vivian's brow to the base of her skull.

She breathed deeply, swallowed hard, and walked on.

Olvir glanced over at her every so often, grave with worry. "I don't want to break your concentration," he finally said, "but you're clearly not well. Can it be helped?"

"Not until we get out of here, but thank you. I'll live. I've certainly felt worse."

That was true. Vivian had never felt more *ill*, but there was no point splitting hairs.

"I'd say you should lean on me, but if we're attacked—"

"Bad idea. No, I'll be fine."

Fine was extremely subjective just then, but neither of them needed to state the fact. There was no option except to press on, trying their hardest to ignore their surroundings.

Before they'd been walking much longer, Vivian stopped being able to tell how long they'd been walking. Outside of the Battlefield, she could generally judge by how tired she was or how sore her muscles had gotten, even when the sun and stars provided no clues. The throbbing pain in her temples skewed that estimation. So did the effort of keeping her footing on the ever-changing ground. Nothing about the Battlefield resembled the world outside—not initially.

The first exception was a song: quick, cheerful, the words in the stonekin's language, the voice a clear tenor. It didn't sound at all like Olvir, but Vivian glanced at him simply because nobody else was present. He stared back, as puzzled as she was.

When Vivian turned toward the direction she thought the song came from, its origin shifted to a point a little behind her right shoulder. She spun toward the new origin, and it shifted again. The merry verses continued with no pause.

"Do you hear somebody singing?" she asked and hummed a bit of the tune. The Battlefield was strange enough that music for her could have been screaming for Olvir.

But he nodded and pointed behind his right shoulder. "From there, for me."

"Do you understand any of the... Oh, you're a knight. What does it say?"

He stood and listened, a calm figure amid the dazzling lights. "It's about roads. The verses are how they change with the seasons, and there's a subtle shift with the chorus, too, but it'd sound awkward if I translated it."

"A clue?"

"I don't think so. Just...celebration. High spirits."

An echo, Ulamir said. *Or likely so.*

"Veryon?" Vivian thought of the most famous stonekin, tragic as that fame was.

"Or one of his friends. I don't—" Olvir frowned. "I don't *believe* there's actually a soul behind it any longer."

"Ulamir agrees."

Olvir hesitated. "In case we're wrong," he said and turned to bow to the empty air behind him. "Thank you for the music, and I hope you've found peace."

"So do I." Vivian made a quick bow of her own. "Thank you," she added to Olvir as they began walking again. "I wouldn't have thought to do that."

The song ended, or they passed out of its range. Olvir sighed as the last of the notes died away behind them. "He was very happy, whoever he was," he said.

"I suppose Veryon would've been, for a while," Vivian said, the idea strange to her. "I don't remember many of the temple stories when I was a child, and the Sentinels don't dwell on much except for Thyran and the first storms. We got a sentence or two about Gizath and Letar, that was all."

"We learned more, though not very much. It's still odd to remember that Veryon was a person. He's always been—" Olvir shrugged. "A reason for the shape of the world. A face in tapestries or on temple windows. We hear the echo, maybe, and we don't listen for the voice."

"It would be hard to, after so many years."

Now Vivian was considering the man and the story behind the clipped facts as the Order had presented them. She'd heard tales and poems herself over the years and a bit of theology. She'd rarely given them much consideration.

"It's a pity that joy didn't last, that's all," Olvir said.

Vivian reached out and took his free hand. "Yes."

Chapter 35

AFTER THE MUSIC, THEY CAME TO A ROSEBUSH WHOSE BLOSsoms were women's faces.

The…roses…didn't look distressed, for a mercy. Olvir thought the best word for their expression would be peaceful, or perhaps drunk. They were roughly the size of his palm, and all appeared young, though not close to childhood. All the colors he'd ever seen on roses appeared in them, and each was different. The first Olvir noticed had pink skin and hair the variegated colors of a sunset, shades that extended to the long lashes around her violet eyes.

"I don't think this ever existed," he said, gesturing to the rosebush. A dozen pairs of eyes half focused on him, following the motion hazily, and Olvir shuddered. "Or I truly hope not."

"I'll stand that round," said Vivian, shaking her head and giving the bush a wide berth as they passed it. "There'd have been notes about…this…in some history or bestiary, surely. If it's an echo, gods grant it's a distorted one."

The roses watched them leave. None of them spoke. Olvir didn't know if air passed those slightly parted lips, and he had no wish to draw close enough to find out. The elder peoples had passed down tales of the world before Gizath's betrayal. Most of them were recorded in fairly obscure scholarly manuscripts. Olvir chose to believe that mentions of plants with human faces would have made it into popular legends, had there been any truth to them.

He was almost entirely certain that the river of fire hadn't existed before the betrayal.

The land, such as it was, gave him and Vivian no advance view of the river. It simply appeared a few feet in front of them, a broad slash through the shining colors with the sort of clear-cut sides no real river actually had. Flames danced in its midst, flaring up every moment or so.

Both he and Vivian stopped in their tracks, staring at it, until Vivian swung her pack off her shoulder and pulled out her spare tunic. "I wish I'd thought to bring a stick along," she said as she sliced a strip off the hem. "We're going to be naked by the time we're done, and while that's an appealing prospect in some senses, it'll be uncomfortable traveling."

She put the tunic away, shouldered the pack again, and reached forward, dangling the strip from her fingers.

Flame surrounded her hand. Sick anger rose up in Olvir at the sight, half at her for not consulting him first and half at himself for letting the woman he loved go into such danger. He reached for her arm.

Vivian stayed in place, completely rigid. Despite the sparks in her eyes, her gaze was pure ice. "Really," she said, each syllable distinct, each reproachful. Very deliberately, she looked back at the fire, where neither her hand nor the fabric was showing the least sign of harm.

"How was I to know—" Olvir started to protest.

Then he forcibly closed his mouth on the words. He still knew what was just, and they wouldn't have been. He dropped his arm to his side.

Neither of them had known that the fire was illusion. Olvir could, in theory, have argued that they couldn't be sure Vivian would withstand fire in the odd landscape of the Battlefield the way that she could with normal flame, or that he hadn't seen her stick her hand directly into a fire before.

He'd still known that she was a Sentinel and a woman grown, with a mind free of outside influence. They'd been traveling together for weeks, working together for longer. She knew as much about the fire river as he did. Vivian's decisions hadn't always been right, but they'd always been sound. That should have been all he needed.

"No," he said, facing her squarely. "You're right. I'm sorry."

Vivian pulled her hand back, deliberately slow. "Thank you. Let's get across and hope it doesn't turn real midway through. I'll go first."

"All right," said Olvir. Whether his impulses came from the Sundered Soul or not didn't matter, he told himself. He wouldn't give in again—not least because he'd seen Vivian's expression as she tucked the fabric into her belt.

Behind the cold anger, there'd been grief.

Illusion or not, blessing or not, walking into fire had never appealed to Vivian before.

It might have been the least painful option at that moment even if the flames had been real. She was glad to leave Olvir behind for the first time in their journey, and not because she was still angry.

Vivian would have welcomed that clean, righteous wrath. People had let her down in the past, turned out to be less than she'd hoped. She'd forgiven them or not, as the situation merited. It was simple, relatively speaking.

She'd have forgiven Olvir normally: he'd seemed genuinely contrite. In a way, it was easier to do so knowing that the fragment of Gizath could have pushed him to actions he'd never take otherwise.

But that was worse in the end.

They were in the Battlefield, approaching its center. If Olvir wasn't quite himself now, there was a good chance he'd be less so before they reached their goal. The world would suffer for that and would suffer worse if Vivian didn't recognize the change and carry out her duty. She had to mark every detail even while she ached at what it could mean.

The fire crackled on every side of her, sounding realistic while giving off no heat at all. Under cover of the noise, she asked Ulamir, "Can you use my body the same way you used my voice when you summoned the rocks?"

With your consent, I likely could, yes. Do you expect that I'll need to?

Behind Vivian, half-hidden by flames, Olvir stood waiting alone. His back was straight, he didn't hang his head, but there was an air of dejection about him as well as patience. Vivian spoke around a thickness in her throat. "No," she said. She had her duty. Neither she nor Olvir, as he really was, would have wanted her to put that aside for a man. "But I won't doom us by confidence any more than by sentiment."

Ulamir spoke less crisply than before. *I could plan to be the mind behind your arm, should you so wish. It need not be your will that kills him, if that comes to pass, even if that will would be sufficient.*

Vivian turned her gaze forward once again. The phantom flames parted in front of her, revealing more of the Battlefield's uncanny ground, which she'd never thought she'd be glad to see. "It may not happen. Even if he is a little influenced, there's a fair distance between being obnoxious and being murderous."

She knew the truth of her words but also the motives behind them and loved Ulamir for not addressing that directly. *It may not,* he agreed. *But my offer remains.*

Olvir waited behind the fire. Vivian understood that he was watching her. She could see his expression of relief in her mind, despite the flames obscuring his face. "No," she said again, with as much difficulty as before. "If he doesn't get out of this, then I should be there."

Chapter 36

Next came shades.

They printed themselves across the intact portions of the sky. Silver-white lines formed enormous shapes, blurred and featureless but recognizably people: two arms, two legs and a single head each. Three of them stood together, facing each other. Vivian couldn't tell whether they seemed friendly or angry.

She drew closer to Olvir as the two of them walked, feeling a little embarrassed about it until they nearly collided and she realized that he'd done the same. Then she glanced at him and had to smile, despite everything.

"I'm sure they're probably harmless," she said. "And it's odd to be scared of pictures in the air, considering the fights I've been in. The size of them, though…"

A fitting representation, Ulamir put in. *Two, if not all, are almost certainly the images of gods.*

"That's not entirely reassuring," Vivian told him. "We all know the gods are greater than we are, but it's not comfortable to think for long about how *much* greater. Not for me, at least. Maybe priests are different."

"Not in this sense, or I'm a poor example," said Olvir.

"You're human too." She chose to ignore, for the moment, what else he was. She tried not to let that evidence of humanity give her hope. "We never knew the gods like the older peoples did. Maybe that's why Ulamir seems less nervous."

My state is a great source of tranquility as well.

"I'm glad there's some advantage in being a sword," she said, responding, explaining, and avoiding the word *dead* all at once. It was a sadly clever bit of verbal footwork. "But I doubt either of us can draw much inspiration from that, even if we are each weapons of a sort."

"We're supposed to be shields first. Losing mine so early in this may have been a bad omen. Or maybe a sign that I didn't need to worry about protecting the helpless, since there weren't any nearby." Regret was plain in every syllable Olvir spoke and in each line of his body.

Vivian couldn't sustain even a fraction of her anger in the face of it. She had to keep being suspicious, but she could let that become part of the background, akin to the ache in her feet.

You have me for a skeptic, Ulamir put in.

She sent heartfelt thanks his way and replied softly to Olvir. "This whole damned business is protecting the helpless, isn't it? As for me…we guard each other, don't we? When we need to?"

"We do our best," Olvir said. "Not that I expect being close to each other would do much good if any of those *did* turn mean on us."

"Probably the reverse, although I could argue that getting squashed quickly might be a mercy in that case. I admit I hadn't followed through that far. It's only…instinct, I suppose."

That much I would call human: to be afraid, in the recesses of your mind and the base of your gut, of that which is large. The sea is far greater than any of those images, and so, too, are mountains.

"I have felt similar things when I was out on the sea," Vivian said after summarizing for Olvir, "but not as strongly. And I'm glad I didn't consider it in the mountains."

"Gods, so am I," said Olvir with an uneasy laugh. "But those look too lifelike, as though they could move all of a sudden. That's probably part of the problem."

So speaks one who knows neither the sea nor mountains well. We live, all of us, side by side with titanic forces, and all our strength cannot ward them away completely. Does it matter what form they take?

"I'm going to have to try and forget this entire conversation if we go back," said Vivian. She tried to sound amused, even to be so, but the line between humor and unease was very thin, and she wasn't sure where she landed. "Never make it across the Serpentspine again, otherwise."

"We should've packed more wine, perhaps. Or lignath," said Olvir, referring to a foul and potent drink of the waterfolk.

"I could simply hit my head against a rock a few times."

With as little warning as the Battlefield ever gave, the ground turned slippery. Vivian hissed as she slid off-balance, teetering with her hands spread and her footing uncertain.

Olvir grabbed her by the shoulders. His face, suddenly only an inch or two from hers, showed all his concern plainly, but he never faltered as he helped Vivian stabilize herself, and he spoke easily. "It wouldn't do you much good to start the process now, would it? And this seems a bad place to fall."

"Yes." She'd grabbed for him automatically as well. Beneath his armor, his shoulders were granite against her palms. "Thank you."

"Of course. Are you all right?"

"Nothing broken but my dignity. You?"

He nodded. "Wearing plate during winter battles trained me for this, it seems."

"I'm glad." Time was pressing. They needed to let go of each other and start walking again, but Olvir was staring at her, all earnest concern and clean-cut handsomeness even after weeks in the wilderness. Vivian *was* human.

She kissed him: not for long, nor with any demand in it, but lightly, quickly, savoring the moment when Olvir stopped being surprised and started to respond. When he pulled her close, Vivian relaxed against him. She took in the gentle pressure of his lips against hers, each rise and fall of his chest, and the quiet sound he made in his throat, surprised and pleased.

That had to suffice. They each pulled away at the same time,

Vivian knowing that they'd lingered as long as they could and that Olvir realized it too.

She'd never thought, before, in terms of first or last, not with any of her other lovers and not even with Olvir. The future was generally clouded. Vivian had always been content to let it remain so, until she turned away from a tall, chestnut-haired knight and set her attention on the strange landscape ahead of her once again.

Then the words *last kiss* grew in her mind, brambles with iron thorns.

As far as Vivian could tell, the Battlefield had neither weather nor day and night. It was a pity. She badly wanted to weep.

———————

It wouldn't be a bad memory to take into Letar's Halls, that kiss, if matters ended badly. Every kiss Olvir had shared with Vivian had been good, granted, and other activities had been better, but that latest had been the sweetest as well, maybe because it had been tinged with sorrow.

Vivian felt the sorrow of it more than the sweetness, Olvir suspected. She walked along silently beside him with her face like a mask. Grief echoed every careful footstep she took.

He couldn't offer direct comfort without putting them, and perhaps the world, in more danger. Whatever it occurred to him to say as a means of distraction seemed either painful or absurd. Physical reassurance was also out of the question, since they both needed to keep walking and to have free hands in case of an ambush.

Not fair, he thought, glaring up at the phantoms in the sky.

Olvir hadn't spoken the phrase aloud, not as a protest, since he'd become a squire. He'd tried to keep from thinking it. Life was frequently unfair, which was not the same as unjust. It was the knights' duty to restore justice where they could. When they couldn't, complaining about unfairness was petty bordering on blasphemous.

Nonetheless, he watched Vivian march onward, holding herself together with her own duty, and silently raged against the world that had put her in that place. He could have rebuked himself, too, for not keeping more distance from her—for responding to her as he'd done—for not rejecting her for her own good.

But that would've been the same error he'd made at the river of fire. Vivian had known her hidden mission, likely long before Olvir had guessed at it, and she knew her own heart. Denying her will to spare her pain would have been wrong. For himself, he didn't regret a second.

He, after all, would have the easier end, even if their quest went wrong.

Vivian spoke quietly with Ulamir, or the other way around. Sensing that soothed Olvir a little: Vivian wouldn't be alone if the worst happened. He sent silent thanks to the sword-spirit, though he doubted Ulamir could hear it.

"We should eat," he said, finally coming up with a halfway useful statement. He also managed not to sound hoarse. "I don't know how long it's been, and I can't say I'm hungry, but it'd probably do us good."

"Right," said Vivian and managed a bleak grin. "We'll be better off if we don't confuse seeing things from hunger with seeing things because they…sort of exist."

So they ate rations and drank water. They *didn't* sit down. Olvir suspected that the ground probably couldn't do more harm through cloth than it could through boot leather. "But that only makes my feet feel off," he added when he said so aloud, wiggling his toes and grimacing.

"And we might as well not test it," Vivian agreed after a mouthful of bread. "Isn't that why you caught me?"

"I wouldn't have wanted you to fall regardless."

"The perfect knight," she said with another smile. She clearly tried to keep grief out of that one.

"Far from it," he replied and bled for her inwardly.

If the moment they were fearing did come, Olvir hoped maybe he could retain enough of his will to spare her the worst. He had his own sword and knife. It wouldn't take long.

Try hard to stay yourself, he thought in the manner of Nahon lecturing an over-dramatic young knight, *and you may both be spared, not to mention a number of others.*

That was true. He wasn't sure how to win that fight, though, save by watching himself closely for any hint that he might be acting out of the ordinary—and what was ordinary in such circumstances? It was trying to battle fog, and it became all the harder as they went farther into the Battlefield.

Their surroundings were still strange then. More distressingly, they began to feel familiar.

Chapter 37

VIVIAN HAD NEVER MET A KNIGHT WITH A TALENT FOR gambling. Serving the god of truth apparently left its mark, and Olvir was no exception. If she'd been closer when he pretended to consider the Twisted mage's offer, or the wizard itself had been better at reading humans, there would have been no delay at all.

She knew it immediately when he was uneasy—or more uneasy than both of them had been since they'd crossed the border. When she asked, "Are you all right?" it was only because "What is it?" would have sounded too harsh.

"Fine in body," Olvir said, brows knitted. "But…I'm beginning to recognize this place."

That could further their goal, Vivian reminded herself. The whole situation reminded her of some of the field surgeons' herbs or the Mourners' power when an illness was grave. Healing lay cheek to cheek with death. She had no real ability to predict which direction this particular development pointed. "How do you mean?" she asked carefully. "Do you know where we're going, the way I do? It isn't as though there are landmarks."

"There aren't any longer. Or they've changed. Or…"

Olvir fell silent, but it was the expectant silence of thinking out what came next. Vivian waited, walking along cautiously even though the terrain had gone back to normal, for what its version of "normal" was worth. There'd be no warning sign before it became ice again—or fire or spikes, for that matter.

Eventually, Olvir gestured to a section of the Battlefield. To Vivian, it looked no different from the always-different world they were walking through: light blue one moment, black the next, eddying like a slow river. "There was a fruit tree there," Olvir said. "Plums, or maybe pears. That's not clear—but I know it was just in that spot and that lightning hit it once. It took off half the branches."

She stared at the spot. No suggestion of a tree emerged.

I sense no such thing myself, said Ulamir, *for what that may be worth.*

"It's not a landmark, really. I couldn't tell you how to get here if we were a mile away or where to go from here. But...there are patterns, and they mark places. Or I see the shape of what was. I don't... I wish I could put it into words better."

"Do you remember being here? Or eating the fruit, climbing the tree, anything like that?"

"Not...quite. Or yes, a little." Olvir looked like he would curse, if he'd been a cursing man. "I remember seeing it. But not seeing it on a particular day or what I was doing or felt. What he was doing or felt," he hastily added.

The correction came as a relief. Vivian wasn't sure what to make of the initial fault. It could be the sort of slip anyone could make when seeing visions, manifestation of the Sundered Soul or not, but she hadn't met many prophets.

"Recognition, but no context," Olvir went on, "except that it seems closer than if I'd seen a picture in a book. Not that there'd be one." He made a face. "This is why I didn't tell you right away. I was trying to figure out how to phrase it so that it made sense outside my head."

"I can follow you so far," said Vivian, feeling the *right direction* pull her onward and knowing that she could never have defined exactly what sense it used to do that.

She took in their surroundings, the soap-bubble shimmer and constantly changing motion. "Do you think you could change things here?" she asked and then made her own swift correction: "I'm not saying you should try!"

"I wouldn't if you ordered me," Olvir replied with an incredulous laugh.

In that we are all agreed, chimed in Ulamir.

Olvir walked in quiet contemplation for a few yards. "I suppose," he eventually said, "that I could make things change. But I doubt I could direct the form those changes took except in a very rough sense, and maybe not that much."

"You could pull a stick out of the tower and see if it crashes," said Vivian, remembering games she'd played in her training. "That's all?"

"That'd be much simpler. Here, there's…" He made several vague gestures, describing shapes in the air that never quite resolved. "There's too much, too entangled with itself. If I pulled a stick out, the tower might remain or crash, but it could also go sideways or levitate or burst into flames. One of the gods themselves might be able to sift through the whole mess, if They had a year or so of leisure to do it."

"I can't say I'm all that surprised." Vivian should have been far past the point of regarding the Battlefield with fresh revulsion, too, but Olvir's description worked an unfortunate miracle in that respect. Now she pictured strands of force writhing beneath her feet, rotted and snarled with centuries. "Are you all right, having to feel all that?"

"It's kind of you to ask, but yes. It's not pleasant, but I don't have to stare at it, so to speak, unless I try. It's not intruding on my mind, thank the Four."

"Very much," said Vivian. She imagined having the Battlefield anywhere near the inside of her head, shuddered, and made the sign of the gods.

Olvir touched her shoulder lightly. "Remember, I'm used to some amount of divine strangeness from what I chose to be, as well as my birth. You don't need to worry. Not about my comfort."

She couldn't help it, but he didn't need to hear that, so Vivian only smiled back at him. "Just tell me if it does get worse," she said, though gods alone knew what she'd find to do in that case, "or if you do start getting memories. Or emotions."

"I promise," he said, and she chose to believe him for that moment.

Silver shimmered ahead of them. Unlike the rest of the Battlefield, it stayed silver for more than the span of two breaths. It was too broad to be a river, nor did it move as water usually did. Olvir had to admit that water in the Battlefield probably wouldn't have moved as he expected it to, either, if there had been any.

They had crossed a stream recently, or what had been a stream. It still was, somewhere. He could discern the shape and the nature of it, buried inside twisting layers of power, but he couldn't have said what it looked like. On spring evenings, the sound of its water had mingled with a chorus of little frogs. It had been icy even at noon in summer.

Knowledge rose up without reference. Olvir tried to get out of its way and at the same time to hold on to himself: he was Olvir Yoralth, Tinival's knight, Edda's fosterling, Vivian's companion and lover. Silently, as he walked, he repeated the vows he'd made to Vivian after his meditation, striving to summon the feeling of Letar's statue under his hands.

As they came closer to the silver patch, the Battlefield's changes began to slow down. Sections became rigid and sharp-edged: a square of blue, a triangle of purple. The ground stabbed up into the sky in hedgehog spines for a while. Their footsteps rang out, and the surface they were walking on felt harder than stone.

"I'd hate how conspicuous it makes us," Vivian said, "but I don't think an ambush is what we need to worry about."

"One fewer thing for the list," Olvir replied and was glad to get a chuckle, even a brief one.

When he looked up again, the trio of silver-white shapes had vanished from the sky. A face had replaced them, etched in the same color, with almost as little detail. The hair was long, the chin was tilted back, and the eyes were almost shut.

Weeping? Laughing? Screaming? Olvir couldn't tell, any more than he could recognize a trace of the person's identity—and legends alone made all three activities possible.

All three had happened on that spot. He was suddenly certain of it.

His throat was dry with dread.

"Problem with my promise," he got out and watched active alarm replace mere wariness on Vivian's face. "I'm not sure I'll be sure. With emotions."

"Ah. Hmm. I would have thought it'd only be… No, you're right." She gestured to Ulamir, indicating that the sword-spirit had spoken. Olvir had felt the communication too. "He says I should remember we're not dealing with Gizath as he is now. Fear?"

Olvir fumbled for his waterskin and took a drink. It helped his throat, if not the root cause. "Obvious, is it?"

"The most likely candidate. If we weren't both terrified, we'd be stupid. But it's worse all of a sudden?"

"Or I've merely been holding it off better until now. Or it's that." He pointed at the face in the sky. "Or the fragment's remembering when the Sundering happened and where. I wish I could tell you more definitely."

He wished, watching Vivian, that he hadn't promised to tell her any part of what he felt. It did no good, it wasn't right that she should be worried needlessly, and he'd probably only made it worse. But he had given his word.

"I'm not sure the specifics matter in this case." Every syllable Vivian spoke was clearly measured, considered: stones in the bridge over what she didn't say. She paused, listened as Ulamir spoke, then let herself settle back toward being merely watchful. "But I'm glad you told me. It's good to keep track. Thank you."

"Of course. I did promise."

"You did," she said, and the warmth Olvir glimpsed in her face was enough reward to overcome his earlier regrets. "A knight's vow. But appreciation's nice, even if it's for duty."

"Do people thank you for yours?"

"Sometimes."

He would have pressed Vivian further on that, but she spoke first as they entered a moss-green patch where the ground rose up on both sides. It towered over their heads, but sunlight—or light that appeared to be sunlight—reached them exactly as it had before. Olvir saw no shadows but their own.

"The places that stay the same aren't as hard to look at," she said. "I have to admit it doesn't make me like them much better than the others."

Most of the patterns in that spot weren't familiar to Olvir, or the distortion was too great. He had a vague impression of motion, of multicolored bodies sleek with scales, which could have been dragons or snakes or fish. Size and shape both eluded him.

There was no motion now except for theirs. All the rest was rigid, changeless, bound in a single senseless form.

"No. There's nothing good here," said Olvir.

And the sea of silver, whatever it was, waited.

Chapter 38

It was a mirror.

Olvir and Vivian stood where the last colored patch of the Battlefield ended, feet still on featureless black ground, and stared across the expanse of silver glass.

Lines marred its surface every yard or so. They were the same thin crevasses that appeared when a normal mirror cracked, but Olvir had never seen glass break so straightly. Each fracture was a smooth ray heading toward the center. None intersected until they got to the middle, where a slim object stuck up a few inches above the ground.

"Can you tell what that is?" Vivian asked.

"No. I should be able to from here, but then, we should have been able to see all this more clearly from farther away," Olvir said, indicating the mirror-land. "And we would certainly have noticed the sky, if any of this place made sense."

Where they stood, the sky was blue. It even stayed the normal distance from the ground. That changed just over the border. A wall rose up as far in front of Olvir as he could see, one fashioned of flashing darkness and light. It filled the world above the mirror. The cracked glass gave back its reflections, blazing bright and then vanishing in darkness that he couldn't see through, despite the power Tinival gave him.

Olvir tried to find the point where radiance became shadow and swiftly gave it up. He might channel the power of one god by dedication and hold part of another by birth, but his eyes were mostly human. Searching for the joining point made them feel about to fall from their sockets.

"I'd give quite a bit for you to tell me that this is only a diversion and our real path is off to the right," he said, "but I suspect we're not that lucky."

"I'm afraid not. For one thing, there's no 'off to the right.'"

That was true. Just as the flashing sky went up forever, the mirrored ground ran to both right and left without ever stopping. If there was any land beyond it, then Gizath and Letar's fight had severed it completely from the rest of the world. Maybe a dragon could have flown over it or a stonekin army tunneled beneath, but Olvir greatly doubted it. Scars ran deep.

Besides, he and Vivian could neither fly nor tunnel.

Forward and backward were the only options. Back meant failure, the ruin of the world, and very probably their own deaths. Forward might not end differently, but that way lay at least a chance—if Sitha's prophecy held true, and if they'd interpreted the spider correctly.

Olvir wished he'd never heard the word *if*.

Gingerly, he took the first step onto the mirror. He heard a series of snaps, exactly the sort of sounds he would have expected, and froze, waiting to see what would happen.

Nothing did.

No new cracks appeared. The mirror held him. Only the sound acknowledged what would have taken place under normal laws.

"This is not going to help my headache," said Vivian. "At least I still have a head, I suppose."

She flinched at the sounds anyhow when she stepped onto the mirror. Olvir wasn't sure either of them would stop doing so before long. Everybody learned young to react to that sort of noise: whether prized glasses or thin ice, it meant something important had broken.

That remained true, he supposed. It was just nothing either he or Vivian could help.

"Are you ready?" he asked.

"No, but that won't change for waiting. You?"

He forced himself to smile. "The same."

They began to walk. The thunderstorm sky closed in behind them.

———————

"Knife," said Vivian, peering as best she could across the mirrors. They reflected the light overhead in dazzling flashes that left green and pink flecks swimming in front of her, while the darkness in between bursts of radiance was almost absolute. It made vision difficult.

Nonetheless, it hadn't taken much walking before she got a better sense of the shape in the center: about hand-length, with a curved guard and a square hilt. She thought that it was metal and that some of the blade might have showed beneath it, but it was hard to say. There was too much other light, too much of the landscape itself that shone.

"A hilt, at any rate," Olvir said after Vivian alerted him to the object. "And it does look too small to be from a sword."

Both of them spoke softly, with reverence bordering on horror or the other way around. Only one knife went with the Battlefield, the one that had shed the first blood in treachery.

And Veryon's grave, said Ulamir, *for the stories say he left no body behind.*

"Would the mirrors have come from him? Glass is a sort of stone, isn't it?"

Here, it's hard to determine what came from which source or even what was real when it happened.

"I don't think he turned into them." Olvir's eyes were shadowed, his voice half-dreaming. Hearing him made Vivian's muscles tighten, getting her ready for action she hoped would never come. "He vanished. The dagger went into the ground. The

Threadcutter came just in time to see, and then she threw herself across the mirrors, but they weren't Veryon. He was beyond her reach."

"Gizath, then," she half whispered, feeling the old peasant's fear of saying the Traitor's name.

"Not meaning it. Not minding it. The mirrors appeared because of his actions, because of his mind, but not from his intent. He… No. I'm sorry," Olvir said, sounding alert once again. "There's nothing else. I don't know if I should apologize for *that* or for speaking in the first place."

Vivian put a hand lightly on the nape of his neck. "I wouldn't say you need to apologize at all right now," she said, and she meant it, even while her nerves sang with tension. "You're doing what you can. Besides, I asked."

Nor can we predict what knowledge may prove useful in the end, said Ulamir, and then, as close to wry as he could manage, *and in truth, should this quest not undo us, the world, or his mind, the knight could likely be a scholar's dream.*

That was undoubtedly true, but Vivian wouldn't praise the day until nightfall, as the saying went.

Darkness took its turn, leaving her with only the sound of creaking glass as she walked. Her eyes, with the stupid persistence of instinct, kept trying to make out shapes, though she understood that it was futile.

It was unnecessary too. Even her blessing wasn't exactly crucial any longer. They knew where they were going—unless—

She didn't let the idea become hope, but she did speak. "Since you're remembering more and you're sensing more, do you think you could make the storms stop just with that and not bother going the rest of the way? The spider didn't mention grabbing the knife specifically."

"I don't know," Olvir said after a moment of silence. "I can't even tell one way or another. They're building up on the other side of the mountains, you understand, and there's so much…noise here, so to speak. When I try, I can tell a bit of what the storms are doing and how, but only a bit, and I could be remembering some of that from what I did earlier. We'd have to go a good distance back before I could try."

Should we do that and fail, we'd have very little chance of making it this far again. No, Vivian, said Ulamir. *It was a clever idea, but our fate lies where Veryon met his.*

"It was a long shot anyhow," she said.

"I'd give my right eye if it hadn't been."

Every feature of Olvir's face was sharper in the flashing landscape. Vivian could see what he'd look like in ten or twenty years or after a long illness: handsome, still, but gaunt, a man whose bones were wrapped as much in willpower as in flesh and skin. "Olvir—" she started and came up with nothing to say.

He turned toward her, just a little. "I know. I'll see it through, don't worry. And I still consider it our best chance—but no part of me wants to go near that knife, let alone touch it."

That was, in its own way, reassuring.

———————

Olvir spoke only a tenth of what he felt aloud, not out of shame or concern about Vivian's opinion but because he was afraid even to put his terror into words.

He couldn't be sure of its source. He wasn't even sure how separate he and the fragment were any longer. The moments of recognition had felt like his own, and so had the memories he'd told Vivian about. Those images—the dagger's swift entrance and the woman's anguished countenance—had carried with them grief, not triumph. That had been some relief, but it gave Olvir no clarity.

Each step he took was a trial of his will. That much was clear.

Every inch forward was one closer to…what? The unknown fate that he, the mortal man, might have good reason to fear? The spot where the divine portion of him remembered a hideous crime? He couldn't tell.

What waited at the center was irrevocable, whether it had been so in the past or would be in the future or both. All of Olvir understood that, and all of him feared it, even as he walked.

There should have been a drum, he thought, like the ones that beat out the journey to the headsman's block.

Instead, he heard steady breath and breaking glass. He watched the horizon, where the shape of the knife became ever clearer. After closing some distance, he noticed the gem in its hilt: large, square-cut, and red-orange. Below the guard, the blade tapered dramatically for the inch or so until it entered the mirrors, and the light glinted on two razor edges.

Death would have been quick for Veryon, if the Traitor had aimed at all truly.

Olvir couldn't yet remember that moment. The blank patch in his memory was a fair-sized blessing, one that let him keep going until he and Vivian were only a few feet away from the knife.

Then he stopped and turned to her. "You should stay here."

In the moment of light, he saw Vivian make the same calculations he had: how quickly she could cross the ground, how much longer the distance would give her to react. Behind that, he saw all that neither of them had time to say. It blazed forth at him, so blatant that speech wasn't necessary.

"All right. Gods—" she began and then stopped, rigid, cocking her head to stare upward. "Do you hear that?"

Darkness descended. Vivian's hands did, too, grabbing Olvir and yanking him sideways. The air itself screamed above them, a rending shriek that actually sounded pained.

He knew that noise from Oakford. It had come with dark fire, worse than the spells the Twisted mage had used.

In the silence after it ended, Olvir heard the flapping of gigantic wings.

Chapter 39

Tactics took over. Vivian and Olvir scrambled up from the mirrored ground and bolted apart, drawing weapons. Out in the darkness, the new arrival—surely not who'd first come to Olvir's mind when he heard the spell distort the air over his head, please, gods, no—landed with a thud.

Light flashed, illuminating the form that was gathering itself. Wide wings grew from the being's shoulders and spread out, tattered in some places and blotchy with tumorous flesh in others. They cast strange shadows on the mirrors, in the light that came from every direction and none. Olvir couldn't see the figure's face at first.

He didn't need to. The gray-and-orange silk robe gave a lot away. So did the gems that glinted from the shadows around the person's head and glared from one of their hands. The sight of the other hand alone would have let Olvir recognize its owner, though. It was spatulate and skinless, girdled by three metal circles with a blackened jewel at the center of each.

Thyran had arrived.

His countenance, revealed when he folded his wings, was as horrible as Olvir remembered from the final moment of their last encounter. A bone crown had fused to Thyran's head, melting over one eye, and the cheek below that had vanished. So had his lips. He hadn't grown wings when Olvir had last seen him, but it wasn't surprising that he'd had the will to reconfigure his own form. His remaining pale-blue eye stared at Olvir with all the fury that had led the man to murder, then conquest, and finally apocalypse.

Power danced in the scorched jewels. Olvir had seen it before. He'd survived it once, with the help of a whole circle of other people. Those companions were far away now.

Maybe he could dodge a strike or two. Maybe Tinival could shield him again, even against Gizath's high priest and in the middle of the Battlefield, where the Traitor had changed the world itself.

He doubted it.

Olvir set his sights on the warlord's wings, coiled his body for the charge—and Vivian was at his side, in a burst of speed that clearly startled even Thyran.

She didn't really pause, any more than the wind paused when it ruffled the leaves on a tree. Olvir heard her whisper in his ear, almost silent and all the more emphatic for it, before she was gone.

"Get the knife," she told him.

Then she hurled herself at Thyran.

Love, honor, and every impulse of the power within him all shrieked at Olvir to follow the dark armored shape that hurtled across the mirrors, to protect Vivian with his life or at least to ensure that she wouldn't die alone.

He dropped his sword and ran for the knife instead.

Vivian dashed forward at nearly her top speed, two or three times as fast as a normal mortal, and lunged with almost all her weight behind the blow. Her aim was clear and true, her arm straight: she would've run any other enemy through.

This was Thyran.

When Ulamir barely pricked his chest before hitting a thick, clinging mass of flesh, Vivian was ready. The fraction of force she'd held back became the lever she needed to turn herself around, putting all the thwarted energy of her blow into a backward roll over one shoulder. She held Ulamir close to her body, she saw one of the half-molten jewels in Thyran's crown flicker—

The edge of the warding spell, expanding in a corona close to the warlord's body, clipped her. She went sprawling on her face, barely managing not to land on Ulamir.

One of her own eyes stared back at her from the mirror-ground. Then darkness surrounded them again.

Thyran's breathing was loud, distorted as it rasped through his half-melted nose and mouth. His steps were louder. Vivian's would be, too, she realized. She couldn't hear Olvir's any longer. She hoped that meant he'd reached the damned knife.

Vivian gathered herself but didn't stand. She crept sideways on her knees, a hair's-width at a time, listening simultaneously for the ground creaking beneath her and for any sign that would tell her where Thyran was headed.

When the light returned, Vivian sprang again.

This time, she didn't charge. She got a quick glimpse of Thyran, allowing her to see the power gathering around his hands and where he was aiming it, and leapt out of the way. A stench like rotting meat reached her nose, burning as she inhaled, but Vivian was already darting toward clearer air.

Olvir was a few feet from the pair of them, she saw, kneeling and gripping the knife. His chain mail glittered. His head was bent, auburn hair falling over his brow. That was all Vivian could make out.

She wasn't between him and Thyran any longer. A few swift steps took care of that. Then she darted inward, slashing at one of the sorcerer's wings.

That stroke did get through. Ulamir arced down, leaving a silver trail in the strange radiance around them, and carved off a chunk of patchy pink and gray meat. Vivian saw what nobody had in a hundred years or more: Thyran's blood was still red.

He opened his misshapen mouth for the first time since he'd

landed. The sound that emerged, a thick, throaty *hhhhhaaaahhhh*, was equal parts anger and pain.

"Bitch," he said when the scream ended.

It took Vivian by surprise—not the vulgarity or the malice but the simple commonplace nature of the insult. Thyran of Heliodar, the world's near doom, spoke like any drunken idiot she'd met on the road, like a village boy who'd just lost at quoits.

"Yes," she said, laughing. "And?"

He snarled, not quite a word but a pattern of sounds. Sickly fire whipped from his fingers and directly toward Vivian, far too fast to dodge.

———

Olvir didn't look behind him.

He couldn't, not even when he heard the blast, then the heavy thud and cracking. That meant a person's whole weight had hit the mirrors. He hoped that person was Thyran, doubted it, couldn't let himself check. To turn, no matter how briefly, would destroy all his resolve.

He concentrated on the knife's hilt, put his head down, and ran. He welcomed the darkness, though it made the sounds more vivid.

Do your job, Vivian had said. *Trust the people you're with to do theirs.*

She knew what she was doing. She knew what price she might pay, just as well as Olvir did, and she'd decided to take the risk. Olvir wouldn't dishonor her decision now.

But gods, he wished they could have traded places.

When the landscape went radiant again, the knife was right in front of him. The mirror had closed on the blade an inch or so below the guard. Olvir thought that the cracks nearby might have been redder than the others, but that might only have been a trick of the light.

He fell to his knees in front of the knife. Trying to brace himself, not sure he even knew what he would be preparing for, he reached out and wrapped one hand around the hilt, then put the other on top of it, covering the gem.

And he remembered.

He had distance from the worst of it. The fragment wasn't Gizath. Although the Traitor had left some of himself on the Battlefield, that part didn't completely share his perspective. There was a hairsbreadth of separation between Olvir and the memories, adequate space to let him be aware that he wasn't the one feeling tainted by what the Traitor viewed as his sister's willing degradation, nor the one bent on saving her from her chosen fall.

In one sense, that fall had already happened by the time Gizath-he waited for Veryon in the early morning, with the sky turning pearlescent above the trees. Letar had already lain with the mortal—sickening notion—but more damage could be done, and thus more could be averted. Free of her attachment, she would come to regret her choices.

He, Gizath, could give her that gift.

Through a god's memory, Olvir recalled the stonekin's bright smile and cheerful greeting, both a little strained. There had been words before. Gizath had given him and Letar both a chance to turn away from their error, and his effort had failed. Despite that, Veryon wouldn't insult his lover's family, and he'd never suspect them.

Treachery was still a moment or two away from entering existence, after all.

It was easy to get Veryon to turn, easier still to sink the knife into his back. Olvir saw the stonekin's emerald eyes, wide with confusion, as he turned in his final moments.

Then he witnessed the breaking of the world.

Red light shot up in front of Vivian, its bright, honest color a vivid contrast to the orange-gray strands of power it deflected. They whipped off at an angle, leaving Vivian unharmed.

Against that, Ulamir said faintly, *I cannot protect you for long.*

"I know," she replied, watching Thyran, saving her strength. The air near him started to flicker orange-gray. His one good eye was fixed on her chest. She doubted he was appreciating her figure.

If Vivian had been certain it would work, she'd have used her lethal blessing. Gods knew Thyran had been amply hurt—but he hadn't died of it. He could have wards, and if the spell didn't kill him or leave him unable to fight, Vivian would be left defenseless.

So she kept Ulamir in reserve, and he didn't suggest otherwise. She shifted around Thyran, staying on the defensive, aware of the power he was gathering as well as how long the two of them had been bathed in light. Their shadows stretched, distorted, on the shining glass below them.

Thyran stabbed a finger outward just as the world went dark again.

Vivian dropped, deliberately this time, flattening herself against the ground. She listened as the spell went over her head, then sprang to her feet.

The pattern began again: strike, dodge, attack, retreat, every move in either pitch blackness or bright glare, with the mirrors sending the light back to blind the unwary. Vivian got another scratch in, this one directly above Thyran's hip. A little while afterward, a burst of pure pain tore through one of her legs for a few seconds as she failed to evade a spell and Ulamir blocked the worst of it.

She couldn't win. She and Ulamir both knew that. Thyran was not one of his minions, whose stores of power had been relatively limited. There was no outlasting this man, except in one sense, and that had nothing to do with anybody currently in the fight.

So when Vivian saw Thyran look past her toward Olvir, she broke her own rule and talked during a battle.

"You're losing, aren't you?" With satisfaction, she saw him turn his full attention back toward her. The single eye narrowed. Vivian continued, circling sharklike around him. "That was why you summoned the storms last time. You weren't confident in your army. I wouldn't have been either. And that's why you did it now."

"No matter," he rasped at her. "A tool is a tool."

Vivian shrugged. "An ineffective one."

He held up his melted hand. *Earthquake*, said Ulamir, and Vivian jumped into the air a second before the ground where she'd been standing shook, then split. Another too-regular crack shivered through the mirrors, this one wider than the others, but she landed easily out of range.

"You killed some of us," she said, taking a step toward Thyran. "Many, I'll grant. But we survived. We rebuilt, and the ones who died left their marks before they went to Letar. They didn't know that was what they were doing, maybe, but they accomplished it anyhow. And now we live because they left caves, or we learn because they told stories, and the seeds that the wind carried have become trees to hold it back."

Thyran lashed out with more grayish fire. "Amris *cheated*," he snarled as Vivian scrambled away from the blow. "It won't work this time."

The power raked down her side, a ladder of pain that Ulamir could only partially shield. Vivian felt it eating into her arm, saw her skin ripple and bleed.

She caught her breath, looked up at Thyran, and said, "Then we'll find another method. We've known what you are for a hundred years. You can't surprise us any longer, you stupid, petty little man—and neither can your stupid, petty little god."

Fury split Thyran's jaws and creased what skin he had. He gave it physical form with a gesture, sending a barely visible ripple through the air toward Vivian, who tried to spin away again.

It was Thyran's blood that hindered her, slick on the surface of the mirror. She didn't fall, she mostly evaded the spell, but in catching her balance, she was a few seconds slow with her right leg.

That was enough. Vivian saw Ulamir's light flicker around her, fending off the very worst, and heard his anguished mental cry as he came to the last of his strength. Then agony consumed her as her leg broke from the inside out in half a dozen places.

Vivian had the presence of mind to bite down on her scream. Her teeth drew blood when they sank into her lower lip, but they trapped her cry, and the pain served as some feeble balance to the overwhelming anguish spreading through her leg. That equilibrium let her pull herself onto her left knee and hold Ulamir up in front of her.

She couldn't die on her feet any longer, but she'd come as close as she could.

Chapter 40

THE SPLINTERING WAS SO PROFOUND THAT OLVIR BRIEFLY forgot who and where he was.

Impressions came to him, flashing like the bursts of light in the outside world: the knife in a pool of blood, a scream so full of pain and rage that human ears couldn't have withstood hearing it, and a dark-haired woman who threw herself at a blond man, grabbing for his throat. The two of them appeared more solid than the ground where they fought. Grass and earth faded as the gods struck it. Other shapes, less constant ones, took their place.

He was watching from the outside now, not only as Olvir but as the fragment itself. That was another break, one that hurt the heart as badly as the shifting landscape hurt the mind. In the second when he'd raised the knife, Gizath had cast aside the part of him that might have been better. It lay invisible, bleeding in its own way.

Olvir called to it.

The voice of his soul was quiet compared to what the fragment had lost, but it was there, and Tinival's will was behind it. From the moment of heartbreak eons past, the power responded, joining the imperfect version that had taken form in Olvir. United, they filled him.

And having seen the world shatter, he could now figure out how to fix it.

There, in the present, Vivian knelt, holding Ulamir up in one last and lovely gesture of defiance as Thyran gathered force to strike the death blow. Olvir sensed her pain and ached to set it right but turned his attention to the warlord's ravening soul.

Chains stretched off from Thyran, overwhelming chords with faint screaming woven through most of them. One, the loudest, lacked that chorus of pain. In its place was frustrated, all-encompassing rage—and the hunger Olvir had sensed in Thyran's storms.

He recognized the Traitor God's touch at once. As Olvir alone, he'd have been terrified: Thyran was channeling more of any god than he had ever witnessed a mortal touching, far more than any human should have been able to endure. Only Olvir's union with the fragment let him inspect that snarling flow of power, identify it, and then draw his consciousness back in an instant to see the larger picture.

That tie would be the hardest to break. The others were to mortals—whether Twisted minions or sacrifices, Olvir couldn't tell. All of them together maintained the warped knot of power and hunger that Thyran had made of himself. All were, to Olvir's new awareness, desperately wrong: they were to the normal bonds of friendship and worship and love as a mangled limb was to straight bone.

He reached out, as he'd reached for the wind when he'd been in the stonekin's cave, grasped one of those bonds, and snapped it.

Part of the world fell back into place, no longer forced into distortion. Thyran, in the midst of his final, lethal spell, jerked as though struck by lightning.

The force that would have killed Vivian flew off into the distorted sky instead. Its wielder recovered his composure and spun toward Olvir. The Sentinel was on the ground, no longer a distraction from the real threat. Thyran began to charge.

Olvir broke another chain. It was easier than the first had been: with every person that he freed, the others became harder to restrain. A third followed, even while Thyran tore across the ground toward him, and each shock slowed the warlord's advance. The others began to unravel themselves, just as the storm winds had done when he'd touched them from the cave.

That left the link between Thyran and Gizath. Not only the Traitor's raw force gave it strength; both parties had forged that bond willingly. It didn't want to shatter as the others had—it was vile, but the shape of it was true.

Still, as Olvir bent his will upon the link, he felt it begin to crumble.

The Traitor God roared at the contact, blasting Olvir's mind not just with hatred but with affront too. In all the long aeons of his divine life, Gizath had never been subject to a mortal's will, nor had he ever imagined the shard of his own being turning against him.

Thyran echoed his liege's fury. He didn't bother with a spell but sprang for Olvir's neck—

And Vivian, rising in agony on the remains of her leg, hurled a dagger into his back.

It struck Thyran under his right shoulder, not a vital hit, but those few seconds of unexpected pain were all Olvir needed. The sorcerer's connection to the Traitor, the source of both his power and his survival after Oakford, finally broke.

Thyran collapsed to the ground, all the gems that he wore and all that had grown into him shattering in that moment. He screamed. It wasn't very loud: he didn't have much of a throat left.

Kneeling in front of the knife, Olvir turned his awareness from the wreckage of Thyran. He sent it a few feet away instead, following the golden strands that ran between him and Vivian.

If Thyran's chains had resembled mangled limbs, then there was a similarity Olvir could use. He focused on that, on the way bones should fit together and the way the ones in Vivian's leg didn't, and guided them back into their proper places. That was more effort than stopping Thyran had been and the limit of Olvir's abilities. Healing had never been Gizath's domain.

Anger followed that thought. It seemed natural for a moment that it was Olvir's own. Who could gaze on Gizath's works and those of his chief servant and not be angry?

But then the rage vanished. Confusion took its place. A very faint voice spoke in the back of Olvir's head. It creaked with disuse, but once it had clearly been beautiful.

Not him. You are him and yet not him. How can this be so?

It came, Olvir realized, from the topaz in the knife's hilt.

━━━━━━

She was alive.

Vivian had braced for death. Its absence knocked the prop out from beneath her mind. Her thoughts stumbled to a halt.

Thyran was screaming, then gurgling. His body twitched on the ground, bits of it falling in, the ruin of his face crumpling in on itself.

Pain pierced her leg again, without movement on her part or warning on its. The sensation was different from the agony of Thyran's attack, though. Vivian had gotten bones set on a few occasions in her life as a Sentinel. She knew the feeling of having them yanked back into place, the sudden reunion that strained flesh. Now there were no hands on her leg, and many bones snapped into their proper positions at once, but she recognized the feeling nonetheless.

Tears blinded her. She blinked them away. Thyran lay motionless in front of her. Past him, Olvir knelt by the knife.

The world yet remains, Ulamir said, his voice growing stronger, *and healing bodes well.*

It wasn't a definite answer. Vivian didn't need the sword to tell her that. Her leg, and Thyran's undoing, could be victories in a war Olvir lost in the end or bribes for his good behavior. The vilest people had pets.

She didn't know. She had a job to do.

Her leg was set but not really healed. She kept her weight off it as much as possible, bit back oaths of pain, and staggered forward, clutching Ulamir.

Thyran lay without moving or breathing. His face no longer looked like it had ever belonged to a human, and his throat was halfway caved in, but Vivian didn't believe in taking chances. Kneeling so she didn't fall, she took his head from his body, then stabbed Ulamir through the spot where his heart had been at some point. The bones put up no greater resistance than paper.

Everything was smaller after it had died.

That was one task done. She didn't want the next one, the most vital, and what she wanted had very rarely mattered.

The few feet of mirrors between her and Olvir stretched to miles. He was in the same position, but light began to flicker around his hands where they clasped the knife.

Vivian couldn't make out the light's color, nor did she know what message she would've taken from it if she could have. Would Gizath's power indicate the Traitor's personality? Would Olvir just use what was available, unchanged? Was his mind slipping away as he sat there, with Gizath's influence or not?

Another few limping steps left her sweating, out of breath, and dizzy from the effort. She suspected she'd sobbed in the process a few times. Tears were running down her cheeks. She only realized it when she tasted the salt.

Olvir was less than a foot in front of her. He didn't turn at her approach. His hands were glowing orange. Vivian thought it might be a brighter shade than she'd seen from Gizath's servants. She knew that she could be seeing it through the prism of her hopes.

There wouldn't be a lot of time, if she was wrong about him.

She started to raise Ulamir, to hold the blade ready for the downward stroke. It wouldn't be easy with a wounded leg, but it was the only method Vivian could see. Her arms screamed as she began to lift the sword.

No, said a voice in her head. It was a low alto, not remotely close to Ulamir's, and yet familiar.

Her leg was healed in an instant, whole as if Thyran's arts had never touched it. Vivian froze. Reflexes and training both told her to shift her balance, to find a firmer stance now that her body would let her. Amazement and confusion held her still.

Wait, the voice said.

Vivian had never heard the speaker before. The voice filled her mind, drowning out all else, but she knew it was only the faint shadow of a greater force. She wasn't built to bear more than that. That echo was already power far in excess of any she'd ever encountered.

She'd felt a hint of it once, though. The presence had been far less immediate, it had been watching rather than speaking, but it had been with her at her Reforging.

Olvir recognized the speaker almost as soon as he'd worked out where he was. The confused distress in the mental voice struck him before any sense of awe could. Veryon, ancient or not, legendary or not, sounded similar to a dozen people Olvir had heard stunned by fire, flood, or banditry.

A lifetime in Tinival's service told him how to respond.

"I'm not," he said to the gem, calm but emphatic. "I'll explain, I promise, but I've an urgent duty to perform first, one that I swear will harm nobody."

He was still mortal: the effort he'd used to kill Thyran hadn't left him seriously depleted, but Olvir could tell that his power was finite. Time was finite too. Each moment the storms lasted was one of more potential destruction.

I cannot doubt you, said Veryon, speech seeming as though it came a little easier now. *I know not why that should be either. Yet I will wait.*

"Thank you," said Olvir and turned his attention to the task for which he'd come to the Battlefield.

The patterns of wind, rain, and cold were obvious now, as were the ways Thyran and Gizath had twisted them out of their natural paths. They shrieked at one another in reverberating echoes that fed on themselves and gained strength. Only a whisper had made it over the mountains, but following that back to its source was an easy matter.

Silencing the discordant core of the storms would simply require Olvir to shout louder than they did. The force was channeled into much more complicated forms than Thyran's ties had been, though. Severed, those strands could lash about, uncontrolled—perhaps leading to some portion of the destruction that had happened after Thyran's first defeat, perhaps causing other sorts of damage, perhaps dissipating harmlessly.

Olvir couldn't take the chance. Slowly, clumsy at first but becoming defter as he went on, he found one of the individual notes and hushed it, then followed to the next. He felt Veryon within his consciousness during the whole process, observing with wonder as well as with disgust that the tangle existed in the first place.

The storms' fury settled as Olvir worked. In distant lands, blizzard winds died. Patches of blue sky appeared among the clouds. People in camps or on battlefields peered up at them, wondering, not yet daring to hope.

One after another, the strands of stormy air drifted away.

That was nobly done, said Veryon at the end. *Craft that any of my people or the Weaving Lady could be proud of—or healing that—*The voice faltered.

"Thank you," Olvir said again.

He sat back, only then aware of the Battlefield and the knife.

He knew that Vivian stood behind him, waiting. Ulamir was in her hand, but she held the sword by her side, not ready to strike.

The blade might have reassured her, or she might have heard Olvir talking. He wished he could give her some other sign, but he would collapse the moment he stopped working. He didn't want to stop, not just yet.

Other patterns, other bonds, had become obvious.

Those ties lacked the angry finesse Thyran's work had possessed, because they had been formed unintentionally. Gizath hadn't meant to stick Veryon's spirit in the knife any more than he'd meant to leave the best part of himself behind. Actions had simply resonated when the world was new and the gods had walked with mortals.

Veryon's trap was to the Sentinels' delicately crafted soulgems what fermented windfall apples was to good wine: accidental, not nearly as good, but the similarities were there. As with the soulgems, the jewel was the center of the bindings. Unlike the soulgems, it hadn't been reinforced.

Olvir bent his head closer toward the polished stone. The magic there was another howling din, but he didn't have to worry about being delicate with that one.

"Silver Wind, guide your servant," he said, "even now."

He lifted his spirit, lifted his voice, and sang a single note with all the skill that Edda had ever taught him.

Veryon's prison shattered.

Chapter 41

JOY, INCREDULOUS AND OVERWHELMING, FLOODED VIVIAN. Even at a distance and secondhand, it swamped her mind. She stood frozen. Ulamir was a faint presence, as awed as she was, Olvir knelt in front of her, and that was as much of existence as Vivian could take in just then. In the shadow of that great elation, she was barely aware of herself.

It would kill her to stay too close to the joy's source for long—normal humans had never lived side by side with the gods, and she was no priest—but that knowledge brought no fear, only floated within her as an unimportant fact. Such a death was more than Vivian could ever have asked for.

So she didn't bat an eye when the world glowed before her, taking on a brightness that dwarfed the mirrors and the lightning. A rainbow of colors spread themselves in front of Vivian's sight, forming stars that dissipated, re-formed, and melted once again into the ever-changing spectrum. It was as hard to keep track of as the Battlefield, but Vivian felt no discomfort observing it.

Within her or around her or both, Letar withdrew slightly. The sense of the goddess resolved itself into words again.

Thank you.

One of Letar's symbols was a teardrop, like those that marked Vivian's cheeks. She sounded as if she was weeping now, or would have been had she been a mortal woman. These were tears of joy, though, which the Dark Lady had never shed in any legend Vivian had heard.

Thank you, she said again, and now her voice was flavored

with quiet mirth as well. *Words have grown smaller in my absence, or I larger, but I doubt they would have sufficed for this moment if I'd spoken them at the beginnings of existence. My children—my saviors—not my mother herself could have foreseen this last act.*

Wherever they were was not quite the living world any longer, Vivian realized. Among other differences, Ulamir kept flickering in both appearance and location: the sword she held, then a lithe stonekin man at her right side. He was kneeling, long ruby-red hair falling across his face.

"Cutter of Threads," he said, and despite being sure she'd come to the limit of her capacity for astonishment, Vivian still blinked when she actually heard his voice. "Lady of Mercy. It was our duty and our honor."

And your service not least, blood of my beloved, said Letar. *You, who turned from my halls for duty, without whom my sorrow would have perhaps never ended.*

It was the work of many, said Ulamir, *and my companions most of all, here at the last.*

Vivian hadn't, couldn't have, forgotten about Olvir, but hearing the plural from Ulamir yanked her attention sharply away from even the goddess's presence.

The knight still knelt as he'd been kneeling all along, hands on a knife whose hilt now held a shattered stone. Vivian could see his chest rising and falling as he breathed, but otherwise he remained immobile.

She stepped—or moved, since her feet worked oddly— forward and put a hand on his shoulder. It was like touching a living statue.

The pain of her broken leg had been nothing in comparison.

"Olvir," she said, choking on the second syllable of the name. Then she looked up, though the sky overhead was no different from the world in front of her. "Lady—"

I understand, said Letar gently. *He went beyond his strength at the last. A shard of our power may burn its vessel, if used too long and hard. But healing is mine to command, and you love him.*

She didn't bother asking, but Vivian said "Yes" anyhow.

Then there is yet work we may do.

"Anything."

Suddenly, Olvir was facing her. His hands were empty now, but his head was still bent. He stared at his interlaced fingers and the colors shining in the air beyond them. Clearly, he saw nothing.

I have helped to make you a weapon, said Letar. *Will you be a vessel for me, in this moment, on this ground?*

Vivian wanted to repeat *anything*, but she recognized a ritual question when she heard one. "Yes," she said.

It will suffice. Lift his head.

She did it gently, fingers light under Olvir's chin. There was almost no resistance anyhow, and her heart broke a little more to feel how easily she could move him.

And now, the goddess said, *a kiss.*

———————

He was broken. Scattered. Lost, and becoming more so by the minute. His mind was many minds, many pieces streaming off in different directions, following voices that shrieked and babbled. Olvir could almost understand the words. He had almost forgotten his name.

Each fragment of him tried to resist, tried to reunite with the others, but to no use. There was no center to which they could strive to return. Without it, their struggles remained directionless, chaotic, and the voices led them ever onward to dissolution.

Once, he had been different. That knowledge remained, but little more. His name was Olvir. He'd freed somebody. He could remember the mind that had flowered out when all the pieces had broken, the sense of release and reunion he'd gotten. He, Olvir, had done that.

Before, he'd done other things.

He believed he had fought. He was sure he had served.

He knew he had loved.

Suddenly, there was another with him, a sound that was not the screaming voices. At first, that presence was only there, new but familiar. Then it began to call to him.

The voices kept going, shrieking outward to gods knew what destinations, but the scattered pieces of Olvir had another goal. The new arrival had become steady, powerful: a soaring melody laid over a regular drumbeat, calling to mind the best marching songs he'd once learned.

He remembered marches. Training. Singing.

A cave.

Vivian.

The newcomer was her but not only her. A vast power anchored her call, amplifying it and keeping her from losing herself.

If Olvir had possessed a body, he would have been kneeling. He remembered that he was, somewhere.

He gladly turned to answer Vivian's summons, each piece of him retreating from the voices that had been leading it outward. Those voices didn't try to reclaim him; they didn't seem to notice but simply passed further out, heading toward the boundaries of his perception and reason, then beyond.

Free of their grip, with the strong, unwavering rhythm of Vivian and her divine patron to focus him, Olvir began to put himself together.

Vivian was the core: she was there to guide him, reminding him of their moments in the cave, of jokes shared on the trail, of slaying the geisbar and sitting by campfires, of taverns and villages and dark manors. Going beyond themselves, she gave Olvir the memory of the army camp, of long watches staring out over snow. That led to Nahon, to the men Olvir had commanded, and then his own consciousness found a bridge to Tinival's service and Edda, who had prepared him for it.

Bit by bit, he filled in the gaps. The Sundered Soul went in there, too, part of Olvir even if he'd exhausted its power—his power—for the time being. So did Darya, Emeth, a thousand faces met in the course of duty or pleasure. Songs and sunsets filled him, blood and bread, all the horror and beauty of the mortal world.

He was a mortal man, Edda's fosterling.

He was the lost child of Verengir, the incarnation of what Gizath had left behind.

He was Olvir Yoralth, servant of Tinival.

Fingers gently tilted his chin up, and a pair of lips pressed against his: warm, soft, yet urgent in, for once, a manner that had nothing to do with physical desire. Olvir recognized the touch and took the only sensible action. He wrapped his arms around Vivian and pulled her close.

He hadn't thought about his position or hers, and they toppled backward almost immediately. Olvir was briefly surprised that he hadn't hit his head on the mirrors—the surface beneath him was barely solid enough to hold him up—but Vivian was lying on his chest, kissing him, laughing and crying at once.

Nothing else was important.

Chapter 42

BEFORE OLVIR HAD SUFFICIENT PRESENCE OF MIND TO TRY figuring out where he was, he wasn't there any longer. The yielding surface under his spine solidified at some point while he embraced Vivian, but Olvir didn't notice the difference until a rock jabbed him just above his right kidney.

"Oof," he said, and Vivian immediately lifted herself off him.

"Sorry. I should've been more careful, considering."

"You're not to blame at all." Olvir sat up. The world was suddenly full of facts: he was sitting, and Vivian standing, on red grass. Overhead, the sky was blue, with a few wisps of white cloud near the mountains. He was mortal, sore, and incredibly tired. "Besides, when it comes to physical injury, you were the worse off by... Should you be standing on that leg?"

She didn't appear as though it pained her in the slightest. Vivian's eyes were red and her cheeks showed the tracks of tears, but she looked perfectly happy in that moment, and her smile at the question had more than happiness in it. There was an awe there that Olvir recognized very well.

Remembering the anchoring power he'd sensed when Vivian had brought him back, he wasn't all that surprised by her answer. "The Threadcutter is merciful."

"She is." Reflexively, Olvir made the sign of the Four. "Was She the one who brought us out of the Battlefield?"

Vivian nodded. "She left almost as soon as you came back. You were handling contact with two gods—or one and a half—far better than most humans would manage, She said. There was no sense in risking a third, and the window we opened was closing fast at any rate. The window you opened, really."

Olvir lacked the strength or the wit for embarrassment. "I'm honored," he said. "And thankful. And I rather hope the Dark Lady didn't mean for us to start walking now."

The air echoed with Vivian's laughter. "I doubt it. She didn't give us a schedule, but She did say that nothing in this land would harm us. I interpret that to mean we can make camp as we choose—and I think we're past the point where a few hours will make a difference at home."

"You know the storms are gone," Olvir said, realizing only then that he hadn't told her earlier. "Did the Dark Lady tell you?"

"No." Vivian settled herself down onto the grass at his side, sitting with her legs folded and her pack in front of her. "But if you hadn't, and you were still you—which I have it on good authority that you are—you'd still be trying. Probably while your brain melted in the process. I can't imagine you relaxing in the face of duty."

It was Olvir's turn to laugh. He reached out, although his arms felt limp as dough, and took one of Vivian's hands. "And you should know, my love."

―――――――――

Vivian was content simply to sit there for a while, Olvir's hand in hers, watching him. His smile and the pressure of his fingers gradually pushed back the memory of his previous vacant expression. Experience said that she'd probably still recall it on particularly restless nights, but experience also said she could live with that.

He was there, after all: body, mind, and soul.

After that fact had finally started to sink in, Vivian leaned back and took a real look around. The grass had dried in their absence to a lighter red, the black and silver outlines of trees rose against a deep-blue sky, and the sun was turning a rich gold as it set in the west. Between Vivian and the sunset, the Battlefield lay, iridescent in the light.

"Odd," she said. "I would've expected it to vanish or change when you freed Veryon."

Olvir shook his head. "He was only trapped there. He didn't have much at all to do with creating it. And what—" Modesty still made him clear his throat before he could say the next words. "What I did just set matters closer to right now. Veryon still died there, he still suffered, he's still changed from it, probably. I couldn't make that not have happened."

That is almost certainly for the best, Ulamir put in. *I wouldn't wish pain on the Queen of Death, nor on my ancestor, but the world's spun itself out quite a length since that moment. To reverse it... I have not the slightest idea what changes it would make.*

"Ulamir says that's a good thing," she summarized. "He understands magic—and time—better than I do, so I'm inclined to agree."

"I think I am," said Olvir. "But I'm very glad I wasn't in a position to decide. Changing history would be considerably beyond my judgment, even if it were possible."

"I'm fond of your judgment. But...yes. Above all our pay grades, I'm convinced." Vivian thought of scars, of memories, of legends. She remembered abandoned caves and a weary, wise voice all around and through her. Off in the distance, the Battlefield glimmered. "So it'll stay there forever."

"I can't see that far. But I can't imagine any reason it wouldn't remain." Olvir studied her expression. "That doesn't mean we have to stay here and watch it. I can walk now, though I can't promise I'm good for many miles."

The strange landscape swirled, colors dancing across its surface, edges melting and then re-forming. Trying to follow its changes hurt, but Vivian no longer felt any urge to try. Neither did she have the dizzy, sick feeling that had come over her when she'd first seen the place.

Scars were always startling. Most were uglier than this one.

"No," she said. Turning away from the horizon, she focused on Olvir instead and raised one hand to cup the side of his chin. His skin was rough with a day's growth of beard, the bones of his jaw solid and strong. "No, I think we're fine right here."

Later, under the rich purple twilight of an evening in late spring, they roused themselves enough to spread out bedrolls, to shuck off boots and armor, and to eat. They drank the last of their water too. Olvir luxuriated in the knowledge that the creek was close, just as he did the clean air on his feet.

They would start walking in the morning. Then they'd refill their waterskins, pick some of the silver apples that grew by the stream, and make for the mountain path. Olvir expected the journey back to be faster, with neither storms nor undead bears likely to present obstacles. Whether it was or not, he was content. Speed mattered far less now.

Vivian agreed when he mentioned it. "Without Thyran and the weather, the army should be able to send the Twisted scurrying north, especially with Amris's reinforcements coming from the west. And if they can't, the two of us won't turn the tide. Well, probably," she added, after a comment from Ulamir. She gave Olvir a curious once-over. "Do you think you could instantly make them disintegrate, like you did Thyran?"

"Sadly, I doubt it," said Olvir after due consideration. "Thyran was...what I did was similar to your lethal blessing, as a matter of fact. He should have died already. I just cut the ties keeping him alive. The Twisted are what they are. I doubt I could reverse that, any more than I could get rid of the Battlefield."

"Mmm. I suspected as much. We'll have to set up watches when this is over—train a new cadre of spies or wizards or I don't know what, make sure we're not caught by surprise again." Vivian dusted biscuit crumbs off her hands. "The Adeptas will have plenty to do, and I'm sure Letar's priests will take an interest."

"Oh, we'll have our fingers in that pie too," said Olvir. "It'll be work for everyone, rebuilding—but better work, to my way of thinking, than we've had for the last few years."

"I'd drink to that, if we had wine left."

"I'd say it deserves better wine than we brought."

"Another task for later, then." Vivian tipped her head back to see the stars as they began to come out. "That's the only reason I'd hurry—that, and I'd like to learn how they're all holding up in Criwath. Even if I can't change what happens."

"So would I," said Olvir. He thought of Nahon—and almost immediately had a sense of the marshal. It was the same sort of awareness he'd had of the storms, as if he heard a melody from far away. This was more complex than the storms had been, more solid, and so it stood out more despite being smaller. "I...think I could discover that."

"*Without* risking yourself again?" Vivian asked sharply, returning her focus to Olvir in an instant. "My curiosity isn't worth losing you."

"No danger," he said, recognizing her worry. It was a good one: the memory of being lost would chill him for a good while. "I'm only observing, not trying to make changes. And I won't look very deeply at that. I don't want to read anybody's mind by accident."

"You know what you're doing," she said and leaned against him. "Tell me if I can help."

Olvir breathed in the smell of her hair. Her weight rested solidly on his side. Thus anchored, he closed his eyes and sent his mind out again.

Geography wasn't important or wasn't the same. Instead of

following paths over the mountains, he traced the bonds that connected him to Nahon, to Emeth, to everybody that he'd left behind. He could sense Vivian's, too, giving him a clearer impression of many Sentinels and their companions.

"Nahon's near to Darya and General var Faina," Olvir said, taking in their signatures and learning what he could without intruding. "They're all in decent shape, more or less. Tired, of course, and wounded. I suspect Darya's missing an arm, or maybe an ear. It's odd, but I can't tell which." There was an absence, a major one, that she hadn't gotten used to yet. That was all Olvir could determine without coming too close.

"Under the circumstances, that's not bad," Vivian said.

She was holding her tongue, Olvir knew, not wanting to suggest more for fear she'd inspire him to go beyond his strength. He hugged her tighter. "Katrine's fine. Emeth's…she's weak but recovering. A close brush, I think." The Mourners would have worked hard in a case such as that, whatever had happened, and Letar's power left its mark when used in great quantities.

Thinking of the Dark Lady drew his consciousness slightly beyond the group he'd sensed before, into another gathering. "Branwyn… You mentioned a letter from her… She's there. No serious harm, though there's a Mourner with her, and—" He paused. The man, as tied to Branwyn as Olvir himself was to Vivian, was familiar, yet Olvir was certain they'd never met. "I believe we're related."

"Zelen Verengir, I'd imagine. Lord Verengir, if he weren't a Mourner. Hmm." Olvir felt mirth shake Vivian. "They may want you to assume the title, you realize."

"Gods forbid." Knights weren't barred from titles as Letar's priests were, but the idea held no appeal at all.

"Oh, consider it. I'd make a wonderful mistress for a nobleman."

"Would you want to be?" Olvir had already been drawing his consciousness back. Despite his reassurance to Vivian, his strength was limited, and he had no desire to test it. At her comment, he returned fully to the spot where they sat and opened his eyes to watch her reaction.

Vivian tilted her head upward so that she could meet his gaze. "I want to be with you," she said, "as much and for as long as our duties allow. I couldn't care less about the circumstances."

"Oh," said Olvir. His chest was too tight suddenly. It was anything but comfortable, and he wouldn't have changed it for the world. "Then neither do I."

When they moved to the bedrolls, not much later, Vivian curled up against Olvir as she'd done the first night they'd kept each other warm. He wrapped an arm around her shoulders, rested his other hand on her waist, and watched as she yawned and closed her eyes.

He kept his open for a few minutes. He looked from Vivian, rapidly slipping into sleep, up to the star-filled sky over a land that nobody else had seen for a hundred years.

All his prayers were thanks that night, and he knew his dreams would be sweet.

They were going home.

Epilogue

I regret to inform you, my lady, that House Verengir will have to be content with its current choice of leader. Young Danica has my sympathy, I completely understand her reluctance, but the knights have only recently regained Sir Yoralth. They have no intention of losing him to a lifetime of politics in Heliodar.

Besides, the man and his mission have already become the subject of much rumor here. If he can disrupt a camp where everyone should be better occupied cleaning up after Thyran's defeat, think of how he'd set Heliodar on its ear! I find the prospect almost appealing enough to try and persuade Marshal Nahon, though I know it wouldn't help, but I doubt you and the rest of the High Council would find it so delightful.

Perhaps I can persuade him and Commander Bathari to come along for a visit when Branwyn and I return. I admit I also would enjoy seeing society deal with two Sentinels.

P. S.: No, I won't confirm the rumors. Nor will I deny them. I wish you luck in your new role, as I do Danica in hers, but a greater Lady than both of you commands my loyalty now.

—Mourner Zelen Verengir

And though the study of sympathetic magic retains significant hazards for the unwary, I am convinced that it's no longer the snare it once was. Gizath's influence over connections is significantly less than it was before Thyran's demise.

We're cautioned against inquiring too deeply into the reasons for this change. I respect this. However, that prohibition doesn't extend to exploring the effects, and it is for this reason that I'm seeking potential colleagues to join me in the ruins of Klaishil, where we will conduct experiments...

—Notice from Tebengri, Wizard of Criwath

Call: Who is the Remnant Saint?
Response: *The union of a mortal knight and the conscience that Gizath cast off. He lacks the Traitor's might, but he ever seeks to repair the bonds that are broken, to free those held against their will, and to oppose the Fifth God and his servants. Through him, the pattern of the world changed once more.*

—Catechism of the Temple of Sitha, Revised, c.
24 Years after Thyran's Second Defeat

Acknowledgments

I'd like to acknowledge my editor, Mary Altman; my agent, Jessica Watterson; and everyone at Sourcebooks for helping me finish this up in the midst of general 2020ness.

About the Author

Isabel Cooper lives outside Boston, where she spends her days editing technology research and her nights doing things best not discussed here. (Actually, she plays a lot of video games.) She likes road trips, but camping is best left to fiction.

You can find her sporadically updated blog at isabelcooper .wordpress.com.

THE KINGMAKER CHRONICLES

Amanda Bouchet's bestselling,
award-winning fantasy trilogy

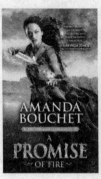  

An NPR Best Book of 2016

An Amazon Best Book of 2016 and 2017

A *Kirkus Reviews* Best Book of 2016 and 2017

Catalia "Cat" Fisa lives disguised as a soothsayer in a traveling circus. She is perfectly content avoiding the danger and destiny the Gods—and her homicidal mother—have saddled her with. That is, until Griffin, an ambitious warlord from the magic-deprived south, fixes her with his steely gaze and upsets her illusion of safety forever.

"A heart-pounding and joyous romantic adventure."
—NALINI SINGH, *New York Times* bestseller

For more info about Sourcebooks's books and authors, visit:
sourcebooks.com

THE LEGEND OF ALL WOLVES

For three days out of thirty, when the moon is full and her law is iron, the Great North Pack must be wild...

The Last Wolf

Silver Nilsdottir is at the bottom of her Pack's social order, with little chance for a decent mate and a better life. Until the day she meets a stranger and decides to risk everything...

A Wolf Apart

Only Thea Villalobos can see that Elijah Sorensson is Alpha of his generation of the Great North Pack, and that the wolf inside him will no longer be restrained...

Forever Wolf

With old and new enemies threatening the Great North, Varya knows that she must keep Eyulf hidden away from the superstitious wolves who would doom them both...

"Wonderfully unique and imaginative. I was enthralled!"
—Jeaniene Frost, *New York Times* bestselling author

For more info about Sourcebooks's books and authors, visit:
sourcebooks.com

Also by Isabel Cooper